Love Always, Kate

d. Nichole King

Love Always, Kate

Limitless Publishing, LLC
Kailua, HI 96734
www.limitlesspublishing.com

Formatting: Limitless Publishing

ISBN-13: 978-1-68058-192-8
ISBN-10: 1-68058-192-9

Dedication

For all those who've been touched by cancer.
Your strength is an inspiration.

Chapter 1

The expression on Dr. Lowell's face said it all.

I sat back against the chair in his office, nervously playing with a lock of my thick auburn hair. Stretching it under my nose, I inhaled the coconut scent of my favorite shampoo. Already, I missed the sweet aroma.

"Your lab work came back, Kate." Dr. Jackson Lowell's eyes fixed on me then shifted to my parents. He paused. "The white blood cell count is twenty-two thousand."

I didn't have to glance over to know what my parents were doing. My mother's eyes squeezed shut, and my father's hand rubbed her back. The soft breaths escaping my mother filled my ears.

I stared blankly at my feet. What seemed like hours passed before anyone spoke.

"What options do we have this time?" Dad asked, his voice cracking.

I lifted my eyes to Dr. Lowell. His gaze drifted to his desk. He removed his glasses and laid them on top of my file.

"Another round of chemotherapy." Turning his attention to me, he continued, "And we'll need to put you back on the bone marrow transplant list."

I nodded, not knowing what to say. The lump in my throat made it hard to breathe. I'd heard this spiel twice before, but it didn't get any easier. Sitting up higher in my seat, I put on my brave face.

"When do I start treatment?" I asked, tucking my hair behind my ears. My focus stayed on Dr. Lowell. If I so much as glanced over at my parents, I'd break down. And I couldn't do that.

"Monday."

Leukemia had forced its way back in my life, and just like the last times, I needed my coping mechanism from the store—my new best friend since I didn't actually have one. As soon as I left the hospital, I drove into the parking lot of Target.

I walked to the stationery aisle and saw it immediately. It didn't have my name printed on it like my first one, and it didn't have the intricate cover of my second. This one was perfect: black with a red rose on the front. Black for the cancer and the red rose for me defeating it.

When I got home, I collapsed on my bed and flipped it open.

October 29
Dear Diary,
One year. That's it. One measly year of

remission and now it's back. I don't know if my body can handle another round of chemo. Not only that, but can I mentally withstand the emotional turmoil that goes with it...again?

It's not just about me, though. Seven years of on-again, off-again chemo treatments has taken its toll on my parents, too. They've sacrificed so much for me; how can I ask for more? I know it's stupid, but I wonder what their life would have been like if they'd had a whole daughter instead of a broken one. They love me. I hate to disappoint them after all they've done.

My red hair has finally grown back and hangs past my shoulders. I don't want to wake up every morning to chunks of it on my pillow. Already I miss the feeling of my fingers running through the tresses. What good is clean hair when it's clogging the drain in the shower? Soon it will be gone. Every. Last. Strand.

I'm seventeen; I've survived leukemia since I was eleven. But I don't know long I can keep fighting. I'm trying to be brave. I don't want to die. I've never even been kissed.

I closed my eyes and fought the oncoming tears. Feeling sorry for myself wasn't an option. Yeah, I had cancer—nothing I could do about it besides accept the fact. But that nagging voice in the back of my head kept pushing.

I felt fine. Maybe there was a mix-up at the lab.

Could the numbers be wrong?

Why me? Why again?

How could I feel so good, but have cancer ravaging my body?

Sighing, I rolled onto my back and stared at the ceiling. Yep, still white. I swiped the tears from my cheeks. I'd just started to have a life. And now, I was back to being an outcast. Life sucked.

Instead of wallowing, I attempted some meaningless tasks to keep my mind occupied. I got up and fluffed my pillows on the window seat. When I finished with that, I smoothed out my sheer curtains and picked some fuzz off the floor in the corner. It didn't help.

During dinner, I noticed my mom's puffy eyes. I hated the stress my disease caused. She tried so hard to be strong—to be positive. But those eyes gave her away. Fighting was my job, surviving was hers. Dad didn't throw any chairs, a good sign that he was taking this lapse better than the last one. He sat quiet and reserved.

No one ate much. Our appetites, like our vacation fund, had disappeared with the test results.

The weekend moved slower than a funeral caravan—sorry, bad joke. Slipped into a daze, we all seemed to be dealing with the news by avoiding it, which was fine by me. Dad went to work in downtown Des Moines. Mom read her *Better Homes and Gardens Magazine* and worked outside

4

in the flowerbeds. I penned a few pages in my diary before deciding to veg-out in the kitchen. I'd be puking my guts out soon enough, so I figured I might as well enjoy something sweet and totally unhealthy. I mixed up a batch of cookie dough and ate it by myself.

Making friends required being around *people*— not hospitals. I'd missed so much school because of treatments that I enrolled in summer school to try and keep up. It worked, but only to get me into tenth grade—one year behind. Pretty much all the kids at school knew I had leukemia. They felt sorry for me, so they didn't say anything. I don't think they knew *what* to say. I was "the girl with cancer who used to be bald." I understood.

"Hi, Kate," Leslie said as I walked into the tiny hospital room Monday afternoon. I was on a first-name basis with all the nurses and staff members on the floor. "I really hoped I'd never see you in here again."

"Me, too." I sat down on the reclining bed.

My mother had allowed me to come by myself. Having her there wouldn't make things any easier, and I was old enough now to go to my own appointments. No need for her to take the hours out of her week.

I squeezed my eyes closed as Leslie rubbed alcohol on my hand before inserting the IV. Watching made my stomach crawl. Feeling the needle go in felt bad enough, seeing it just reminded me how real it all was. The central line, my first of many visual reminders, would soon be attached to my chest.

"All done," Leslie announced. "Dr. Lowell will be here in a few minutes. I'm sure you don't, but I have to ask—do you have any questions?"

I had no questions. In fact, I could probably write a textbook of procedures by now.

I shook my head.

Leslie sat down on the bed next to me and ran her fingers through my hair. "Your hair is beautiful, Katie. I really like this cut on you."

My hair fell in layers, framing my full, round face. "Thank you." Last time, when my hair started falling out, Leslie sat with me, holding my hand as I cried. I knew it was just hair, but it was *my* hair. Soon, I'd look like a little bald old man. Wigs itched. I had one that matched my own hair color, but I hated wearing it. People stared when I went out in public because they felt sorry for me. And that was annoying. It wasn't the stares or the whispers, or even the silence. I didn't want people to feel sorry for me. I was a warrior. I'd beaten cancer twice, and I could do it again—at least, that's what I told myself.

Dr. Lowell walked in and gave us a slight grin. He held my chart in his hands, but he didn't look at it. He probably had it memorized. Another nurse, one I didn't know, stood next to him. She was young and pretty with dark brown hair and a reassuring smile.

"Hey, Kate," he said, flipping on the overhead lights. "This is Tammy. I'm sure you two will get to know one another soon enough."

"Hi." I nodded at her.

"So, are you ready?" Dr. Lowell asked.

"As ready as I'll ever be, I guess." Who was ever ready to be sliced open and have tubes put inside their veins?

Leslie patted my shoulder. "You're my hero," she whispered.

I slipped my right arm out of my bra strap and tank-top sleeve. The procedure happened while I was conscious, but I really wished they'd knock me out. Because of the local anesthetic, I didn't feel pain. I felt the tugging, though. Oh, and I could hear the little tools and the clanking on the metal tray. Those sounds alone were enough to make me nauseous.

Leslie smoothed the skin on the right side of my chest with an alcohol wipe. The scent of rubbing alcohol would forever be burned in my nostrils, like someone's initials etched on a silver flask—which I was pretty sure wasn't used for *rubbing* alcohol.

"You're going to feel some stinging," Dr. Lowell said.

Stinging? I didn't think stabbing someone with large needles multiple times in the chest qualified as "stinging."

I took a deep breath.

Leslie held my hand, and I squeezed it harder each time the local anesthetic pricked me. Tears formed behind my lids, but I fought them back. I could be strong. This was nothing.

When Dr. Lowell finished, the bed started moving. My head slowly sank down as my feet began to rise. Next to me, Leslie never let go of my hand. Her soft expression gave me strength. I balled my other hand into a fist as hard as I could, then slowly let my fingers fan out. I concentrated on breathing steadily. My eyes stayed closed.

Dr. Lowell started working. I knew exactly what he was doing. First he'd insert the needle into a vein in my chest. Then, with Tammy's help, he'd put a guide wire into the vein. Next, he'd cut one small slit in my chest and another in my neck. That part I didn't mind. I felt nothing when they cut me. It was the next part I dreaded. Leslie knew that, being in Tammy's position last time, so she grabbed the small white garbage can and held it up to my mouth—just in case.

Dr. Lowell slid the central line in the lower cut on my chest and came out at the slit in my neck. I felt the pressure it caused. My stomach started to churn, and my mouth exploded with saliva. I tried to hold back. Really, I did. But I couldn't help it.

"Go ahead, Kate," Dr. Lowell assured me.

I puked in the basket. Thankfully, the nurses on the third floor of Blank Children's Hospital were used to people throwing up. Leslie wiped my mouth with a wet paper towel she'd grabbed before she sat down. She swiped my hair back and sighed. I nodded to her.

The rest of the procedure happened quickly. I didn't open my eyes until the stitches around the new cuts had been put in place. Already, the central line felt weird, but I knew it would become just another appendage once I got used to it.

"All done," Dr. Lowell said as he straightened out the bed. "Can you sit up?"

Leslie, still holding my hand, helped me up. I felt dizzy and light-headed. The room began to spin. I shook my head, and Leslie guided me back down. Feeling the burn rise in my throat, I squeezed Leslie's hand twice—our code. It was the price you paid for having the hospital nurses as your best friends. As soon as I rolled to the side, Leslie had the wastepaper basket ready. The worst part wasn't the upchuck, actually; it was the lingering bile aftertaste.

I released my grip of Leslie's hand and swung both of my arms over my eyes. Inhaling deeply, I let the air out in a small stream. I just needed a minute.

The first time, Dr. Lowell had showed me a video of the procedure, and I panicked. I'd almost run from his office screaming. And I would have… if I hadn't passed out first. When I came to, the central line had already been placed.

The second time, I cried and threw up during the entire procedure. All things considered, I aced it this time.

I reached down and touched my new appendage involuntarily. I knew what it felt like, but my hand went to it anyway. Feeling it there, protruding from my chest like a lamp cord, made everything more real. Until now, it hadn't been hard to convince myself that the last few days were just a dream. In a dream, you can pinch yourself and wake up. Now that I had needles and wires pushed through me, I couldn't pretend anymore. This was real.

"Are you ready to head down to X-ray?" Dr. Lowell asked.

I sighed and let Leslie help me up. Dr. Lowell had a wheelchair ready. I hated being rolled all over the hospital, but honestly, I was in no condition to be walking. I sat down like a good patient and allowed Leslie to wheel me down to the second floor where the technicians would X-ray my new decoration, making sure of its correct position. I had no doubt of its perfect placement, though. Dr. Lowell was one of the best pediatric oncologists in the nation. That's why we'd moved here.

After confirming the line's faultless position, Leslie taped it down. She wheeled me into another small room with a couple of reclining chairs, a bed, and a sixty inch TV hanging on the wall. I moved myself to one of the leather recliners and got comfortable. My black diary lay in my lap, ready for my next entry. Leslie attached the chemo drip to my newly placed central line.

"Apple juice or orange juice?"

"Orange."

"You need to drink it all, Kate," Leslie warned. "I know you. No one else is here today for you to give it to, and I hate cleaning out wastebaskets filled with juice."

I rolled my eyes. "Fine. I'll drink it."

"And I'm bringing you some crackers, too." She walked out the door before I could argue.

Alone, I opened my diary and read the last entry. I needed to write about how I felt, but right now, I just felt numb—and a little hungry. Even though I didn't want to admit it, I was thankful to Leslie for offering crackers. I hated inconveniencing her.

I toyed with my pen, bumping it on the paper and then sticking the end in my mouth. I didn't know what to write. My mind was blank. No, I didn't want to be here. Yes, this really sucked.

That's all I had. Maybe I could blame it on my empty stomach. I felt detached—another reason to side against the dream—like a ghost watching a complete stranger. There was no connection. That was probably what they meant by an "out-of-body" experience.

The click of the door brought me back from numbness-world. Maybe the crackers and orange juice would help stir some real emotion to write down.

"Thanks, Leslie," I said, looking up.

My heart had never technically stopped before, that I knew of (and I'm pretty sure I'd know *that*), but at the sight of him, I wondered if it just had. It was like one of those movies where the woman dies, and the super-hot guy started performing CPR. Then, her heart suddenly began to beat, her eyes flew open, and the first thing she saw was the man of her dreams giving her mouth to mouth. Unfortunately, the gorgeous dirty-blond with sapphire eyes standing in the doorway wasn't kissing me. The rest of it was accurate, though.

"Oh, sorry. I didn't know anyone was in here." He smiled. "Hi. I'm Damian."

Chapter 2

November 1

Dear Diary,

Damian, Dr. Lowell's son, is volunteering at the hospital. Apparently, he got lost and ended up in the chemo room with me. I didn't mind. At. All. Granted, his sandy-blond hair is spiked with too much gel, but he looked hot. Way hot. Even in his oversized sky blue scrubs.

He stayed in the chemo room long enough to ask my name and where the storage room was. His eyes kept darting to the chemo drip hanging from the IV pole beside me. I don't know, maybe since he's the son of an oncologist, I expected more. He seemed uncomfortable, like he didn't want to be there. I guess I can't blame him for that.

I wonder how often he's there. If I'll get to see him again. Yeah, I know, it's stupid, *but I can't seem to help myself.*

Is it too much to hope that maybe, just maybe, he could look past the cancer and see me?

~*~

On Thursday, I almost skipped into the hospital. That was a first. As I walked down the hall to the dreaded chemo room, I kept glancing around, hoping to catch some glimpse of spiked blond hair. I saw nothing. No sign of over-sized sky-blue scrubs, either. I noticed that the spring in my step disappeared, and I entered the chemo room, ready to be hooked up like a hose.

Leslie grinned at me when I walked in. "How are you today, Kate?"

"Eh," I answered as I sat down in the blue chair. "Alone again?"

Leslie nodded. "For now."

"That's good, though, right?" I asked as Leslie snapped the tube to the line imbedded in my chest.

"Yeah. It's good. Lots of kids in remission."

I debated asking Leslie about Damian. Would she even know? I didn't want to seem like I was overtly interested, but Leslie had been there for me for years. Holding my hair back as I puked my guts out had to count for something, right?

"Do you know anything about Dr. Lowell's son, Damian?" I asked, not meeting her eye, and not watching her hook the tubes together either.

"You don't want to get mixed up with Damian."

"Why not? What's wrong with him?"

Leslie sat down in the empty recliner beside me. "Damian is here so his father can keep an eye on him. Dr. Lowell's wife and oldest son, Liam, died in a car accident two years ago. Damian's been unraveling ever since."

The wedding photo of my doctor and his wife that sat on his desk flashed through my mind. "Oh, I didn't know..."

A wave of pity washed over me. How horrible it would be to lose your wife in such a tragic, unexpected way. And even worse to have to bury your son at the same time. I had appointments with Dr. Lowell during that time. His pain never showed. Dr. Lowell was a pediatric oncologist, though—his job centered around dying kids and trying to save them. It was horribly ironic that he could save others' kids, but not his own. How devastating.

And Damian? He had to be my age. Fifteen back when it happened, and to have suffered so much loss. My heart ached for him. Of course he would be unraveling. Who wouldn't?

"Um, maybe, if he's still hurting, then—"

"Katie," Leslie interrupted, "it's more than that. He's...well, he was kicked out of Dowling High School, and now he's been expelled from Lincoln. It's only gotten worse. He's been arrested twice this year."

Arrested? Damian's a criminal?

"What did he do?"

"I'm not sure what he did to get booted out of Dowling, but his father had to leave here to bail him out of jail for stealing a car two months ago. Last week, Damian got picked up for public intoxication and destruction of private property—here at the hospital, no less."

"The window down the hall?" I asked, remembering workers there the day Dr. Lowell had told me my latest numbers.

Leslie sighed. "Courtesy of Damian Lowell."

I nodded, taking it in. He didn't look like a troublemaker. I thought about his smile and the way the deep dimples on his cheeks gave him an innocent look. Imagining him in a jail cell wearing an ugly orange jumpsuit entered my mind. It didn't fit. My image of a bad boy included black leather jackets, motorcycles, tattoos up and down his arms, more earrings than me, and a cigarette poking out his mouth. But what did I know? I'd spent most of my life in a hospital on drugs. And because of that, I was invisible at school. *I* was the person to avoid.

Leslie interrupted my thoughts. "Orange or apple?"

It took me a second to realize that she spoke. "Uh, apple," I said without looking up. After the door clicked shut behind her, I sunk into my seat. I tucked my legs underneath me and pulled out my diary, staring at it.

When Leslie came back in with my plastic cup of juice, I thanked her, still lost in thought. If Damian was hurting, why did that mean I had to stay away from him? Maybe he needed a friend, someone to relate to.

Granted, I didn't know what it was like to lose a parent or sibling, but I knew about pain—and how in one single moment, your entire life could be flipped upside down. And I understood about being an outcast. How everyone felt so sorry for you, and the only way they knew how to respond was to ignore you or give you sad looks and sympathetic smiles.

I watched the door, hoping he'd get lost again. But the only person who walked through was Leslie at the end of my two-hour treatment.

I went to bed that night thinking about Damian and feeling guilty for ever being sorry for myself. He had lost so much more than I. At least I still had my whole family for support. Damian only had his dad left, and maybe that wasn't enough for him.

The sickening effects of chemo punched me in the gut over the weekend. Energy drained from me like water down a sink. I was tired and weak, barely wanting to get out of bed. My stomach began to turn early Saturday morning and didn't stop until Sunday night. Mom helped me to the bathroom and kept the small wastebasket next to my bed empty for when I couldn't make it to the toilet.

She also brought me a stack of books from the library, but they remained untouched on my nightstand. A few times I reached for my diary. I jotted down some notes about not feeling well and tried to stay strong, especially in front of my mom.

Damian crossed my mind a few times. When I pictured him in my head, he silently reminded me of how blessed I was. I barely knew him, yet that weekend he gave me strength. Maybe, somehow, I could return the favor. Even though Leslie said not to get involved with him, that didn't mean I couldn't talk to him if I happened to run into him.

It's not like he'd ask me out on a date.

What does 'involved' *even mean?*

On Monday I felt decent enough for half a day of school before my next treatment. I didn't see Damian that day or on Thursday. Finally I was resolved to speak with him, and now I hadn't seen him. I wandered the corridor with my IV pole traveling around with me like an unwanted companion.

I had stopped at the nurses' station to talk with Leslie. Part of me wanted to come out and ask about Damian, but maybe that wasn't such a good idea. Like Leslie had said, the only reason Damian volunteered was so that Dr. Lowell could keep an eye on him.

"How are you feeling, Kate?" Dr. Lowell asked on his way to make rounds.

"The weekend wasn't good, but I'm feeling better today."

He studied me over the rim of his glasses. "Well, don't forget I have you on a more potent dose than two years ago, so it's very important you take it easy."

Yeah, I thought. It didn't get any easier than lying in bed, throwing up all weekend. I didn't want to strain myself with over-activity or anything.

A small snicker escaped me. "Okay, I will."

Dr. Lowell made a humming noise in his throat. "I mean it, Kate. Your immune system won't be able to handle much more than a very basic cold."

"I know," I insisted. "I'm taking it easy."

"All right." Dr. Lowell sighed, and then asked Leslie about someone's test results.

Leslie followed me back to the chemo room where she unhooked me, forced me to drink another glass of juice, and reminded me of what Dr. Lowell had said earlier. I rolled my eyes.

I never found Damian. Maybe he avoided the cancer floor. Or his father.

Disappointed, I walked out to my car. Surely Dr. Lowell hadn't expelled him from the hospital. That would be counterproductive.

I swept my fingers through my hair, knowing I had a couple more weeks with it at the most. The cold wind blew, and I caught a whiff of cigarette smoke. My stomach started rolling. *Just make it to the car*, I thought. *Almost there*. Even as I said it to myself, I knew I wasn't going to make it. And what if I did? I couldn't puke in the backseat of my yellow Volkswagen Beetle. Instinctively, I twisted my hair back. I ran toward the small patch of grass just a few feet ahead of me. Luckily, I only had apple juice in my stomach. It didn't take long to empty. When I straightened up, I looked around, hoping no one saw.

That's when I noticed him.

Walking toward me, stepping on his cigarette, was Damian.

I had two options: pretend I didn't see him and beeline to my car, or wait for him to acknowledge he'd witnessed my little episode.

Our eyes locked, and I couldn't move. Crap. Too late for option one. Since our first meeting, I had worked out a whole conversation in my head about mundane things, none of which centered around vomit. Now, he'd seen me throwing up in the hospital parking lot, and I had caught him smoking on a smoke-free hospital campus. Not great conversation starters.

"Hey," he said, stopping in front of me. "You okay?"

I nodded, wishing my breath didn't smell as horrible as I thought it did. "Yeah. Thanks."

He cocked his head to the side in recognition, dark lashes partially concealing the blue behind them. "I know you."

"I, uh, showed you the store room a couple weeks ago." As I said it, I seriously turned around and pointed to the hospital as if he didn't know it loomed behind us.

Nope, definitely not how I had imagined this little chat. I felt awkward, but Damian looked completely at ease, standing casually in faded blue jeans and his oversized hospital scrub top.

"Oh, yeah. Kate, right? You sure you're all right? I can take you inside or something."

"No. It's fine. Thanks." I smiled. He was concerned. How sweet. And he remembered my name. Even sweeter.

"You sure? It's kinda my job." He tugged on his uniform for emphasis.

"No. Really. It's okay." I cleared my throat. He wasn't walking away. "So, do you volunteer here every day? I haven't seen you around."

"Every damn day," he sighed, not offering more.

"You don't want to be here, do you?"

He shook his head. "I don't like hospitals."

"Me neither," I said too quickly, biting my lower lip. "It's boring, smells bad, and there's lots of needles."

He grinned. "I eat supper here every night. Trust me, there are worse things in that building than needles. Hopefully you haven't had the pleasure."

I chuckled, and Damian started laughing with me. Just like that, the tension disappeared.

"You're right. I've never been able to keep hospital food down," I said, still giggling.

"Maybe it would be more bearable if I had some company." He brushed a wind-blown strand of hair out of my face. My breath caught at his touch. It was surprisingly gentle.

I blushed. "Yeah. Maybe. Distract you from the taste, at least."

He curved up the corner of his mouth. "You here often?"

"Every Monday and Thursday for the next ten weeks."

"Ouch. Well, I guess I know where to find you on Monday."

Chapter 3

November 12
Dear Diary,

I woke up this morning to a large clump of hair on my pillow. Even though I knew it was coming, I wasn't prepared. The first time my hair started falling out, Mom kept a little of it in a bag and put it in the FIGHTER scrapbook she'd made for me. This time, I balled it up in my hands, stared at it for a few minutes, then threw it in the trash. I keep telling myself, "It's only hair. It will grow back." Because sometimes, the mini pep talk actually works.

In the shower, I took great care washing it. I used extra conditioner and brushed through it as lightly as I could. My efforts weren't enough. More hair than usual ended up in the drain. When I got back in my room, I changed my mind and yanked *some strands out of the garbage. I placed them in a plastic bag for Mom.*

It's only hair. It will grow back.

I cried.

A girl at school asked me how I was feeling today. I didn't know how to respond. No student has ever asked me that before. I told her I felt fine and thanked her for asking. She nodded politely then walked off to her next class. I wish now that I would've asked her for her name.

I hope I feel good this weekend. Mom wants help getting ready for Thanksgiving, and I don't want to sit on the sidelines. Besides, my Pinterest-inspired mother has a way with helping me keep my mind off things.

Curiosity got the better of me, and Friday night I spent the evening in my room with my laptop searching the archives of the *Des Moines Register*. Sometimes it reported on fatal car accidents in the state. If not, it would surely have an obituary.

I found a small article dated two years previous on April 21. The *Register* said that a vehicle with two passengers, Nora Lowell and her son, Liam, had lost control during a thunderstorm and hydroplaned into the interstate barrier. Both passengers were killed on impact.

I also found their obituaries in the paper dated a few days later. Liam was eighteen when he died. A year older than me now. He had just been accepted into the pre-law program at Yale. Mother and son had a dual funeral service.

I stared at the screen. Even in black and white, the picture of Nora showed a striking resemblance to Damian, and even more to Liam. The brothers looked so much alike that they could have been twins. I traced my fingers over Liam's picture on the screen. Were he and Damian close, like I imagined brothers being? A lump rose in my throat, and I stifled a sob as I closed my laptop. I threw back my violet comforter and fell asleep with my jeans still on.

On Saturday, I felt surprisingly good, health-wise, anyway. I helped my mom bake pumpkin pies from scratch to put in the freezer for Thanksgiving. For some moms, putting decorative piecrust leaves around the edges and in the middle was a bonus. For my mom, it was a necessity for the perfect pie. As the three pies baked, I helped her make a beautiful centerpiece for the table. My mom was so crafty—I could barely cut a straight line. But I think I did a smash-up job placing the glue dots in precisely the right spots on the homemade cornucopia.

Knowing the stupidity of it, I hung onto Damian's words of a visit on Monday all weekend—even if it was just his job. I kind of wished I'd left my gloves at the hospital so that I'd have an excuse to see him sooner.

~*~

Leslie left the room for my orange juice. I settled in for the next two hours, wondering if Damian would show up. My wondering didn't last long. Damian, wearing sky blue scrubs that brushed nicely over thick biceps, walked in holding a plastic cup of orange juice.

Don't stare!

"Leslie said, 'no peach schnapps.' Sorry," he said, smirking and handing me the cup.

I smiled, half-surprised to see him. "Thanks for trying. It's probably better for you this way. I'm not sure how well that would mix with this." I pointed to the bag hanging from the pole.

"So, what is that stuff, anyway?" Damian shot a glance up to where I pointed.

"A very potent chemotherapy drug."

Damian sat down beside me. I could smell the smoke on his clothes. He tried to cover it up with too much cologne. I ignored the slight stir in my stomach.

"Does it hurt? Having cancer?" His eyebrows furrowed.

"No, it doesn't hurt. I can't feel that I have it. I just feel the side effects. It's sort of like having a flu that doesn't go away."

"How long have you had it?"

"Dr. Lowell...I mean, your dad, diagnosed me with ALL—Acute Lymphatic Leukemia—when I was eleven. We did chemo for almost six months, and I went into remission, so my white cell count was back to normal. Then it came back two years ago. We did another round of chemo, and again I went into remission a year later. Now it's back."

"You talk about it like you're okay with having leukemia," he said, confused.

I shrugged. "I've tried crying, screaming, throwing things, avoiding people. It is what it is. I didn't choose to have cancer, but it happened."

He let out a puff of air as his eyes drifted over me. "Damn, I couldn't do it. Being here all the time, letting the nurses poke and prod you like you're a cadaver."

"You would if you had to." I shifted in my seat.

"You've been doing this for, what, seven years? Wouldn't it be easier just to give up, live while you can, do whatever the hell you want, and not be held back by shit like drugs and appointments?" His voice rose as he spoke.

I fidgeted with a tube, giving myself a second to try and figure him out.

"Sometimes I think that," I answered calmly. "Every time I go out of remission, getting back in gets harder. I've gotten sicker each time. The chemo gets stronger while I get weaker. So, yeah, it would be easier to say I don't want to do this anymore." I looked around the room. This wasn't the conversation I had envisioned. Yet, somehow I didn't mind it.

"I could go to Disney World. See Greece. Climb Mount Everest. Swim with dolphins. Watch a volcano erupt. And not be sick for any of it. Enjoy the time I have left. Or be sick and then die, and not do any of those things. But I hang on to the hope that I can do it all, not be sick, and not have

25

cancer."

"I don't think the statistics are on your side."

I opened my mouth to retort then closed it. Most people, when they learned I had leukemia, grimaced and told me they were sorry, and encouraged me. Other than with the hospital staff, I'd never had a conversation like this before. I appreciated his bluntness.

I sighed. "I know the stats, and they get scarier every time I have to come back here. But I have people counting on me. Someone fills that small percentage. Why shouldn't it be me? Staying positive is medicine, you know."

Damian looked solemn. He was the son of my doctor, and I wondered how much he knew—how much Dr. Lowell talked about his work and the survival rates of patients.

Damian's gaze settled on me. "Your file was sitting on Dad's desk, so I flipped through it."

My eyebrows shot up, surprised and actually a little thrilled that he took the initiative.

"It says you're on the bone marrow transplant list."

I cringed. During my last lapse, my best friend was Molly, a nine-year-old girl who had her chemo treatments the same days as me. When I went into remission, she wasn't showing any signs of improvement. Dr. Lowell put her on the bone-marrow transplant list, a list with over ten-thousand names. No suitable donor was ever found. I went to the hospital during her treatment times to keep her company until one day, she wasn't there. It rained the day of her funeral. She would have liked it—she loved the rain.

"Yes," I said, pushing Molly's memory away. "It may be my only chance. And if I get it, my stats increase."

He scoffed. "It's one helluva list."

"It is. But there's always hope."

"Your folks aren't a match?"

I swallowed. "No, they're not. They got tested last time. Their HLA type isn't compatible."

"So, how do you get a compatible HLA?" His dimples deepened when he talked. It was hard to ignore.

"The best matches come from siblings. I don't have any."

His playful grin faded. "Yeah, me neither."

The words hung in the air for a moment. I stared at the linoleum.

Damian spoke quietly. "I admire you. You're strong."

I was strong because cancer is resolute, and I didn't want the beast to win.

"Now you know me. How about you? What's your story?" I asked.

Damian sighed and adjusted his nametag. "I'm the son of Jackson Lowell, Doctor Extraordinaire. That means I have a lot of time to myself. I play the guitar. Write music. I've beaten every *Assassin's Creed* game. And I don't live up to my father's expectations. Hell, I don't know if I live up to anyone's expectations."

"I'm sure your dad just wants you to be happy."

Damian grunted. "Whose definition of happy? His? Mine?" His eyebrows rose. "Yours?"

I shrugged. "Doesn't happy only have one definition?"

"Does it? Are you happy?"

I thought about it for a few moments. I had beaten my disease twice before, and I was determined to do it again. More than anything, I was happy just to be alive. "Yeah, I am."

His eyes narrowed. "Having a tube sticking out of your chest, being hooked up to toxic drugs, getting sick—that makes you happy?"

"Oh, well, no. But…"

"Not that easy, is it?" The edge in his voice pricked at me. I couldn't tell if he was talking about me or himself.

"The outcome of—"

"You don't *know* the outcome." He sounded angry, his eyes blazing. "You only *hope* it will make you happy, when it might kill you. That's reality."

I pulled my lips tight. "True, but it makes my parents happy to see me fight."

"Bullshit. They're not happy having a daughter who has to battle cancer. And if you die, well, how can they be happy about that?"

"If—"

Damian cut me off. "Yeah. If. So much is based on that word, and there are no fucking guarantees attached to it. What makes you happy now may be what destroys you later. Or those you love. Then what? Sometimes, being happy isn't worth the risk."

"And sometimes it is," I said quietly.

Damian brightened again, offering a slight smile.

"See what I mean? Nothing in this shithole life is easy."

"Just because it's not easy, doesn't mean it's not worth it."

"So tell me then: *is* it worth it?" His blue eyes searched mine. "Worth all the time in this place?"

It was a question I'd asked myself many times. One I didn't have an answer for. Sometimes it didn't seem worth it. If I fought and lost, no one gained anything. I'd have wasted the last years, months, weeks of my life on hoping. I'd be dead, my parents would be heartbroken. No one would win. If I stopped fighting, went off the chemo and accepted my fate, I could enjoy my last moments on this earth. My parents could enjoy them with me, making memories they could cling to long after I was gone. But if…

What if I kept fighting? And won? Then we all won. The chances were slim, I knew that. Wasn't it worth holding on to, though?

I stared at the wall in front of me. "I don't know."

"I could do what makes me happy now and risk being miserable later." I felt Damian's gaze on me as he spoke. "Or I could please the good doctor and be miserable now. Choices come with consequences, some good, some bad. It's risky, and it's always, *always* based on if."

I swallowed hard and took a sip of my juice before lifting my eyes to him. "Does your dad want you to be a doctor?"

Damian scoffed. "I'm sure he would. He had his career picked out when he was my age, med school and everything. Me, well, I'm just hoping to graduate." He tugged up the corner of his mouth, showing off his gorgeous dimples.

My stomach tightened. *Not now. Not in front of Damian again.*

His smirk faded. "Hey, are you okay? You're white. I can get Leslie."

I shook my head. There was no time. I shot my hand down beside me but the wastebasket wasn't there. Oh no! I leaned forward and heaved. When I'd finished, I noticed Damian on the floor in front of me, holding the basket with one hand, his other resting on my thigh.

His eyebrows shot up. "Feel better?"

I nodded, surprised that he was there. His gaze was kind, his expression soft.

"Can I get you some water or something?"

"Yeah. Please."

The door opened and Leslie walked through. It only took her a millisecond to analyze the scene before she rushed over.

"You all right, Katie?" She picked up the full garbage can. "Do you need some water?"

Damian appeared next to her, holding a Styrofoam cup. "I've got it."

Leslie watched as Damian handed me the cup. She looked sideways at him and then at me. Her mouth opened as if she was going to make a comment then decided against it.

"We're fine." He took the empty cup from me, then faced Leslie.

What? Did he just say "we" were fine? As in, him and me together?

"Well," she drawled out. "Uh, I guess if everything is under control, I'll just…"

Leslie looked at me and sighed. I nodded, hoping to reassure her. I knew what she thought. The look in her eye said, *Be careful, Katie.* Leslie took a final glance at Damian before she walked out.

"I'm real popular with the nurses around here," Damian jeered at the closed door. "Especially that one."

"She's just protective. This is the last place she ever wants to see any of us who've been here and left."

Damian sat down beside me and grunted. "I doubt that."

"You doubt what?" My eyebrows furrowed. "She cares about us, Damian."

"I didn't say she didn't," Damian snapped, his blue irises drilling into mine.

"Then what did you mean?"

"The last place she wants to see you is in a coffin." His words were hard and fell to the floor. As soon as he said them, his sad gaze shifted to his feet.

Was he thinking about the last place he saw his mom and brother?

I didn't say anything. We sat in silence for a few minutes until he shifted his eyes to my lap. "What's that?"

"My diary." It sounded so childish when the words came out. "Uh, cancer diary. It's my cancer diary."

Yeah, nice cover-up, Spaz.

"So, you write down stuff about cancer?"

31

Damian asked, glancing at me.

"Yeah. A nurse in my mom's support group suggested it when I was first diagnosed."

"So, you've always written in one, huh?"

I wanted to brush it off like it was no big deal. Just a dumb diary thing. But, honestly, it was a big deal. It helped me more than anything else. "I know it sounds stupid, but the diary gets me. I can talk to my parents, or the nurses, but none of them have to go through this. In reality, I'm alone. So I write down how I feel about having cancer, about the treatment, the side effects, about stares and whispers from kids at school. About anything. It helps me cope—like three-dollar therapy between two pieces of cardboard."

Damian chuckled. "Cheap therapy."

I tilted my head to him and chuckled. "Yeah."

The door creaked open, and we both jumped. Dr. Lowell cleared his throat.

"Sorry to interrupt, but, uh, Damian, can I see you for a few minutes? In my office?"

I couldn't see Damian's face, but his hand curled into a fist. "Sure."

Dr. Lowell nodded at me, then the door closed. Damian shook his head and muttered something under his breath.

"Are we still on for dinner in the cafeteria?" he asked, standing up. "Crappy food, but hey, I'm paying."

I laughed. "Okay."

"When are you done in here?"

I glanced at the clock. "Forty-five minutes."

"I'll pick you up."

"See you then."

Damian flashed me a dimpled grin before he disappeared out the door.

Unable to stop thinking about him, I opened my diary and wrote about our conversation and how he had sat right there while I puked. His expression showed the normal reactions of concern and worry, but there was something else, too. Something I didn't recognize. I wrote about the feel of his hand on mine. How I couldn't decide if the butterflies were because of the chemo, the fact that I just finished throwing up, or because his touch felt amazing.

I was so engrossed in writing that I barely noticed Leslie standing next to me. When I looked up, I jumped.

"Sorry, Kate. I didn't mean to startle you."

"Oh. That's okay. I didn't hear you come in," I said, taking a deep breath.

"Do you mind if I sit?"

Odd. Leslie had never asked before. "Go ahead."

"I wanted to speak with you," she started. "About Damian." Leslie was older than my mother with two grown children of her own. She'd always treated me as an equal, but this was going to be a "mom" conversation, I could tell.

"I know you said to stay away from him. Really, it just happened. Nothing is going on, though. We're just friends." I fidgeted with the corner of my diary as I fumbled over my words. "I don't know if we're friends. I mean, we're not more than friends." I flushed.

Leslie's voice was soft. "Kate, Damian is in a lot

of pain."

"I know, but I don't think that's a reason to stay away from him."

"No, it's not." Leslie placed her hand over mine. "That's not why I said that."

"Maybe him getting into trouble is his way of reaching out."

"It is," Leslie agreed.

I was confused. Last time, Leslie tried to scare me into having nothing to do with him. Now, she suddenly agreed with everything I said.

"Then what? Why did you tell me to keep my distance?"

"I don't want to see anyone get hurt."

"I'll be fine. Like I said, there's nothing going on."

Leslie sighed. "Kate, I saw the way he looked at you. I've never seen him actually interact with a patient before. What he did for you in here, well, that's what scares me."

I shook my head. "It was just a kind gesture. Anyone would have done it."

"You're strong, and you can handle it."

"Okay…?" I didn't know where she was going with this. The expression on her face morphed from concerned to sad.

"Oh, Kate. I'm worried about what *you* might do to *him*."

"What…what do you mean?"

She glanced away, but not before I saw moisture in her eyes. Turning back to me, she cupped my hand in both of hers. "Damian is still mourning his mother and brother's death. It's destroying him.

34

He's destroying *himself.* Damian isn't as strong as you are."

Leslie fell silent. I watched as she pursed her lips. She squeezed my hand inside hers. "If he falls for you, and something happens to you..." Leslie swallowed hard. That's when I knew what she was going to say. That's when I understood her warnings.

I dropped my head, closing my eyes as Leslie finished. "If you die, if you don't recover...Katie, it'll kill him."

Chapter 4

"They might look like mashed potatoes, but I guarantee, they're not. I think they come from a box and are mixed with some sort of mashed turnip and white sand. May I suggest a baked one, instead?" Damian picked up a foil-wrapped baked potato and plopped it on my tray. He grabbed a dollop of butter in a paper cup. "The butter is actually real." He winked at me.

I giggled. In the back of my mind, Leslie's words repeated over and over again. *I saw the way he looks at you. He's never interacted with a patient before. If he falls for you and you die, it'll kill him.*

I just wanted to enjoy dinner. Okay, maybe *enjoy* wasn't the right word. Tolerate dinner. Enjoy Damian. But how could I enjoy being with him, stare into his ocean-blue eyes and not think I could kill him?

No. I shrugged inwardly. Leslie was obviously exaggerating. Still…Would I have one more person to disappoint if I couldn't fight hard enough?

One step at a time. Just concentrate on keeping

this meal down in front of him.

"Corn or broccoli?" Damian asked.

"Hmm." I shifted my eyes between the two. "I'll go with corn. Is that safe?"

Damian laughed. "Well, none of its safe." He scooped up a heap of corn for my plate and dumped another on his. Like with school cafeteria food, there was no end to the horrible hospital food jokes.

We found an empty table and sat down. "I still think you're risking your life with that meatloaf," he said.

"Well, I wasn't sure if that was chicken or cat meat." I nodded to the chicken strips on Damian's plate.

"It's hospital food, not Chinese!" He looked offended.

"Either way, I think we're doomed." I laughed.

"Cheers." Damian held up his glass of Mountain Dew.

Our glasses clinked as we hit them together, then we both took a sip.

"So, tell me about life before cancer," Damian said, taking a bite of his turnip and sand potatoes.

I tilted my head and eyed his spoonful.

He laughed. "I'm immune. Besides, I like sand."

"Well, during remissions, my dad and I would go to the country club and golf a lot. I don't think I'd mind joining the LPGA. My dad says I'm pretty good," I said, tipping my head up. "I really wanna make the varsity golf team at school this spring."

"Ugh. Country club brat, huh? You probably do everything your parents say, don't you?"

I forced a smile. After all they'd done for me, it

was the least I could do. "Your dad's a doctor; I'm sure you've swung a club or two in your day."

Damian grunted. "Cliché."

I raised my eyebrows at him and smirked. Damian licked his lips slyly, shook his head, and gave in. "Private golf lessons. Every summer. Since I was seven."

"I knew it!" I sat up.

Damian laughed. "I haven't set foot on a golf course in over two years."

"Why not?"

He shrugged. "I never played with my dad. It was sorta me and my brother's thing. And now…" Damian eyes clouded over, and his voice softened as if he just realized what he'd said. "Well, I don't play anymore."

Damian's head lowered, and he took a bite of his corn. I averted my eyes, embarrassed about bringing his brother to his attention.

"Maybe we can play together sometime?" I said, wondering if it would be enough of a topic change.

"I dunno. You'd probably kick my ass." He shifted his weight in his seat. Then he cleared his throat. "God, I need a cigarette. Uh, I'll be right back." He almost tipped over his chair as he stood and hurried out of the cafeteria.

I felt stupid as I watched him go. Alone, I plopped my elbow on the table and picked at the food. I ate a few bites then put the fork down.

Part of me wondered if he would come back. I'd hit a nerve, a memory of Liam. "*He's not strong like you, Kate.*" What a great first date. Was that what this was? No. I pushed the ridiculous notion from my mind. A guy sitting next to me in the chemo room and afterward meeting in the hospital cafeteria hardly counted as a date.

I ran my fingers through my hair, mulling it over. When I looked at my hand, it was full of auburn strands. I stared at it. Why did I do that? The hair was soft and beautiful, but it wasn't supposed to be intertwined in my fingers. What would Damian think of me with nothing but skin on the top of my head? "*I saw the way he looks at you.*" Would he look at me like all the kids at school? Feel sorry for me? Avoid me? I wouldn't blame him if he did.

Time passed at warp speed. I didn't remember him sitting back down as I was still staring at my hair-covered hand."It starts happening that quickly, huh?" Damian's voice was soft.

For a few moments, he didn't say anything, and I didn't look up. All I could think of was why I hadn't tossed the hair away. Now, not only had he seen me balding, he'd also seen my insecurity.

I lifted my eyes to him, nodded, untangled the hair out of my hand and wadded it up.

"I'm sorry," he said. "Some people do wigs, don't they?"

"Yeah. I don't. They itch," I said, dismissing how much it really bothered me. "It's just hair. It'll grow back. It always does."

"But you still have to deal with it falling out all the time until it's gone. That's just a reminder of what's happening."

Did he really just say that?

"Side-effect of chemo." I shrugged, hoping he

39

hadn't heard the crack in my voice.

I wanted to tuck my hair behind my ear, but I worried that another clump would fall out. Instead, I picked up my water and gulped it down.

Damian's phone rang—an old Journey song, something my dad listened to. He grabbed it then touched the screen. He tensed and shoved the iPhone back in his pocket.

"If you have to go…"

"No. It's just the old man. He can wait." Damian shoved a spoonful of food in his mouth. "So, where do you go to school?"

"Roosevelt." I hesitated. "You?"

"I'm between schools right now. I'll start at Valley in January."

I wanted to ask why he'd been expelled. Instead I blurted, "Why did you steal a car?"

Damian's eyebrows shot up faster than a rocket. "My favorite nurse told you, huh?"

"Sort of."

"Bitch," he muttered to himself. Then he grinned. "To see if I could."

Damian's phone rang again. This time he jerked it out, cursed, and switched it off. "I'd better go before the asshole pages me over the intercom."

"Yeah. That'd be embarrassing."

"Thanks for eating with me tonight," he said. "I'll see you Thursday."

He pivoted and walked away before I had a chance to say anything. I watched him until his sky blue scrubs were just a small speck down the corridor.

I shoved my tray aside and laid my head on my

arms, taking a deep breath. I wished that my life recorded itself like a DVR. The rewind button looked real good right now.

If only I had chucked the hair.

If only I hadn't run my fingers through it in the first place.

If only I could stop Leslie's words from repeating in my mind.

If only I hadn't mentioned golf.

The list went on and on. The rewind button would have been busy.

I sighed and dug through my bag, finding my diary.

November 15
Dear Diary,
Worst non-date ever!
What did I get myself into? I have no idea what I'm thinking! Sure, Damian pulled me in with his amazing eyes, and well, let's face it—he's gorgeous! But he's carrying around more Dixie cups than the medication cart.

Oh, and he's so not my type. Agh! Well, I guess I don't have a type. All I know is that I never dreamed I'd have a crush on a guy who smokes, apparently hates his father, has been arrested, and Lord knows what else. I think I've lost my mind. It's the only explanation.

Unless...hmm. I never thought of that. Do I see him as my charity case? Someone

41

I can fix? I don't know. At the same time, he held the garbage can while I hurled in it, for crying out loud. What teenage guy does that? I must be crazy.

I do like the fact that he's not afraid to challenge me. He doesn't treat me like I'm going to break. Or like I have cancer. I feel almost normal around him.

He knows my hair is falling out, and he didn't make a big deal of it. He knows who I am—the cancer patient—and still talks to me. I care about what he thinks and how he sees me. What I might mean to him. I wonder what he's doing now. If he's thinking about me. If he worries about me.

This makes no sense. I've never been more confused in my life!

~*~

Going bald in the winter was nicer than in the summer. I could usually find cute hats that went well with my outfits, and I was thankful that the administration at school made an exception for me to wear them to class. It cut down on the stares and sorry looks I got from my classmates. Generally, I took it off for treatments, since I didn't feel awkward on the cancer ward. In fact, it might be about the only place I felt somewhat normal.

My hair had thinned so much I was beginning to look like Gollum. I kept my black hat on at the hospital because Damian said he'd be there. Leslie didn't say much as she hooked the IV into the tube sticking out from my chest. I tapped my fingers on my diary and watched the clock. At four-thirty it crossed my mind that maybe he forgot or something.

At four thirty-five, I had given up on him, and at four thirty-eight, Damian twisted the knob and let himself in.

"Nice hat. I like the little, uh, flower thing." He pointed at my head.

I laughed at his odd hand gestures. Seeing him standing in the doorway lifted my spirits.

"Can you leave this room?" he asked. I peered around him and noticed the black bag he held behind his back.

I looked at him sideways. "Yeah. But the pole has to come with us."

"Eh. I suppose, if it must." Damian held out his hand to me. Reluctantly I took it, and Damian helped me to my feet before letting go.

"Where are we going?"

Damian held the door open. "One of the empty rooms."

I stared at him for a few seconds, biting the inside of my cheek. He had a quirky smile across his face, and his eyes danced as they stared at me.

"Oh, come on." Damian reached out and grabbed my hand again, tugging me forward. An odd-looking caravan walked down the hall: Damian pulling me and me dragging the IV pole. I wasn't thinking about where we were going or about the bag slung over his shoulder. I just enjoyed the feel of my hand in his. Never before had a guy who wasn't related to me or treating me held my hand. Damian didn't hesitate as if I were contagious. He just reached out and took it, and didn't let go.

We rushed past the nurses' station. I felt three pairs of eyes follow us—including Leslie's. Damian didn't seem to notice. We rounded the next hallway and swept into the second room on the right. Damian let go of my hand to close the door behind us, and I wanted the warmth of his touch back.

"What are we doing?" I asked as Damian took my hand again.

Oh, good!

"In here." He led me into the bathroom and locked the door. "Sit."

"On the toilet?" I looked down. "There isn't a seat."

"That or the floor." Damian put his bag on the counter and unzipped it.

"Are you going to tell me why you've locked us up in the bathroom?"

He grinned, facing me. "Your hair."

I shifted my weight. "My hair? What do you mean?"

Dinner on Monday flashed through my mind— me staring at the strands woven through my fingers and Damian's sympathetic eyes as he watched me. My growing feelings for him made me even more self-conscious. Now my hair was the reason we were locked in a bathroom together. Fantastic.

"I saw how you looked at it during dinner the other night. It must be annoying having to lose it little by little like that." His eyes were soft. He

44

pulled out a pair of scissors and an electric razor from his bag. "I thought it may be easier if you got rid of all of it in one shot. Then no more worries."

I had nothing to say for a few seconds as his words sunk in. He had been thinking about me. He'd come up with a plan. Wow.

He took a step closer. I felt his breath on my forehead. It smelled like smoke and spearmint gum. "What do you say?" he whispered.

I peered up into his beautiful eyes. I couldn't form words to tell him how wonderful I thought he was. How much I appreciated him thinking about me this way. I loved his idea.

I nodded.

Damian grinned, reached down, and slipped my black-knit hat off my head. After running his fingers through my hair a few times, he wiped a tear from my cheek.

Tingles shot up my spine, and I shivered at the touch.

He motioned for me to sit. I moved the IV pole behind the toilet and sat facing the tub. I felt Damian comb through the strands. He cut the hair, and I watched my auburn locks fall to the floor. Then he picked up a chunk and handed it to me.

"Here, do you want to keep some of it?"

I took it, purposefully touching his fingers. "Thanks."

I heard the clippers come to life and felt the metal against my head. My eyes closed, and I listened to the buzz as Damian shaved each individual hair from the top of my head. After a few swipes, he rubbed his hand over the bare skin. He repeated this gesture until all of my hair laid lifeless on the floor.

I spun around and peered into the mirror. Damian was putting the clippers back into his bag. I swept my hand across the top of my head. The reflection looked normal to me.

I glanced up at Damian. He had a glob of white lotion in his hand, and began to rub his hands together.

He grinned. "I wasn't sure if I should bring lotion or aftershave."

I laughed, thankful he chose lotion, and wondered if he'd really considered aftershave. His hands moved gracefully over my head. I cringed from the cold at first, but his warm hands caressing my head soon relaxed me, and I closed my eyes to enjoy the sensation. He rubbed the lotion in for a few minutes. His fingers moved down behind my ears, to my shoulders, and down my arms. His lips pressed against the top of my head. I swallowed. A wave of emotions washed through me. My hands were settled in my lap and his came to rest on top of mine. I didn't know whether to move or not. Should I flip my hands over and take hold of his?

When I opened my eyes, he was kneeling in front of me, gazing at me. "You look beautiful."

My eyes searched his. If it weren't for the butterflies flying around my stomach telling me otherwise, I would have wondered if he was being a jerk.

He reached up and caressed the side of my face. With a gentle tug on my hand, he lowered me down. I slid off the unromantic porcelain throne and sat on my knees on the floor. Damian placed both hands on either side of my face, his eyes locking with mine. He leaned in closer.

Were my lips dry? Were they supposed to be? What if I sucked at it? I hadn't brushed my teeth since that morning, and…

Before I had a chance to finish my thought, Damian's lips were pressed against mine. I closed my eyes, 'cause that's what happened on TV, and let my shoulders fall. More questions ran through my mind, the old ones forgotten. Was I supposed to breathe or hold my breath? What should I do with my hands? Should my lips stay closed or open? *Please, oh, please don't throw up!*

I kept my hands on my lap for a moment, but as Damian's mouth opened and sucked my lower lip between his, my arms wrapped around his neck on their own. He responded by moving his hands to my shoulders and sliding them down my arms. His lips moved over mine tenderly, then he folded his arms around my waist and hugged me against him.

When the kiss ended, I stared at him. Small shivers still raced down my spine, and my whole body tingled. Damian smiled. He kissed the tip of my nose, and his fingertips trailed over the side of my neck. My insecurity dissipated at the expression on his face.

"I saw the way he looks at you."

Now I could see it, too. It was the sparkle in his eyes. The way the corner of his mouth curved up in an impish grin. He leaned in and kissed my neck where his fingers had been.

"You taste good," he whispered in my ear.

It could have been the chemo dancing its way through my bloodstream because I was suddenly light-headed. Then again chemo didn't typically make me feel good.

Damian kissed me on the neck again, and I had never felt the little pin-pricks that covered my body before. I ached to have him kiss me again. I wanted him to envelop me in his arms and draw me into his body and keep me there forever.

"Damian isn't as strong as you are. If he falls for you, and you don't recover, it'll kill him."

I couldn't speak for Damian. And whether or not it was a good idea didn't matter. I knew the moment he pulled out the clippers and looked into my eyes that I was in danger of falling for Damian Lowell.

Chapter 5

November 18
Dear Diary,
He kissed me! A real kiss. One that left me breathless.

I can't get Damian's touch out of my mind. I can still feel where his fingers treaded over my skin, where his lips pressed against me. I'd give anything to have them there again. I've been lying in bed for the last three hours, staring at my ceiling and picturing Damian's Caribbean blue eyes. I don't want to get him out of my head, but I would like to fall asleep.

It felt so good to have him want me like that. I felt...normal.

I wish I didn't feel like this, though. We're different in so many ways. I hate that I love being swept up in him. I hate how much I want to be with him. I'm opening myself up to get hurt.

He's not good for me, I know that. But I also can't stay away from him. Maybe if I wasn't sick, then...

On the flip side, he's giving me another reason to fight this as hard as I can. Is that what I want, though? Someone else to disappoint?

My parents are counting on me, too. I don't want to let them down.

~*~

This time I really did forget my gloves at the hospital. Technically, I had another pair that I *could* wear, but retrieving my favorite ones gave me a great excuse to see Damian again. I didn't think I could wait until Monday, anyway. His face filled my dreams, and I woke up once in the middle of the night kissing my pillow...okay, twice...

I half-ran inside and took the elevator to the third floor, a giant smile plastered across my face. Would he be happy to see me? Would he kiss me again? Probably not in front of everyone. Maybe he'd walk me back to my car and kiss me there? It didn't matter; I just wanted to see him again. I hoped he wouldn't be too weirded out, it not being a treatment day and all.

The elevator ride to the third floor took forever. When the metal doors finally opened, I got out and walked to the nurses' station.

No one was there. I checked the chemo room, hoping to find Leslie. It was empty, too. I walked the length of the hall and found no one. All of the doors to the rooms were closed; they were usually open with the sounds of televisions and family members wafting into the hallway.

I opened the door to the Commons. Two young boys were playing *Mario Kart* on the Wii, and a little girl, receiving her chemo treatment, was sitting on the sofa reading a book. She wore a pink infant headband on her bald head.

She looked up. "Hi."

"Where is everyone?" I asked.

She shrugged. "Leslie just told me to stay in here. She said she'd be back in a little while."

"Oh. When was that?"

"I don't know, ten minutes ago? Dr. Lowell is in his office yelling at his son, though, so all the nurses are probably listening in. You know how they are."

My heart sank. "Thanks," I murmured.

I twirled around and rushed down the corridor to Dr. Lowell's office. As I rounded the corner, I saw Leslie, Tammy, and two other nurses attempting to look busy in the same spot. Leslie noticed me first and shook her head. I glanced away and stared at the cracked-open office door.

"What the hell do you care? You're never around, anyway." Damian's voice boomed down the hall.

"I'm doing the best I can. You're not making this any easier. At least *I'm* trying," Dr. Lowell yelled back, though not as loudly.

"You call working sixteen hours a day *trying*? Bullshit, Dad."

"I asked you to be here with me."

51

"No. You want me here to fucking baby-sit me."

"What else am I supposed to do, Damian? You got yourself kicked out school, I've bailed you out of jail twice, you show up here drunk, and now you're skipping your therapy sessions. I can't trust you."

"I'm such a goddamn disappointment to you, aren't I? If only Liam were here instead."

Thick silence filtered down the corridor.

"I didn't say that." Dr. Lowell's voice was quiet.

Damian jerked the door open. All of the nurses twirled their heads in different directions. My eyes stayed transfixed on Damian.

"No, Dad, you don't have to say it. You make it perfectly clear."

Damian spun on his heel and slammed the office door closed. He started walking down the hall—no way he wouldn't see me. He paused slightly, his eyes set on mine. His expression was hard and unreadable.

I opened my mouth to speak, but he pushed forward, swept past me, and swore under his breath. Leslie came up behind me as I watched him disappear down the hall.

"What happened?" I asked, still staring at Damian's wake.

Leslie shook her head. "It's not the first time. Before you, Damian showed up drunk every other day or so."

"That's what this was about?" I faced her.

She sighed. "It was about a lot of things."

"Thanks, Leslie," I said and started jogging after him, I'm not sure why. It wasn't as if I could do anything about the situation.

The look in his eye as he'd passed me in the hallway scared me. The voice that had spoken so softly to me turned cruel and edgy as he yelled at his father. I'd never dream of speaking to my parents that way.

I checked the cafeteria first. He wasn't there. I wandered around the first floor, poking my head into each of the waiting rooms. It was a large hospital, crowded with visitors and full of patients. Damian reeked of alcohol and probably wanted some place where he could be alone. I knew the third floor well, but the rest of the place was like a rat maze. After an hour of searching, I gave up. He obviously didn't want to be found.

I slipped on my hat and walked out into the cold November afternoon. It had begun to flurry, and the wind stung my cheeks. I shoved my bare hands into my coat pockets and stared down at my feet as I walked to my car.

It was a long trek to the back of the parking lot, the only place I could find a spot. My mind wandered, thinking about the Damian I saw today, drunk and screaming. I touched my lips and remembered the warmth of his kiss. The guy who had taken so much care cutting my hair, kissing my bare head, caressing me, couldn't be the same one I saw today.

"Hey."

I jerked my head up. Damian stood leaning against my car, smoking. He looked different, not wearing scrubs. His black Columbia coat and faded blue jeans fit him much better than his hospital get-up. I swallowed as I made eye contact. Did he look sad or were his pupils that dilated?

"I was looking for you," I said. "In there."

"I don't want to be anywhere near here." He stared off in the direction of the hospital and threw his cigarette on the ground.

"Yeah, I can tell."

"Wanna take me home? Doc confiscated my keys." He had trouble pronouncing the last words.

I nodded. "Sure."

I unlocked my yellow Bug's doors. Damian opened the passenger door as I slid behind the wheel. He stumbled only slightly getting into the car, but fumbled with the seatbelt.

"Fuck it," he muttered.

He gave up and I grabbed it and clicked it for him. He glared at me.

"I don't need a ticket," I said quietly.

"We wouldn't want Miss Perfect to have *that* on her record, now would we?" he grumbled under his breath.

I shifted my attention to the snowflakes circling around us. I didn't know what to say, so we sat in silence for a few minutes, letting the car warm up.

"You'll have to tell me where to go."

Damian didn't say anything. He just stared out the window. I could hear him breathing. Taking my hands off the wheel, I sat back in my seat. I didn't want to push him, so I waited. Eventually, he sighed and turned to me.

"Uh, I didn't expect to see you here today."

"I forgot my gloves."

So lame.

Damian reached down and unzipped his bag. There was a half-grin on his face as he pulled out my favorite pair of gloves. "I was going to give them to you on Monday."

If the smell of alcohol hadn't been burning my nostrils, I would've found the gesture charming. I took the gloves from him, touching his hand. "Thanks."

He bowed his head, refusing to look up when he spoke. "Hey, I'm sorry. Like I said, you weren't supposed to be here today."

"Damian, I don't even know what happened." I reached and placed my hand over his. He started to withdraw it but stopped. His eyes met mine.

"My dad and I haven't gotten along in a long time. Sometimes it just..." he paused and rubbed his forehead. "My mom and my brother died. They went out to get a birthday cake for The Good Doctor, and they never came home."

How drunk was he? Would he remember opening up to me tomorrow?

The idea spurred some bravery within me, and I squeezed his hand. "I'm sorry."

"It hasn't been easy."

"And the alcohol?"

Damian squinted at the floor and scoffed. He shifted in his seat before meeting my eye again.

"I get it."

"Get what?" he snapped.

"Losing everything in an instant. Wanting to run away from the emptiness inside."

Damian didn't say anything for a while. He stared at our entwined fingers. "I live on Lincoln

Place Drive. I'll show you."

We drove in silence, except for Damian giving me directions. I turned into the long driveway to a huge three-story brick house. I gaped at the size of it. It was beautiful, with white trimmed windows and evergreen shutters.

I drove up to the first garage door and shifted into park. Damian grabbed his bag and reached for the handle. The door swung open, and he swiveled. "You coming?"

"Oh, uh, sure." The invitation caught me off guard. I guess I'd assumed he'd rather be alone.

The foyer was bigger than my bedroom. My mouth dropped. No way could my parents ever afford even a fraction of the place. Damian must have noticed my awe as he was halfway down the hallway before coming back for me.

"It's just a stupid house. Come on." He grabbed my hand and yanked me into the massive kitchen. My eyes bugged out. It was Martha Stewart's dream kitchen, aka my mother's dream kitchen. Stainless steel appliances accented the black marble countertops and cream-colored cabinetry.

The grip he had on my wrist almost hurt. I tried to tear away, but he held on even tighter. "Damian, let go. You're hurting me!"

He dragged me over to one of the stools under the breakfast counter. I rubbed my wrist when he let go and plopped down on one of the stools. Glancing over, I saw Damian rummaging through the refrigerator. He yanked out two bottles of beer and started walking over to me.

"Oh no," I said, sliding down. I swiped them

56

before Damian had a chance to protest. "I'll make you coffee."

Damian's eyes shot daggers into me. I ignored him and put the alcohol back in the colossal refrigerator. The Keurig sat at the opposite side of the kitchen. I took a gander and opened the cabinet above the machine. Bingo: K-cups.

I faced him. "What do you want?"

He narrowed his eyes. "A beer."

I spun on my heel, rolling my eyes. "You're getting coffee. What kind?" The sternness of my voice surprised me.

"I don't care," he mumbled, slouching lower in the chair.

I grabbed a random cup and stuck it in the machine. "Coffee mugs?"

Damian scowled and pointed one cabinet over. He lowered his head to rest on his arms. I took two mugs, filling mine with hot chocolate and his with coffee. When both cups were full, I sat Damian's in front of him. He glared at it, glanced at me and took a sip.

We drank our beverages in silence. Every so often, Damian would eye the refrigerator, probably wishing he hadn't invited me in so he could be drinking his way to oblivion by now. He finished his coffee first and watched as I took a slow drink. When I put the mug back down on the counter, he reached for my hand.

"Come on," he drawled.

"Where?" I considered pulling away, but didn't.

"Upstairs." He stood up and tripped over the leg of the stool. I tried to let go of his hand, but he held on too tight. With a grunt, I toppled to the floor and landed on top of him. He started laughing.

"Couldn't wait, huh?" He licked his lips seductively and slapped my butt. "The floor might be a little cold, but I'm game."

Ugh...

He was drunk; I ignored him. He pushed my head down to kiss me. I ducked out from under his grip. Sure, I wanted him to kiss me, but I wanted him to remember it.

I crawled to my feet. Damian scoffed, swearing under his breath as he rolled onto his stomach, dragging himself onto his hands and knees. I offered my hand; he batted it away.

"I'm not a fucking child," he stammered.

If it hadn't been for the wonderful moments we'd shared, I would've been hurt. Instead, I blamed the alcohol and followed him up the stairs.

He rounded the corner to his bedroom. Staggering his way to his unmade bed, Damian slipped off his shirt, dropping it to the floor. My eyes were drawn to the tattoo on his bicep. The design looked Celtic. He crawled into bed and fell onto his back, eyes closed. Another Celtic design in the shape of a cross was burned on his chest. I wondered what they meant.

My eyes drifted over his body. Oh so perfect! My heart pounded, and I forced myself to look away.

I grabbed the black blanket and spread it over him. He opened his eyes, staring straight into mine. Still high on courage, I reached down and touched his cheek, running my fingers down over his lips.

He kissed my fingers, saying nothing. I dropped my hand, and Damian rolled to his side, taking the blanket with him. His shoulders soon rose and fell in a steady rhythm. I sat down beside him, rolling my fingers around locks of his hair.

More than anything, I wanted to take away his torment. Pain, even though it hurt, made us stronger—if it didn't destroy us first. I fought my disease harder each time because of the sting inside. I couldn't allow it to beat me. No matter how loud it screamed, I'd channel all of my energy into defeating it. I wanted Damian to do the same to his. Except right now, his pain was winning. And I didn't know how to even the score.

Or even if I could.

I looked around the room as I toyed with his hair. Two shot glasses and an empty bottle of Tequila sat on top of his night stand. The wall across from his bed was black, all the others were white. Large white stair-step shelving stood at the far left, a guitar leaned against it. Black curtains draped the windows, and a huge television hung on the wall across from his bed. Clothing, CD cases, shoes, belts, towels, and empty bottles of whisky were strung across the floor. It looked nothing like my room, which I kept OCD clean.

Eyeing the mess, I decided to tidy up a bit. At least make a pathway from his bed to his private bathroom. His breathing had steadied, and he started to snore. The soft noise made me smile. I debated for a few seconds, then I leaned down and kissed him on the cheek before I chickened out.

I stood up and started creating a trail by moving

59

stuff with my feet. At best I could get his shoes out of the way. My clean-freak-overdrive kicking in, I grabbed any CDs and Blu-rays I found lying on the floor. With a stack in my hands, I walked over to the white shelving and placed the stuff on it.

I glanced back at Damian; he looked so peaceful. I started making my way to the door, watching my step. My eyes skipped across the carpet. My breath caught when I noticed something on the floor beside the bed. A lump welled up inside my throat. There was no mistaking what I saw.

Nothing Damian did or said that day had stung until now. I was able to excuse it all. But seeing the black lacy bra beside his bed hurt even more than any cancer procedure I'd endured.

Chapter 6

November 19
Dear Diary,
Now would be a great time to have a girl friend to hash stuff out with. I don't know what to think. I mean, I know I'm new at this whole...whatever this is. Are we even in "friend" territory? Is it possible to go beyond friends without ever being friends? If this—whatever-thing—is nothing, then why does my stomach still feel so empty?

I guess I thought there was something behind what we shared the other day. You don't kiss someone the way he did and not feel something, do you?

Maybe I imagined it. Maybe it's been there for a few weeks. It doesn't look like he cleans his room much at all. Or...no, I'm an idiot. It's lingerie! Of course it means what I know it means. Should I just ask

61

him?

But the way he looked at me. And kissed me. And touched me.

I can't get his blue eyes out of my mind. Every time I close mine, I see his. They pour into me with such intensity. Argh. This is crazy.

I wonder how many girls he's invited up to his room. I was probably the next contestant on his list of "Player's Price is Right." I can't believe I fell for a guy like that. So stupid.

Now I have to get him out of my head. Should be easy, right?

Who am I kidding!

How do you stop liking someone? Can I just will myself to let him go? How do I forget his lips? Or his touch? Or how his eyes looked like they were memorizing my every feature? Is it possible to see him again and not burst into tears?

I don't think I want to.

Tears dripped onto the pages as I wrote. The more I wiped them away, the heavier they seemed to fall. Eventually, I gave up. Questions with no answers flooded my mind, making me more confused. My stomach weaved itself into a tight ball. Setting my diary aside, I grabbed the wastepaper basket. I heaved until my chest hurt.

Fire and ice burned in my veins. I picked up my

diary and chucked it across my bedroom. After it smacked against the door, I regretted throwing it. I waited a few seconds, hoping my mother wouldn't come up, wondering if I was all right. When she didn't come, I collapsed face down on my bed.

My pillow sopped wet with tears, so I turned it over and sobbed until the other side matched. No amount of crying would wash away the rejection.

In my mind, I replayed the afternoon. What if I hadn't gone inside? Or upstairs? Why had I wanted to organize his room? I would still be holding onto the false assumption that he cared about me.

My mother knocking on my bedroom door woke me up the next morning. I pulled the blankets up to my chest so she wouldn't see that I'd fallen asleep with my clothes on. No uncomfortable questions that way.

"Yeah?" I flipped onto my stomach to hide the signs of distress.

"Are you hungry?"

"Uh, no. I'm fine. Just worn out from the chemo."

"Okay, sweetie. Come down when you feel rested."

I nodded into the pillow.

As soon as the door clicked, emptiness engulfed me again, and the pain that was forgotten in sleep returned with all its fury. I wrapped my arms around my stomach, curling into the fetal position. Unlike Damian's way for numbing the pain, I would have to suffer through mine. Not fair.

It was past eleven in the morning when my cell rang. I fumbled for it, almost knocking it off my bed. The text was simple.

Thank you.

The number belonged to Damian. I cried myself back to sleep.

If I could have skipped my treatment on Monday, I would have. I didn't want to see him. What would I say? He didn't know what I had seen laying on his floor. He didn't know I knew, and I didn't want to be *that* girl.

I walked as slowly as I could to the third floor of the hospital, wondering why I hadn't just gone home. There were so many times I considered turning back, running to my car and speeding off. But Damian would be there the next time. And the time after that. And the time after that.

"I was starting to get worried," Leslie said as I passed the nurses' station. "You're thirty minutes late. Very unlike you."

"I know. Sorry." I didn't make eye contact.

"Well, let's get started."

I followed her to the chemo room, looking behind me a few times. Where was he? Part of me wanted him to be worried about my lateness, like Leslie. I pictured him pacing the hallway, or sitting in my chair in the tiny room, restless with his phone in hand. In my mind, it would be the proof I needed that he cared, that the kiss was real.

But I searched in vain. I spent my two hours alone, pretending to read my book, flipping through my diary and tapping my pencil on the arm of the chair. Minutes ticked by slower than ever. With flared nostrils, I fought the tears back. I pursed my lips together and made clock-watching my new hobby.

He isn't coming.

I bowed my head and sobbed. His not showing up vindicated the ache in my heart. No matter what I had convinced myself of all weekend, until now I'd held on to the hope that I'd been wrong. I wanted so badly to be wrong.

My stomach turned, and I threw up. Whether from the poison flowing through my veins or the hurt smoldering in my gut, I didn't know. Time stood still, allowing the pain to take over. I curled up in the chair and cried over someone I never had. Ridiculous.

The door didn't move until Leslie returned to unhook the central line. She must have noticed my puffy, red eyes, but she didn't mention it—probably because I didn't give her time. Her lips formed a straight line, and she sighed as she sat down beside me. Understanding her not-so-subtle ways, I jumped to my feet. I fumbled with my bag, stuffing my things in as I started for the exit.

In a defeated voice, Leslie reminded me, "Treatment on Friday this week, Kate."

Thanksgiving. Whatever.

"See you then," I muttered and walked out the door.

Stopping at the elevator, I pushed the down arrow half a dozen times as if it actually helped move the cables faster and waited. Most days the wait didn't bother me, but today, all I wanted was to crawl under my covers. Leslie's words rang in my head: *"You're strong, and I know you can handle it."*

I wasn't handling it. I was falling apart.

I lifted my head to the ceiling. *Stupid elevator.*

"Kate! Wait!"

I jerked around to look down the hall. Tammy, the new nurse, jogged toward me holding a long white box in her arms.

"I'm glad I caught you," she said, a soft smile on her face.

I stared at her. I hadn't really spoken to Tammy since she helped insert my central line. She spent most of her time with the kids who had to stay in the hospital. She handed me the box, which had a large red ribbon wrapped around it that tied in a perfect bow.

"What's this?"

Tammy shrugged. "The florist dropped it off about ten minutes ago. It has your name on it. Happy Thanksgiving."

Sure enough, *Kate Browdy* was scrawled across the top of the box in black ink. I scanned the top, moved the bow to the side, and turned it over. No sign of who it could be from. I began to pull at the satin when the elevator bell rang, and the metal doors opened. Six people already stood inside. Glancing between the bench behind me and the package in my hands, I tipped the box vertical and side-stepped into the elevator.

Not surprisingly, everyone got out on the first floor. Instead of taking my time, I hurried to the car. I tossed my bag in the backseat and laid the box gently on the passenger seat. The bow slipped off

66

easily. Clamping my lower lip between my teeth, I lifted the lid and gasped. Inside laid a dozen red roses. A blank white envelope sat on top of the thorn-free stems. Swallowing, I picked it up and turned it over in my hand.

I studied the flowers; they were beautiful. Someone cared enough to send them.

Who? Why?

The answer waited in the small pocket trembling in my hands. My breaths exited in uneven spurts. What if they were? What if they weren't?

With my eyes closed, I lifted the flap and pulled out the card inside. I held it in my hand for a few moments, hoping, before opening my eyes. The card was white with tiny red roses printed in the corners. I traced my fingers over the handwriting.

Out of town for the week, visiting grandparents. Meet me Saturday? My house. 6pm. Sorry about Friday. ~~I didn't know you'd be there.~~

Damian

I smiled tentatively and slid the card back inside the envelope. Picking up one of the roses, I lifted it to my nose and inhaled. My eyelids fell as the delicate petals glided over my cheeks like velvety satin. The weight in the pit of my stomach lifted a little.

The flowers looked beautiful in the vase on my night stand. When my mother asked, I told her the truth—just not all of it. I said they were from Dr.

Lowell's son who was volunteering at the hospital.

"He keeps me company during my treatments." I swallowed. "Sometimes."

"And?" The eagerness in her irises was crystal clear.

"That's it," I answered, my voice pitched higher than usual. *Crap.*

"Hmm."

I looked away. "Uh, I have some homework. I'd better…" An involuntary smile began to spread across my face. "See you at dinner?"

Before she could say anything else, I scurried upstairs and closed my door behind me.

~*~

On Thanksgiving, I got a text from Damian.

I'm thankful for you.

I didn't know the proper protocol for something like this. *Do I text back?* I decided to leave it alone, though I still thought about it for the rest of day.

Mom and I went Black Friday shopping as we always did, but I drove to the hospital by myself.

"Flowers from Damian?" Leslie asked.

I nodded. "Yeah."

"Kate," she started.

"I know. It's okay."

"That's not what I was going to say." She hooked me up to the IV.

"What?"

"I wanted to tell you that I think you're bringing

68

out the best in him."

Surprised, I turned to her, my eyebrows puckered. Did she seriously say that?

"I don't know…I mean, he's…he's still…It's…" I bit the side of my cheek. *Complicated.*

"Well, whatever it is, I think it might be working." Leslie smiled and left me to my thoughts.

Already exhausted from a day of shopping, I got up from the armchair as soon as Leslie left. Sliding my IV pole along with me, I climbed up on the hospital bed on the far side of the room and lay down. I pulled the diary out of my purse, but my eyes fell shut before I'd written a single word.

Chapter 7

I couldn't sleep that night. All of my insecurities came flooding back. Were the roses, the apology, a farce? Should I go?

When the sun came up, I watched the brilliant rays of citrine and garnet fill the sky. From behind the clouds, sprays of white light poured down to earth. When I was younger, I used to think that was when angels came down from heaven to ferry souls back up to the hands of God.

I wrote about the splendor of the morning skies. How blessed I felt to be able to see even one miraculous sunrise. I imagined what it would look like from the top of a mountain or standing in the sand, peering out over the vastness of the ocean. The sunrise calmed me. At daybreak, there was no room for anxiety, worries, or disquiet.

Feeling calm, I crawled back in bed and drifted to sleep. I awoke after noon to my mother knocking on my door.

"Hey, sweetie," she greeted me with a smile. "I wore you out shopping yesterday, didn't I? We shouldn't have been out so long. With you being back on chemo, I just didn't…"

"No, Mom," I said, rubbing my eyes. "I'm fine. Just didn't sleep well last night."

"I can bring you up lunch if you're hungry."

"That's okay. I need to get up anyway. I can eat with you and Dad downstairs. It's not like I'm helpless and dying."

"Kate." My mother's voice raised half an octave as she said my name.

"Sorry," I mumbled.

When Dr. Lowell first diagnosed me, my parents were overly protective, acting like I was Great-Grandma's priceless crystal vase, which sat wrapped in bubble wrap in a box in the china cabinet. The second time, they relaxed a little, but they never let me out of their sight. This time, my parents went about their business, and I went about mine. I preferred it this way actually—less pressure on me.

But every so often, that worried, sorrowful look would cross my mother's face.

I wanted to go to treatments, stay positive, and forget all the immature white blood cells that clouded my bloodstream. Already, I looked forward to spring when Roosevelt High would start team golf practice—a taste of normalcy.

I took a quick shower, threw on some jeans and a sweater, and headed downstairs. After lunch, I played a dozen hands of Rook with my mother. She had taught me to play when I was stuck in the hospital undergoing tests. Then we'd play during my first round of chemo. And my second. And my third. It became our favorite game. Sometimes Dad would play, and when he did, it was an easy win for me.

I took the bid and reached for the nest, making sure to keep my eyes on my cards. "By the way, can I go over to Damian's tonight?" After the words were out, I held my breath.

"Damian's?" I felt Mom's eyes drilling into me.

I cleared my throat. "Uh, yeah. He asked when he sent the flowers. Red's trump." I threw out the red 1, keeping my gaze down.

Mom played the red 7, and I pulled in the hand. "I thought you said it was just a hospital relationship."

I shrugged, putting the red 13 in the middle of the table. "It was—*is*. It *is*."

"So, is this a *date*?" Mom laid down the Rook, and I added both of our cards face down in front of me.

I shifted my eyes upward to her glowing face. "I don't know." I really didn't.

She played the yellow 8 next to my red 12 and sighed. "Things were less complicated when you weren't old enough to date. Can't you just stay my little girl forever?"

"Sorry, Mom. I don't possess that kind of power." I grinned, taking her yellow 10 and setting out the black 12.

"Be home by eleven." She pulled in the hand with the black 14.

"Thanks." I couldn't hide my smile.

"Dr. Lowell's son. I'd never have guessed," Mom mused.

Damian's house was a good half-hour from mine. Excitement and dread overcame me as I drove. This time, I noticed the towering houses, some with iron gates in front of the driveways, and sprawling brick walls. A few times I considered turning back, but for whatever reason I didn't; it had been over a week since I'd seen him. And he'd been drunk.

My heart pounded as I thought about seeing those blue eyes again. The way they looked into mine...wow! There was nothing about him that didn't make me drool. I mean, I'd already thrown up in front of him—twice!—what was a little saliva?

I pulled into his driveway and parked my car. The enormous house loomed before me like something out of a Wes Craven movie. If it was dark outside, the place would have freaked me out. I checked myself in the rearview mirror, adjusted my hat, threw on a little more lip gloss, and opened the door.

Then I closed the door. I leaned back against my seat and shut my eyes. What was I doing? Was I setting myself up for disappointment? Did the other girl know about me? Oh crap! Was *I* the girl he was cheating on his girlfriend with?

Maybe the kiss was just a mistake. And the flowers just a friendly gesture. And the text...I slumped deeper into my seat. Was the text just to make the bald girl with cancer feel like she was important?

I covered my face with my gloved hands, breathing into the cotton material. The thoughts in

73

my head were spinning in circles. Every part of me wanted to believe Damian genuinely cared for me— as more than a friend. The doubt rolled in thick, and there was nothing I could do to stop it.

When I opened my eyes, I took a deep breath and opened the door again. This time I stepped out of the car before closing it. I stared at the house for a few moments before I walked up to the front door.

I knocked, bit my lip, and almost turned back, but Damian answered too quickly. He stood in the foyer: jeans, a blue t-shirt that matched his eyes, and barefoot.

"Hey," he said, opening the glass door. The slight grin on his face accentuated his dimples. And his voice, oh! My heart melted at the sound.

"Hey." I pursed my lips and inspected the floor as I stepped inside.

"I'll take your coat."

I stuck my gloves and hat in the pockets of my bubble-coat and handed it over.

"Thanks," I replied, still refusing to meet his gaze, scared he'd captivate me more than he already had.

He laid my things on a bench in the foyer. "I almost thought you weren't coming."

I nodded slightly. "Thank you for the roses. They were beautiful." I stole a quick glance up at his face.

Was he blushing? "You're welcome. I noticed the rose on your diary and took a chance. Are you hungry?"

"Um." I hadn't known what to expect. The note hadn't gone into details, so I'd munched on some crackers and cheese on the drive. "Yeah."

He reached over and took my hand. "Come on, then."

His touch surprised me, and I almost pulled back. The warmth sent waves of electricity through me. I didn't want him to let go, but I didn't want him touching me, either. There were too many unanswered questions. I still didn't know if I was angry at him, or if I'd forgiven him.

Damian led me into the den. The dark curtains were drawn and the lights off. The fireplace danced with flames casting a glow over the room. On the floor lay a blanket with a vase of red roses in the middle, and two covered plates of food.

I squeezed Damian's hand without thinking. The place looked incredible, like something out of a sappy romance novel.

"Do you like lobster? You're not allergic, are you?"

I looked up at him. The corner of his mouth was turned up, and one of his eyebrows rose.

"I don't know, actually," I breathed. "Did you cook?"

He laughed. "Take out."

Damian led me to the blanket and motioned for me to sit. He lifted out a bottle of wine and poured himself a glass.

"I...," I started.

"Non-alcoholic." He tipped the bottle over my glass.

I smiled timidly. "Sure." Even though the atmosphere of the room was romantic and...well, gorgeous, I still felt like darting out the door, climbing into my car, and making a quick getaway.

The wine glass was in my hand before Damian put the bottle back on ice. I took small sips, making sure not to make eye contact. The wineless wine didn't taste all that great, but it gave me something to do.

"That good, huh?" Damian asked grinning.

Keeping my eyes on the floor, I said, "Uh, it's all right."

"Look, I'm not very good at this." He scratched his head and sighed. "You know, why don't we eat first—before it gets cold?"

Damian reached over and lifted the silver lid off my plate. Sitting in front of me, staring at me, was a giant lobster surrounded by rice and asparagus. I'd never had lobster before. I picked up my fork and poked at the hard exterior. It sounded hollow. Damian snickered under his breath as he watched me toy with the dead crustacean. I clicked on it again with my fork, this time harder. Sebastian flopped off my plate onto the blanket. Damian, who had just taken a drink, almost spit it out of his nose. I cleared my throat and lifted my eyes.

"Sorry." He bit his lower lip, balled up his hand, and rested his chin on it, covering the smirk on his face.

After lifting the bottom-dweller back on my plate, I jabbed my fork into a string of asparagus and stuck it in my mouth. Damian did the same. When my vegetables and rice were gone, I was left with the bright red bug. Since my host had yet to break into his, I was on my own to try to figure out how to eat the thing. I wondered if that was his plan—wait it out and have a good laugh.

I took a sip from my wine glass. My stomach growled. I didn't want to ask for help, so I took my fork and started poking at the hard shell. A chainsaw would have been helpful, but since I didn't have one in my pocket, I stabbed the lobster with my fork. It worked—sort of. I broke through the shell and small shards of red flew through the air. Damian chuckled, blue glimmers dancing in the light of the fire.

"There's an easier way," he grinned.

I glared at him. "Oh?"

"Want some help?" he asked, trying unsuccessfully to maintain a straight face.

I sighed, contemplating. No, I didn't want help, but I had no idea what I was doing.

Damian didn't wait for an answer. As soon as he'd asked, he was on his feet and sat down behind me, one leg on either side of mine. "Lobster's finger food."

He wrapped his arms around me, running his hands down my shoulders, all the way to my hands where he placed his over mine. At the same time, his lips moved in next to my ear. I could feel his breath on my neck. Instead of tensing up, my whole body relaxed. Without thinking, I closed my eyes, taking in his touch, his breath, his scent.

His lips pressed against my neck, and a soft moan escaped my throat. The noise surprised me. My eyes flew open, and without turning my head, darted to him. In the firelight, I thought I saw him smile.

He used my hands in his to pick up the lobster and pull off its claws. Slowly, he snapped the body in half and started pulling meat out of the tail. He took a small piece and lifted it to my lips. I blushed, opening my mouth. Damian leaned around me as I closed my lips over the white, succulent meat. The buttery goodness melted on my tongue. Apparently the look on my face satisfied him. He kissed my cheek before going back to work. I watched as he pulled the shell apart, alternating between lifting a sliver into my mouth and then his own.

We sat like that, in front of the fire, with Damian feeding me until I'd had enough. Leaning to the side to face me, he slid his thumb over my lips, upper then lower, then repeated it. His eyes followed his own movements. My abdomen stirred, and I shivered. I'd never wanted him to kiss me more than at that moment.

He didn't kiss me. Instead he stood up, handed me my wine glass, then took his and placed it on the end table next to the Victorian-style sofa.

"Wanna see a trick?" he asked, taking hold of the end of the blanket on the floor.

"Is this like the table cloth thing? 'Cause I've seen that one before." I scooted off the blanket and onto the hardwood floor.

"Something like that." He grinned and took the corners of the blanket, lifted, and dragged the whole thing behind the loveseat, revealing a clean blanket underneath. "Ta-da!"

"Amazing. *That*, I've never seen before!" I rolled my eyes, a smile beginning to spread across my face.

"And that's what makes it so special."

He picked up his wine glass and sat in the middle

of the new blanket, beckoning me to join him. I sighed and moved onto the blanket, yet keeping my distance. The talk would be coming. I took comfort in knowing it wasn't up to me to start the conversation; however, I was probably expected to at least say something. I had no idea what that "something" would be.

I hated winging it, but what choice did have? It's not like he sent me a script with the flowers. Surely, he wouldn't be following any of the tête-à-têtes I'd had with him in my head.

I crossed my legs and took a sip of wine. Damian sighed and looked at the full glass in his hands. He tapped his fingers against the bowl, making ripples in the liquid. I watched as he licked his lower lip and pulled it between his teeth. Adorable.

"There's some, uh, stuff, you should know," he said, keeping his head bowed. "About what you heard last week. About…"

The muscles in his jaw clenched. He circled his finger around the rim of his glass, staring at it.

"I like you, Kate. And," he shook his head slightly, cleared his throat, and finally looked up. "And because of that, you need to know…I mean, you already know what an ass I can be. But I wasn't always like that. Not before my mom and Liam died."

He dropped his gaze again before he continued.

"My dad, he, uh, he made all the funeral arrangements by himself. Besides that, he never really dealt with it, you know? It pissed me off, 'cause throughout the whole damn thing he didn't say a word to me. Didn't ask for help or what I thought. He didn't even shed one goddamn tear over them."

Damian's hand squeezed the stem of his glass, and I worried it would snap in two. His eyes drifted to the fire, then back to the clear liquid. I sat quiet, not wanting to interrupt his monologue; I didn't know what to say anyway.

"Liam was his favorite, you know? The apple of Dad's eye. He was going to be a lawyer, Liam was. Valedictorian. He had just been accepted to Yale. Son of a bitch was a fucking genius. And everybody liked him. Hell, there's a plaque dedicated to him at the homeless shelter where he volunteered. Even the homeless guys showed up to the funeral."

When he spoke, his eyes glazed over, and he never looked directly into mine for more than a second before dropping his gaze.

"I look a lot like him. But that's as far as our similarities went, even back then. Dad expected me to take Liam's place. Fill his giant-ass shoes. Become who he was. Instead, I became everything my brother wasn't."

He paused for a second and squeezed his eyes together. When they opened, they were a darker shade of blue.

"It hurt, you know? Every time I went to school, I saw Liam. When I came home to an empty house, I saw Mom in the kitchen and Liam studying at the table. I just couldn't take it anymore. My dad and I, we're each other's punching bags." Damian let out a soft chuckle before he continued. "He drowns himself in work and gets disappointed when I can't live up to his expectations for my brother.

"That's...that's what happened at the hospital when you showed up. I never meant for you to hear that."

The pain radiated off him like the heat from the burning wood in the fireplace. I wanted to reach out, caress his face. There was anger behind his eyes. And sorrow. So much had been taken from him in so little time.

"Were you and Liam close?" I asked, hoping he'd look at me.

He didn't. "He was my best friend."

"If it's any consolation, your dad's a good doctor."

Damian nodded and looked into my eyes. "He is. One of the best. There's no one better to take care of you." He ran his hand over my cheek. His Adam's apple rose and fell. "Come here."

Without thinking, I moved closer. His eyes locked into mine. I sat directly in front of him, my legs folded in front of me. He slid his hand down my cheek, behind my ear, and down the side of my neck. My lips separated as I inhaled, memorizing every touch.

All thoughts about how he felt about me, what I meant to him, if he was with someone else, were gone. This gorgeous bad-boy just opened himself up to me, allowed me into a part of his soul, and shared a piece of his pain.

"I'm, uh, sorry for the way I treated you when you drove me home. I...I was an idiot."

I nodded. I wanted to tell him it was okay, but nothing came out.

Damian's fingertips glided over the base of my

neck like a necklace. I swallowed. My body tingled at his touch. He moved his hand down my shoulder, my arm, and to my hip. The look in his eyes reminded me of the intensity of the first time he kissed me. I bit my lip.

His palm moved over my thigh, and I felt him tug gently under my knee. For a girl with no experience with guys, I instinctively knew what he wanted. I surprised myself when I untucked my leg and scooted forward. He guided it over his and wound it around his waist, drawing me closer as I folded my other leg around him.

I wrapped my arms around his neck. His lips pressed against mine in a kiss so full of passion, I had to hold on tighter. His hands clung to the back of my shirt, clawing at the material. The heat of the fire flushed my face, but the burning inside me seemed hotter. His lips moved to my neck, allowing me to gasp for air.

"Don't leave me, Katie. I need you," he whispered suddenly. "I'm gonna fuck up, but don't leave me. I…"

His mouth found mine again. My fingers ran through his hair with an urgency I'd thought only belonged to him. My body tightened, and my heart raced. When Damian broke the kiss and buried his face in my neck, I wasn't done. I wanted him to keep kissing me, to hold me closer to him.

His lips moved across the base of my neck before they stopped. He pulled me hard against him, his hands clenched in the middle of my back. With my eyes closed, I took several deep breaths, trying to calm myself. Damian's chest rose and fell heavily, his heart thudding.

He didn't look up, he just held me close, every so often kissing my neck. Time passed, and silence filled the room as the fire began to die down.

Chapter 8

November 28

Dear Diary,

My immune system is worthless. Apparently, I've caught the Thanksgiving flu everyone at school has. They'll get over it in a few days. I'll be stuck with it till May—if I'm lucky.

After my amazing date with Damian last night, I came home and went to bed. I awoke a dozen times in the middle of the night feeling like I'd fallen off a three-story building. It's been the same routine with every round of chemo. I get sick from the treatment, then I feel better because of all the pill-popping. After my immune system has been destroyed, I catch a virus I can't kick. You'd think I'd be used to it by now—I wish.

I tossed and turned most of the night, dreaming about Damian and our fire-lit dinner. And, of course, about his lips on mine. I don't have much experience in that department, but holy cow, he's an amazing kisser! There's no way it can get any better than that! It's easy to get lost in him.

I couldn't conjure up the nerve to ask about the bra on his bedroom floor. Stupid, I know. Disastrous, maybe. But how was I supposed to ruin the moment?

I'll ask. I have to, no matter how scared I am of his answer.

I tucked my diary under the pillow. Last night's date with Damian ran through my mind, making me smile.

If only this stupid flu hadn't come on!

It was past noon already. The sun hung high in the sky, peeking through the curtains. My entire body ached. I'd lost everything in my stomach in the middle of the night. A half-drunk glass of water sat on my nightstand, mocking me. My mouth felt full of cotton, but if 5AM was any indication, I wouldn't be able to keep down the other half, either.

The irresistible water called my name, though. My throat burned. I snatched the glass and drank the rest in one swig. It felt heavenly going down; the glass emptied too fast. I swung my legs over the side of my bed and wobbled to the bathroom down

85

the hall.

"Hey, honey," Mom greeted me. She took the glass from me and placed her palm against my forehead. "You're warm. Definitely not from the chemo. I'll get you more water. Go back to bed."

I nodded, mumbled a "thank you" and turned around. My legs almost gave out, and I had to cling to my bed so I wouldn't collapse to the floor. When I crawled between the sheets, I felt like I had just run the Boston Marathon. Not like I knew what that would feel like.

I rolled over and buried my face in the pillow, groaning. It wasn't long before I heard my mom enter and set the glass by the bed. She kissed the top of my head then closed the door behind her. I hated that this was a normal routine in our home.

The glass sat untouched, no longer sweet-talking me. It took too much energy to roll over and reach for it. My eyelids started to fall. Sleep would be blissful, and I wanted nothing more than to drift off. I was almost asleep when my phone rang. Fumbling, I grabbed it off the pillow and squinted at the screen. If the number hadn't belonged to Damian, I wouldn't have answered.

"Hey." I tried to sound chipper.

"Did I wake you?" Oh, how I missed that voice.

Talking hurt my throat. It took effort to push the words out; a few seconds of conversation left me breathless, but I didn't want him to hang up. His voice was already soothing me.

"I...uh. No, I'm still awake."

"Still?"

"No. I...I've been asleep. And..." My throat

scratched.

"Kate, are you okay?"

I sighed. "I have the flu. No big deal." I coughed. "Flu?"

I nodded even though he couldn't see me through the phone. "Yeah. It hit in the middle of the night. It's okay, though. It's…happened before."

"Damn, I hope it wasn't the lobster."

"No. Uh, then you'd be sick, too."

"Right." Silence filled the other end. I swallowed, and my throat burned. The glands on my neck had swelled to the size of golf balls.

"Can I come over?"

Huh?

It didn't seem odd for me to go to his house or have him sitting with me in the hospital. But if he came here, he'd have to meet my parents, and I—

"Kate?"

"Oh, uh. Aren't you worried about getting sick?" I had to stall somehow.

"It's not like I have to go to school. I just want to come and be with you."

"I won't be good company. I'm really tired."

"Then I'll watch you sleep and hold your hand," he answered quickly.

Honestly, I liked the sound of that. Damian's hand wrapped around mine. His body next to me. *Ahh. Yes, come over.*

"I'll have…to call you back." I rubbed the knobs on the sides of my neck. They answered by throbbing.

We hung up, and I sent a text to my mother's phone. Seconds later, she came racing up the stairs.

She knocked before she stepped inside. "What do you need, sweetheart?"

"Uh, would it be okay if…" I took a deep breath. "Damian called. Would it be okay if he came over for a little while?"

My mother's brown eyes widened in surprise.

"Well," she said, drawing the word out. "I think you need your rest."

My mother almost threw me a party when I got my first period. I had to talk her down; she was so excited that "her little girl was becoming a woman!" It made my stomach churn thinking about what she'd do about my first boyfriend. I wouldn't be the one to open the door and save him when he came in.

Yes, I knew what she was thinking. The smile spreading across her face proved me right.

"He said he just wants to be with me," I told her against my better judgment. Her smile grew to a toothy beam.

"How sweet! I knew there was something going on between the two of you! Oh, my little girl is growing up."

I glared at her. We were alone and already she was embarrassing me.

"Well, I suppose he can come over." She rubbed my hand. Then her smile faded, a serious expression replacing the happiness.

"Now Katie. There are boys out there—and I'm not saying Damian is one of them—who only want to be with a girl for one thing."

What? Now? "Oh my gosh, Mom! Please stop!"

"No. No, dear. I need to do my parental duty."

I shook my head. The headache I already had

worsened with the movement.

Distracted by my disease, we'd never actually had "the talk" before.

"I know that being a teenager can be difficult, especially with raging hormones and a boyfriend. I was your age once upon a time too, you know."

'Raging hormones?' Please tell me this isn't happening.

"Just because a boy says he loves you doesn't mean you need to have sex with him. If he truly loves you, he can wait. And I know it's easy to get caught up in the moment, and it feels good, and you might want to…"

I leaned over my bed and grabbed the garbage can. It was only the half-glass of water from earlier, but it was enough to quiet my mother. Oh thank you, Lord.

"You're sick. I guess we can have this conversation later," she said, taking the fluid-filled sack from the garbage can and out of my bedroom.

I heaved a sigh and rolled over. Saved by puke. Lovely.

I called Damian back. He answered on the first ring.

"You can come." I gave him my address.

"Hmm. I was hoping you'd say that."

The doorbell rang.

I smiled thinking about him climbing in his car as soon as we'd hung up.

"I have a movie and a 2-liter of Sierra Mist. That's what you're supposed to drink when you're sick, right?"

I laughed then clutched my stomach in pain.

"Thanks," I whispered.

"See you in a few."

I heard the front door close and Damian's sweet voice float up to me.

"Thank you, Mrs. Browdy," he said as he walked up the stairs to my room.

"Just remember, she needs her rest."

"Yes, ma'am. Of course."

"Marcy. Please call me Marcy."

Mom knocked on the door before she poked her head in. "You have company, sweetheart."

My insides melted when Damian became visible. I hoped my mother didn't notice the quiet sigh that escaped me.

"Hey." Damian's voice sounded rough. His expression was unreadable. No smile graced his beautiful face. No sparkle in his eyes.

Not what I'd expected.

My mother winked at me and intentionally left the door open before she headed back downstairs. I heard her giggle a little too loudly. Damian didn't seem to notice, his gaze focused on me.

I couldn't look away. Part of me worried he'd been drinking. It would explain his stale demeanor. He pulled up a chair next to my bed. His eyes weren't glossy, and his breath didn't reek of alcohol.

"What's wrong?"

His lips began to form a grin. "Nothing. You—"

"You're lying."

Damian's brow creased. "My mom could always tell when I was lying."

I shrugged. "We're gifted. Now tell me the

truth."

"Just surprised, that's all. You're paler than I thought." He cleared his throat and glanced away for a second.

Sure, my skin had the complexion of a polar bear, and according to my reflection, my eyes were decorated with dark circles. Maybe they were a bit sunken in, too, but influenza didn't come with redeeming qualities.

From out of his bag, Damian pulled out the Sierra Mist and poured me a glass. "Drink."

I stared at it, biting my lower lip. *It looks so good!*

"Thanks," I muttered, taking a small sip.

Leaning back on my pillow, I kept my eyes on Damian. He took my hand in his as he slid off his chair and sat down on my mattress. He still didn't smile. My stomach instantly started to churn.

I tried to fight it back, to hold it in. He grabbed the garbage just as the soda flew out of my mouth. If it wasn't for Damian, I would have thrown up on myself.

My body ached all over, my throat felt like a clump of boils, and my head was a ticking bomb. I could barely keep my eyelids open, my vision blurring behind the tears. Damian had seen more of me in gross states the last weeks than most guys ever saw.

"Sorry," I grumbled.

"Kate," he started, hesitant. "Should I…Do I need call my dad? Maybe it's something more?"

"No, really. It's just the flu. I'll be fine. I just need some rest." My words sounded rehearsed.

He sighed as his hand glided over my cheek. I closed my eyes, concentrating on his touch, moving down my chin, over my lips, and across my neck. I drank it in. Every trace his fingertips made across my skin sunk into me like paint on a canvas.

"Damn," he whispered. "You're burning up."

I rolled onto my side, burying my face into my pillow. More than anything, I wanted Damian to keep caressing me. I heard him breathing. His hands never stopped moving over my face, my bald head, my arms.

Damian's phone rang. Sighing, he kissed my head and yanked it out of the pocket of his jeans.

"Yeah?...Tonight?" He let out a nervous breath. "I don't know. I...yeah. Okay."

The voice on the other end rose loud enough for me to distinguish it as female.

I peeked one eye at him. He looked uncomfortable.

"I know. I was busy last night. Fine. I'll call you later." He turned his phone off before tucking it back in his pocket. His eyes focused on the door.

"You all right?" I asked.

His head snapped in my direction. "Oh, yeah. Sorry." He forced a smile. "You need some rest. I'll be right here."

I wanted to ask him who she was, but my head pounded so much I could barely think.

He drew the blankets over my shoulders, touching every inch of bare skin on his way. My body tingled as I relaxed into his caresses. Nothing felt better than this.

Before I dozed off, I felt his body against mine,

and his arms wrapped around me. His lips pressed against my neck.

~*~

I didn't know what time it was when my eyes fluttered open. Light still streamed into my room through the sheer curtains. Damian lay beside me, his arm draped over my stomach. I squirmed under him, but he didn't move. Sweat poured off my brow, and having Damian so close to me made me warmer. I gently moved his arm off me and heard him moan in my ear. Then he sucked in a sigh, vibrations rattling in his throat.

I grimaced as I swallowed. My lungs screamed in protest as I drew in a deep breath.

My head pounded harder than before. I rubbed my eyes, trying to focus on something, anything. The room looked fuzzy with the lines blurring together.

I tried to turn my head, but it cracked and stopped moving. A raspy moan filled my throat. Staring at the ceiling, my eyes teared up. Suddenly, my body began to shake uncontrollably, and I shut my eyes.

What's happening to me?

~*~

Darkness surrounded me when I awoke again. Damian was no longer lying beside me. Heaviness weighed on my eyelids, my head, all over. I wanted to turn my head, call out his name—neither was possible. My head refused to move. In fact, I couldn't move anything except my eyelids. And that took all the energy I had. They fell shut.

I heard my door creak open. My mother didn't address me when she spoke.

"Still asleep?"

"Yeah. Her breathing is sporadic and shallow." Damian's voice answered from somewhere next to me. He hesitated for a second before adding, "Her temp's gone up."

A moment of silence passed between them before my mother said, "I think we need to call your father."

"I already did."

Chapter 9

Dr. Lowell didn't usually make house calls, but he must have made an exception for his son. I heard his familiar voice speaking quietly. His assertiveness had Damian replying with, "Yes, sir," a few times. Somehow I knew Damian's hand was clenched around mine.

My mother's hushed voice sounded urgent. For a short time, the room stood still, and I wondered whether everyone had left or if I had died. Then the frenzy began. Drawers opened and slammed closed. Footsteps beat against the hardwood floor. A chair tipped over. Voices rose.

I tried to open my eyes, but they refused.

In the chaos around me, Damian's hands moved softly over my scalp. His voice whispered close to my ear. "We're taking you the hospital, Katie. You're gonna be okay."

Everything happened so quickly. I slipped in and out of consciousness, never alert enough to catch the details. The scent of my mother's perfume stayed with me during the ambulance ride. She held my hand and spoke to me. I wanted to ask her if I was dying, but the words wouldn't pass through my thoughts.

Needles poked into my skin, and the blood pressure cuff gripped my arm. Usually, I tensed when it squeezed and cut off my circulation. This time I barely felt it.

A horde of voices encircled me, barking out orders. Feet shuffled against the floor. The heart monitor beeped somewhere beside me, slower than it should have been. That familiar hospital smell wafted through my nostrils. I got my eyelids to rise for a split second, and I was rewarded with a blast of bright light stinging my pupils. I closed them immediately. Fear rushed through me. *Where did my mother go? Where is Damian?* I couldn't hear him or feel his presence.

I started to panic as air filled my lungs and pushed against them, making them burn. If I was going to die, I wanted to say good-bye.

The voices around me began to fade. Feeling in my limbs dimmed until there was nothing left.

I tried to speak. I wanted to tell my family that I loved them. That I was sorry I couldn't fight hard enough and that I'd miss them. I wanted thank Damian for the time he'd spent with me. That...

How much did I care about him?

Then, blackness engulfed me.

~*~

When I opened my eyes, I squinted at the clock—4 AM. Damian was asleep in the chair next to me. He was slumped over the side of my bed, his head resting on his arms. It took me a few minutes to realize that this room wasn't my bedroom. I reached over and ran my fingers through Damian's disheveled hair. For some reason, the first thing I noticed was the lack of gel. His head perked up almost immediately. He smiled, and even in the dark, I could see the relief in his eyes.

"Hey, there," he whispered, his smile growing as he spoke. He stood up to move his chair closer and peered at me. For a second, I thought a saw a tear in the corner of his eye, but mine didn't stay open long enough to confirm it.

Damian bent over to kiss me softly. He pulled back and kissed me again, a little harder. I had to push him away to catch my breath.

"Sorry," he said, smirking.

"Uh, um." I swallowed and looked around the room. "I'm…in the hospital."

Damian nodded. His hand glided over the top of my head as he spoke. "The virus took over your system, and, because of the chemo, your body couldn't fight it." He kissed me again. "You've been out for eight days."

My eyes widened. "Eight days?"

I remember watching an alien movie once. The characters noted a space-time continuum where eight minutes of their lives just disappeared. I wish I could say the same. Lucky them.

Damian nodded. "Your mother has been sleeping in the empty bed over there." He nodded toward her.

"And you?"

He cupped my face in his warm hands. "There's no way I'd leave you."

It's weird knowing I was knocked out while people walked in and out, talked, and even touched me. What's weirder, was that it seemed like my mother's life, as well as Damian's, had been put on hold for those eight days as well. They just waited around for me to wake up.

I peered over at my mother sleeping peacefully. Her hair, usually pulled back into a ponytail, fanned out over the pillow. During what I could only assume was a restless night, the sheets were bunched at her ankles. She wore a t-shirt and yoga pants. No make-up graced her face, and dark shadows hung under her eyes.

"Would you like me to wake her up?" Damian asked.

I shook my head. "No, let her sleep."

"I think she'd want to see that you're awake."

"I know. But I don't have the heart to wake her; she looks so peaceful."

Damian nodded. "You should probably go back to sleep, too."

My eyebrows rose. "Apparently, I've been asleep for eight days."

He chuckled. "Okay, but it's still four in the morning."

I patted the space next to me on the bed. "If it's not too much to ask, can you just hold me?"

Damian's dimples deepened. He climbed up on the bed and pulled me against him kissing my temple. "It's never too much to ask."

~*~

I didn't think I'd fall asleep, but when I awoke, my mother beamed at me. Tears streamed down her face as she squeezed me.

In the daylight, lines I'd never seen before filled the space between her eyebrows and hair line.

As she clung to me, I noticed Damian's empty chair. My shoulders fell, disappointed he'd left without saying good-bye.

"Where's Damian?"

Missing him already, I thought about how it felt to fall asleep in his arms last night.

Why does he seem to like me so much?

Mom pulled back, wiping tears from her cheeks. "Oh, he went home to shower. I guarantee he'll be back soon." She winked at me. "He seems to be on very good terms with the hospital staff. Leslie's quite impressed with him."

"Really?"

"He's a good kid. Your father likes him, though he wishes he'd sleep on the chair by the window instead of next to your bed." She laughed and shook her head.

"How are you feeling?" Tammy asked, walking up to my bedside.

"Uh…" *Confused?*

Tammy smiled. "That's okay." She put the blood pressure cuff over my arm. I grimaced when it met its maximum Python squeeze. "120 over 70. Very good." She waved a wand over my forehead. "100.2. You did well, Kate."

"Thanks." They knocked me out, so technically,

had I done anything?

"Dr. Lowell will be in soon to check on you," Tammy said before she left.

An hour later when Damian returned, my mother ran home to freshen up.

My heart almost stopped when he breezed into my room, wearing loose-fitting jeans and a blue and white American Eagle polo. It brought out the color of his eyes.

Damian's face lit up when he saw me sitting up in bed, sipping on some cafeteria soup. He walked over and pulled out eight red roses from behind his back.

"One for each day you missed." He set them on the table next to my bed, then sat down next to me, taking my hand and kissing it.

"Thank you," I said, lifting his hand to my heart and pressing it against me. His smile widened.

"Maybe next time I should bring you some chicken broth made from chicken instead of whatever they pass that off as."

I shrugged and slurped at the spoon. "I think it came from a can."

Damian made a face. "Canned chicken? That might be worse. I'll bring us dinner tonight."

A knock interrupted us, and Dr. Lowell poked his head in. "How are you feeling, Kate?"

Damian shifted his eyes to the floor. Dr. Lowell never looked at his son, keeping his focus on me. Tension filled the small room, and Dr. Lowell forced a smile at me.

They must have been at it again.

"Um…better, I guess."

"Your blood work came back, and it looks like the virus has run its course. I'm still going to suggest you not return to school until January. Your immune system won't be able to take another infection."

I nodded. At this rate, I'd be in tenth grade until I died.

"I'm keeping you on an antibiotic for another week, just as a precaution. All things considered, you pulled through this with flying colors."

"Bullshit," Damian muttered under his breath.

Dr. Lowell shot him a quick glare. "I want to keep you for another couple of days for observation, Kate."

I nodded again, wanting to melt into the bed. "Thank you."

As Dr. Lowell left, Damian rose to his feet, his brows pinched at the closed door. I reached for his arm and tugged. Damian looked down at me, softening a little.

"You're not leaving, are you?"

His eyes flashed back up to the door, then back at me. He sighed, bit his lip, and sat down on the bed.

"He just pisses me off."

"Why this time?"

"He's fucking delusional. You almost died!"

I reached out and slid the back of my hand over the faint indentation the dimple formed in his cheek. "What would you do, then?"

"Not give a false sense of security."

I wished Damian could understand.

Dr. Lowell didn't have to say it; I knew I'd

barely survived. Technically, cancer wouldn't be the disease that killed me. More than likely, it would be a simple bout of the flu, or an infection from a cut—something a healthy immune system could easily fight off. What Dr. Lowell meant was, "I'm glad you're still with us."

"It wasn't false," I said. "It was hopeful. It's a good quality in a doctor."

"Lying is a good quality in a doctor?"

I looked down at my sheets and the standard hospital-grade blue blanket.

Damian moved closer to me, his eyebrows furrowed. He reached out and lifted my chin so that my gaze met his. His eyes searched mine.

"It's not like I don't know. I do. What I don't always get, is that I can pull through."

"You're going to beat this, Katie," he whispered. "I know you will."

He leaned in, kissing me tenderly.

Chapter 10

December 10
Dear Diary,
Dr. Lowell came in and released me to go home today. I'm so ready to get out of this place! I'll miss Damian sleeping next to me every night, though—the last two nights he technically wasn't supposed to be here, but after I begged Tammy, she relented. I guess dating the doctor's son has its perks.

My mom is packing my things, and Dad's signing the paperwork. Damian's arms are full of flowers, balloons and stuffed animals—most of which came from him, anyway. He looks adorable. I don't think he's stopped smiling since he woke up this morning.

Since I'm not allowed to go back to school and Damian's still expelled, I hoped I'd get to spend more time with him.

103

Unfortunately, though, I'm pretty much on house arrest for a week. Not to mention Damian's at the hospital all day. Dad wouldn't let him stay over while I'm alone, anyway, I guess. What am I supposed to do with my time?

"We'll figure something out," Damian whispered.

"Hey!" I closed my diary and glared at him. I hadn't seen him reading over my shoulder.

The mischievous glint in his eye made him look even cuter.

"So you think I'm adorable, huh?"

I nudged him on the arm, heat warming my cheeks. He chuckled.

"No one reads my diary!"

Damian's eyebrows rose. "No one?"

"No one," I said, unable to help smiling at his dimples.

He scanned the room, probably for prying eyes. Then, he leaned in and kissed me.

"You meet their approval, you know." I nestled my head in his shoulder.

His smile faded. "They don't really know me." He sighed and looked at me. "And neither do you."

I dropped my gaze quickly. "Why me, Damian? I'm sick."

He sucked his lip between his teeth and started chewing on it. "You don't expect me to be someone I'm not."

Something told me that wasn't all of it, but it was enough. For now.

I turned his face toward me. Not caring who saw, I drew him close and covered his lips with mine. When he started to back away, I hummed, "Mmm-hmm," and pulled him closer, kissing him harder. He finally relaxed and returned the kiss.

Our kiss was broken by my dad clearing his throat loudly. Damian's eyes shot open. He immediately sat back, glancing over at my dad. I, on the other hand, felt a little daring. Either Damian and I had switched roles or it was the antibiotic's fault. Whichever, I didn't care what my dad thought. I lifted my head, blocking Damian's view so he was forced to look at me. His eyes widened as I kissed him again.

Somewhere behind me, I heard my mom chuckle. When I turned my head, my father was doing his best to hide a grin. He cocked an eyebrow at my mom, silent words passing between them. I looked back at Damian, whose ocean blue eyes seemed brighter.

"All right you two," Dad said, the corner of his mouth turned up. "Time to go."

If I hadn't almost died, I probably couldn't have pulled it off. My tiny moment of defiance surprised even me.

Damian reached from around his armload to help me off the hospital bed. Leslie scooted the wheelchair over.

"I can walk, you know," I said.

"You should take it easy today, Kate," Damian said as I reluctantly took his hand.

Leslie grinned at him. "Plus, it's hospital policy."

"Pfft." I sat down and tried to make myself comfortable. So not possible. "Since I have to ride out of here, I might as well take some of that off your hands," I told Damian.

"I got it. Just enjoy the ride." He winked, and I rolled my eyes.

I hated being outnumbered.

When I stepped through the front door of my house, I half-expected a choir of angels to be singing the "Hallelujah Chorus" in the living room. I took in our den with new, thankful eyes. My dad put his arm around my shoulder and kissed my cheek. "Welcome home, princess." He said the same thing each time I returned home; it never got old.

My mother and Damian took all my belongings to my room while Dad stacked up some pillows behind me on the sofa. I heard Damian's hurried footsteps above me as he arranged the gifts he'd carried in around my room. With an open invitation from my mother, he stayed with me for the rest of the day.

We walked to my room together that evening. When Damian opened the door, it looked as though the flowers had doubled. I gaped at him. He grinned and tugged me close.

"What is this?" I asked. "It looks like a floral shop threw up in here."

Damian shrugged.

"When did you...Why?"

Damian didn't say anything. He took my hand and led me into the room. I closed my eyes and let the scent of the flowers envelop me. In my mind, I imagined standing in a field of roses with the moon shining above me and the breeze sweeping up the long hair I used to have. I pictured Damian walking toward me wearing a tuxedo and holding more roses. He was smiling wildly. I glanced down and like magic, a beautiful gown of gray and white taffeta and sheers covered me and blew behind me in the wind.

When I opened my eyes, Damian stood behind me, his fingers moving slowly over the back of my neck. His lips followed his touch. My eyelids fell closed again, but this time I wasn't transported to the field of flowers. I stayed in the moment, concentrating on each touch, each delicate kiss.

His fingers moved from the back of my neck to my front, his hands gliding over the top of my chest. Air caught in my throat. Damian's lips moved to nibble on my ear. I gasped, and felt Damian grin against my neck.

When I opened my eyes, a chain with a silver heart rested around my neck. Inside the heart were three silver arrowed loops; two pointing out, one straining down. I lifted the charm off my chest and stared at it in the palm of my hand.

"It's the Celtic symbol for hope," Damian murmured in my ear. "Now you'll always know where to find it."

"It's beautiful," I said, remembering the tattoos on his chest and arm. I turned to face him. "Damian, thank—"

He put a finger over my lips, stopping me. Then he kissed me with everything he had.

~*~

Since I couldn't go anywhere, Damian came over the next day. He walked in on a game of Rook between my mother and me.

"Do you know how to play?" my mom offered.

"Uh," Damian glanced at me and snickered. "No, I don't."

I grimaced. "We can't have that! Deal him in, Mom!"

While trying to explain the rules, my dad came home from a Saturday morning at the office. He put the boxes of fresh pizzas on the table and shook Damian's hand.

"They sucker you into playing?"

"Sort of," Damian answered, staring at his hand.

Dad leaned over his shoulder and gave him some pointers as Mom and I headed for the kitchen for paper plates and soda. Holding a glass in each hand, I stopped at the entryway to the dining room. My dad and Damian were laughing together. Mom came up beside me and paused. She watched for a few seconds, then nodded at me.

"Did I tell you that when I was pregnant with you, the ultrasound said you were a boy?"

I cocked my head to the side. "No, you didn't."

She laughed. "Yes. Your father was so excited; he always wanted a son."

Turning my attention back to the dining room table, I noticed my father's hand resting on Damian's shoulder.

"He went all out on your nursery, decking it out in all sorts of sports stuff." She chuckled. "When you were born and the doctor announced that you were a girl, I'll never forget the disappointment on your father's face."

"Disappointment? In *me*?"

Dad gave Damian a high five in the other room. Damian put down his cards, and I was sure that the conversation had nothing to do with the card game.

"But then, I placed you in his arms. You stared up at him with your big brown eyes, and he's never looked away since."

A lump swelled in my throat as I watched my dad interact with Damian. I couldn't help but wonder what if…what if I didn't pull through.

My hand instinctively went to the charm around my neck. *'It's the Celtic symbol for hope. Now you'll always know where to find it.'* I squeezed it. There were no "what if's." I would defeat this thing once and for all.

Holding my head up high, I walked into the dining room and set the two sodas on the table. We laughed, ate, and played Rook until the sun went down; Dad and Damian on a team and me and my mother on the other. Not surprisingly, Mom and I kicked their butts!

Afterward, we all gathered in the den to watch a movie. Mom and Dad sat on the sofa, and Damian and I cuddled on pillows and blankets on the floor.

"Since Kate and I won, you guys pick the movie."

Damian shot my dad a glance. "Bond? James Bond?"

"Old or new?"

"New. Shaken or stirred?"

"Do I look like I give a damn?" Dad said in his perfect James Bond impression.

They both laughed. I just enjoyed being close to Damian and feeling like being part of a normal family.

~*~

I stayed in bed until noon on Sunday while my parents were at church. My head hurt and the room spun like one of those carnival rides where you stick to the side and the floor drops out. I refused breakfast but accepted Mom's offer of Ibuprofen.

When I awoke, Damian had his head resting on my stomach. He was scribbling something in a notebook. I smiled and ran my fingers through his hair, which contained less gel than it used to. He moaned softly and turned his head to look at me. His smile was breathtaking, showing off both dimples.

"Hey, beautiful." His voice stirred the butterflies in my stomach. "How are you feeling?"

It took me a second to answer. From the moment I opened my eyes, the only thing on my mind had been how his hand curled over mine. "A little woozy."

Damian frowned. "I kept you up too late last night."

I shook my head. "No. I wouldn't trade yesterday for anything. What are you writing?"

His smile returned. "Lyrics for a song I'm working on."

"Hmm," I hummed. "Can I hear it?"

110

"Someday. When it's finished."

I puffed out my lower lip. "No sneak peak?"

"Maybe later."

He tossed the notebook on the floor and moved his head to my pillow, pulling me into him. I rested on his shoulder and nestled my face into his chest, breathing him in. The scent of his deodorant filled my nostrils.

And that was it. Just deodorant.

I inhaled him again, then lifted my eyes up at him, confused.

He grinned down on me guessing my thoughts. "I quit. It made you sick."

In response, I touched his cheek and drew him to my lips. He tasted so good. I didn't want to stop, but my body had other thoughts. I closed my eyes and lay back down on his chest, drifting back off to sleep.

My mom brought us dinner in bed. I still wasn't hungry, but I ate a few bites of homemade honey bread and some spoonfuls of soup. After a movie in Damian's arms, he went home, and I dozed off.

In the morning, my headache had vanished. Suddenly, I felt like I could take on the world! Since Damian worked at the hospital all day, I texted him as often as he'd answer. Missing his gorgeous face, I went to the hospital early and sat in the Commons to wait for him.

I threw my arms around his neck as soon as he walked in. We were alone in the room, so he challenged me to a game of *Mario Kart*. Not surprisingly, he beat me with ease.

"Okay, how about a wager this time?" He lifted

his eyebrows.

"No! There's no contest!"

"If you lose, I get to treat you to a Christmas dinner this weekend. And if I win, you...I dunno...have to kiss me?"

I slugged him playfully and accepted his terms. After I lost, I kissed him eagerly.

"Wait! I don't think that bet was fair," I exclaimed, finally realizing what he'd said.

Damian flashed a mischievous grin. "You accepted."

Dr. Lowell knocked on the open door. "Kate?"

Both of us turned.

"I don't want you hanging out here except for treatments, okay? This place is full of germs."

I stole a glance at Damian, then back at his father. "Okay."

Damian grunted and flopped back against the sofa.

I lifted his arm and curled up against him. "How are things between you two?"

Damian inhaled deeply. "Not better, but at least not worse. I guess that's improvement." He kissed my head. "I hate to admit it, but he's got a point. Maybe it's best if you don't come here unless it's necessary."

"I just wanted to see you."

That adorable impish gleam sparkled in his eye. "How about you come over to my house for a swim tomorrow? I'll make up something to stay home."

I bit my lip and sighed. "I don't know. I'm not supposed to leave the house."

"It's just me, and I see you in the evenings

anyway."

My shoulders fell. "My parents said—"

"Do you always listen to your parents?"

I shifted my gaze to the floor. "I can't."

"Rules are meant to be broken, Kate."

"Not for me," I said softly.

"You don't have to be the perfect daughter all the time."

"Yes, I do."

Damian crossed his arms waiting for me to explain.

I pursed my lips together. "My parents gave up everything for me when I was diagnosed. They quit their jobs in Nebraska, sold our house, put Granny in a nursing home, and moved here so I'd be under your father's care. I can't disappoint them." Unable to stop them, the tears began to slip out. "They never counted on having a broken daughter."

"Ah, shit," Damian muttered, folding his arms around me. "You're not broken, baby. You could never disappoint anyone."

He snuggled me into his chest. I sobbed into his shirt, feeling his warmth surround me. He pressed his lips on my head.

"Come on. You're gonna be late." He pulled back and wiped the tears from my cheeks.

"Yeah." I sniffled and forced a smile. "We have to go all the way next door."

Damian took my hand and walked with me to the chemo room where Leslie was unhooking a little boy at the end of his treatment. The child's eyes were sunken in, and he looked pale. He still had a full head of hair.

Damian stood frozen in the doorway, shock visible in his sapphire eyes. I squeezed his hand once before letting go and walking over the boy. He couldn't be older than nine.

"Hey, there," I said, smiling at him. "I'm Kate."

"Hi. I'm Brennan," he said in a raspy voice.

I ruffled his hair. "Hang in there, bud. Leslie's a great nurse."

I didn't see Damian come up next to me. "And you have a good doctor, kid."

Brennan nodded, then walked over to where his mother and Leslie were speaking.

"That was a nice thing to say," I said, looking up at Damian.

He shrugged. "It's the truth."

When Leslie finished with Brennan's mother, she inserted the chemo tubes into my central line. "Thanks for your help today, Damian."

I shot him a quick glance.

"Sure," he said. "No problem."

"Apple or orange, Kate?" Leslie asked.

"Apple."

"Be right back." She walked out the door.

"What was that about?" I asked as soon as Leslie had left.

"I don't know. Just doing my job."

I stared at him but decided not to probe. I searched for a deck of Rook cards in my purse, and we had time for half a hand before Leslie returned with my juice.

"Anything else?" she asked, looking not only at me, but also at Damian.

We both shook our heads.

"I'll be out here if you need me."

Damian and I played cards for a while until I asked, "Could you please find me some crackers? My stomach is turning."

"Sure." He gave me a swift kiss and left for the cafeteria.

As soon as he was gone, I stood up and walked to the door, peeking out. I saw him round the corner toward the elevators. After a couple minutes, my pole and I sauntered to the nurses' station. I felt like a spy, my eyes darting around to make sure he had left.

Leslie glanced up from her paperwork, eyeing me suspiciously. "I just saw Damian walk by?"

"Yeah. I don't have much time," I whispered. "Why did you thank him? What did he do?"

Leslie grinned. "Curious, are we? He helped me clean up after a little girl in the chemo room today. Then he took her to the Commons and played Wii with her until her treatment was over. He's becoming a real asset around here. You're changing him, Katie."

Chapter 11

December 13
Dear Diary,
Leslie said I'm changing Damian, which is good, right? So why do I feel so confused? Are my feelings for him genuine? Am I harboring some idea that I can fix him? If I am, is that necessarily a bad thing?

Yes, it is.

"Dad expected me to take Liam's place. Become who he was. Instead, I became everything my brother wasn't."

"You don't expect me to be someone I'm not."

I don't look at him and see Liam, true. Then, what do I see?

The pressure is too much. Maybe that's why I feel miserable. Everyone's depending on me, and I don't know if I can deliver. I try not to show how scared I am.

Ever since the flu, the headaches have

116

been getting worse. I'm hanging onto the hope that they're just left over from the virus. But I can't get all the "what if's" out of my mind.

What if I fail?

What if hope isn't enough?

What if all my fighting isn't worth it, and I'm lying on my death bed?

What if I let everyone down?

I play with the necklace Damian gave me. Hope. It's easy to believe that hope is enough and everything I'm going through is worth it when Dr. Lowell declares remission, or even maintenance. I reach out my hand and try to grasp it, but I never seem to be able to hold on.

Why does another remission seem like a fairytale that I won't obtain?

~*~

I called my mom at work to ask if she'd seen my black knit hat. It was on my head, but I needed confirmation that she wouldn't come home early.

"See you after my treatment. Bye, Mom," I said, hanging up the phone and taking a deep breath.

I ran to the living room to make sure everything was ready.

Blanket, check.

Pillows, check.

Stuffed picnic basket, check.

Yep, everything seemed set. I paced the kitchen, searching for things to do while I waited. The clock took forever to flip one minute. I even considered moving the clocks forward to ease my nerves.

I was so busy being paranoid that I didn't hear Damian's BMW pull into the driveway. He opened the front door, and I screamed.

"Jumpy, huh?" His dimples deepened.

My heart rate hadn't slowed.

"Come here." He wrapped his arms around me. "Sorry I scared you."

He leaned down and kissed me. I jerked back and glared at him.

"Have you been drinking?"

Damian shrugged. "One beer in the car. No big deal."

I took a step back. "While you were *driving*?"

"One, Kate. One. It was a rough day. Lay off a bit, will ya?"

His tone cut through me, and I dropped my gaze.

"Oh, shit. I'm sorry. I didn't mean to snap at you."

I lifted my eyes to meet his. His lower lip curled between his teeth.

"Just, please don't drink and drive, okay?"

He shrugged. "Sure, whatever."

So not convincing. I'd broken the rules by inviting him over, and I didn't want to fight.

Without taking his hand, I led him to the living room for a candle-lit picnic lunch. He sat across from me, nursing his Coke. I laid out our sandwiches on paper plates and tried to act girlfriendy—whatever that meant.

"You had a bad day?" I tried to sound casual, but it came out rather timidly.

Damian scratched his unshaven jaw. "I didn't sleep well. And El…A friend called. It didn't end well."

"Do you want to talk about it?"

"Not really."

I nodded. "Sure. Yeah, okay."

I took a bite of my sandwich and stared off to a spot on the wall. We sat in uncomfortable silence until Damian pushed his plate away, blew out the candle and stood up. I felt defeated. Setting my food down, I slid my knees to my chest, and rested my head over my arms. My jaw trembled as I fought the tears.

Seconds later, Damian slipped his arms around me from behind. His nuzzled his head against my neck.

"It's not you. I'm being an ass, and I'm sorry."

He kissed my neck, and the tears started to fall. I turned my face to him and folded my arms around him, digging my face into his chest. He chuckled as he kissed the top of my head.

"Why do girls cry so much?"

I let out a soft laugh. "I don't know."

I had a headache again on Friday, so I spent the evening in my room wrapped in Damian's arms. His fingers glided over my skin, comforting me. Somehow, him being there made the headache easier to deal with. I just hoped it was a one night

119

thing.

Since I lost our *Mario Kart* game, Damian planned a Christmas dinner date for us on Saturday at his house. My parents, thankfully, agreed. I was desperate to get out of my cell.

Just after watching the sunrise, I sifted through the clothes in my closet trying to figure out what to wear. I yanked a blue floral dress from its hanger and tried it on.

"Blech!"

I tossed it on the bed. *Maybe a skirt?*

My jean skirt seemed too informal, my petti too girly, and the long black one had a hole in it. They all landed on my bed with the dress. Next I tried on my favorite black dress. The bodice fit snuggly around my central line, digging it into my chest.

At ten in the morning, my closet was empty and my bed cluttered.

"Ahhh!" I screamed, digging through my bottom dresser drawer.

Moments later, my mother knocked on the door and poked her head in.

"Uh…" she drawled, her eyes widening at the mess.

"I have nothing to wear tonight. Absolutely nada." I lay back on the floor with my hands over my head. "I can't go."

Mom lowered herself to her knees and bent over me, grinning at me upside down. "You want me to go to the mall? Pick something out?" Her smile seemed genuine, but a flicker in her irises made me pause.

She shifted her gaze to the pile of clothes on my

bed. "I'm sure we can scrounge up some money to buy you a dress for tonight. It's supposed to be special, right?"

"Yes." I drug the word out. Something wasn't right here.

"Then you need to look special for it." Her eyes met mine again, and she showed off too many teeth.

"Uh-huh." I sat up. "What's going on here?"

"Nothing."

"You're acting...odd."

"No. I'm just excited for you!"

"Uh-huh," I said again, only half-believing her. "Why don't I come with you, Mom?"

Her face turned serious. "Katie, I really think after your headache yesterday you need to rest up for this evening. Don't you?"

I hated that she had a point, but she was definitely hiding something. "Fine."

Mom beamed, and she scurried down the stairs. I swept the clothes off my bed and collapsed on the comforter, not realizing how exhausted I was. Cuddling up with my pillow to rest for a few minutes, I drifted off.

~*~

"Kate."

Mom's voice woke me up. I sat up in bed and rubbed the sleep from my eyes. In her hand, she held up a beautiful red taffeta dress.

"Uh..."

"Isn't it gorgeous!" My mother exclaimed, ignoring the shock on my face. "You have to try it

121

on. Make sure it fits."

"Uh…"

Mom frowned. "What? You don't like it?"

"Uh…I like it," I uttered slowly. "But it's a little…over the top, don't you think?"

"I think it's perfect." She flashed her biggest toothpaste commercial grin.

I pursed my lips together. "You're kinda freaking me out, Mom."

"Trust me. It's perfect."

"But…"

"*Perfect!*"

She hung the dress on the back of my door, then spun around before leaving. "Per-fect."

I offered a fake smile that dropped from my face as soon as the door closed. What was she thinking?

I slipped off the bed and walked to the door. The dress *was* beautiful. I ran my fingers over the top sheer layer of the skirt. Because she'd bought it, I felt obligated to wear it. I didn't want to disappoint her.

For the rest of the day, I did as Mom had said and took it easy. The three of us ate lunch together, Mom and I played Rook, then I went to my room to read. At four o'clock, I hopped in the shower.

I glared at the dress on the hanger before taking it down. The halter top hid the central line sticking out of my chest perfectly. The flouncy skirt hung just above my knees. Included with the dress, Mom had bought me a new pair of red pumps.

I took extra care putting on my makeup; I might as well go all out and make it match the formal dress. I even used the glitter eye shadow I'd never opened. The doorbell rang as I spread on a layer of strawberry lip gloss. My mother hollered up the stairs.

"Coming!" I yelled back.

I wasn't expecting anyone. The clock on my nightstand read twenty to six. I had to hurry; my car had been running, warming up, for fifteen minutes.

Mom stood at the bottom of the stairs with her camera. It flashed with each step I took.

"Really, Mom? Are you making a stop-motion video or something? " I squinted. "It's not prom."

My parents exchanged looks and my dad said, "Pretty darn close."

Damian's gonna laugh at me dressed like this.

I paused on the last step and allowed my mother to take a picture of me with Dad. He held me snuggly to him with a goofy grin on his face. Then he put bunny ears behind my head for the next shot. I pretended to shoot him.

When we were done being silly, he held out my black pea coat, and I slipped my arms inside. We walked arm in arm to the front door where a man in a black suit stood holding a bouquet of red roses. I studied them, trying to figure out who'd sent them, then shot a glance to my dad.

He shrugged. "They're not from me."

My smile faded for a second before it broadened. I thanked the delivery man and gathered the roses in to my arms. The card attached was written in Damian's familiar handwriting.

I can't wait to see you.
Damian

Wow. Just ... wow!

I traced my fingers over the card.

Mom reached over to take the flowers and hugged me too tightly. "I am coming back, you know," I said, doing an inward eye roll.

"Have a good time, honey." Mom beamed.

Dad squeezed me into him next and pecked me on the top of my head.

Walking out the front door, I was surprised to see the delivery man still standing there. Did you tip flower delivery people?

"Are you ready, Miss Browdy?" he asked, a black umbrella at his side.

I toyed with the hem of my too-formal dress. *Maybe...* I skimmed my mom's face. Her nod confirmed my suspicions. *Oh, Mom!*

"This way, miss," the *chauffer* instructed, opening the door. He stayed to the side as he opened the umbrella for me to walk under.

I stepped over the threshold and saw huge snowflakes falling from the gray skies. I started giggling, wondering if Damian had even planned the snow. Then I noticed the driveway. A black limo was parked waiting for me; my yellow car must have been moved back in the garage. My cheeks already hurt from smiling so wide.

The driver took my arm and walked me to the limousine. He opened the door, and I slid inside. I half-expected to see Damian in the seat, but instead there was another bouquet of red roses and a small white box with a red satin bow around it.

The words **OPEN NOW** were scrawled across the top.

I reached for the box as the limo backed out of the driveway. Slipping off the ribbon, I opened the lid. Inside laid an iPod and a set of earbuds. There was no note inside, so I just stuck the plugs in and pressed the screen. It lit up and a playlist entitled "For Kate" appeared on the screen. I hit play and heard Damian's sweet voice.

"Hey, beautiful."

I laughed. *No way! Am I dreaming?*

"Sit back and enjoy the music. I'll see you soon."

The first track started immediately. I'd never heard the song before, and as the singer began the first verse, I realized why. Damian was singing. Probably the song he'd been writing in my room.

Find me in hiding
Writing my own story, tell me is it boring, or is it all the same
Old lines, used lyrics
Or is it unexpected with a happy ending
I'm not there yet
Found it hard to
Finish what I've started
The right words never shot into my mind
Tell me that you love me
Tell me that you hate me
Tell me the world's not over me
The world's not over me.

When his song ended, another came on. There were a few songs I'd never heard before, and as we turned into Damian's neighborhood, Parachute's

"Kiss Me Slowly" filled my ears.

Mr. Dempsey, the chauffer, pulled into the Lowell's driveway. He opened the limo door. On the ground was a red carpet laid over the walkway leading to the front door.

Oh, Damian!

Christmas lights lined the enormous home and the two white pillars that loomed in front of me. At the end of the walkway, Damian, wearing black pants, a black suit coat, and a white dress shirt, unbuttoned at the top, stood holding his guitar. He smiled, his eyes sparkling.

As Mr. Dempsey made the motion for me to take out the earbuds, Damian started strumming his guitar and singing the last song I just had on the iPod, exactly where it had left off. Mr. Dempsey offered his hand, and I took it, rising to my feet. Then he nodded politely and disappeared inside the limo.

Okay, this is too good to be true.

Huge snowflakes floated down from the sky, but I didn't notice the cold. I only saw Damian walking toward me.

He ended the song, a coy smirk on his face. I didn't think; I didn't need to. Every inch of me wanted to wrap around him and kiss him, oh so slowly. And I did, with the snow falling in around us.

Damian led me inside. His full lips formed into a seductive O when he slipped the coat from my shoulders, allowing it to fall to the hardwood floor. He glided his hands down my bare arms and kissed my shoulders. My eyelids closed as his warmth melted into me. His lips moved to my neck.

He took my hand and led me into the formal dining room. I gasped. The massive table and chairs were gone, and in their place sat a small circular table with two black chairs. A black table cloth that reached the floor covered the table, and a single red rose in a vase had been placed in the center. Small candles littered the floor, making it sparkle like diamonds. Mr. Dempsey stood behind the table with a bottle of champagne.

"Non-alcoholic," Damian promised.

"This is amazing," I breathed, sitting down. "How'd you do all this?"

A smirk played on his lips. "Dad helped."

"Really?" My eyebrows shot up, hopeful.

Damian shrugged. "You're the one thing we can agree on."

Excitement drained out of me. "I shouldn't have that much power," I murmured.

Mr. Dempsey poured the champagne in our flutes and walked off.

Damian rose his glass. "To you."

I shook my head. "No. To us."

We sipped on the champagne. Music played from a CD player in the corner, the same songs Damian had on the iPod in the limo.

Mr. Dempsey placed a salad in front of each of us. After a few bites, I looked down at the plate of greens, over the stereo, then back up to Damian.

"Come on," I urged, scooting the chair back.

"Oh, no. I don't dance."

"Everyone can dance." I grabbed his hand.

"Yeah. No. Not everyone."

I yanked harder, and he gave in. "All right, but I warned ya."

He circled his arms around me and held me close. I leaned my head against his shoulder, listening to his heart beat. His lips pressed against my head as he swayed, not moving his feet. I didn't care.

When the last chord of the song was strung, I lifted my face.

"See? I knew you could dance."

Damian grinned, showing off his deep dimples. "All I did was hold you."

"Close enough."

He moved closer, kissing me. I hungered for more, but Damian led us back to our table.

"Not hungry?" Damian asked as he watched me toy with what was left of my salad.

"Uh, not really."

Damian put his fork down, worry lines appearing on his forehead. "Are you feeling all right?"

"Oh! Yes, I'm fine. Just not very hungry," I assured him. He studied me skeptically. "Really. It's just a side effect," I continued.

He picked his fork back up and took a bite, still scrutinizing me. To prove I felt fine, I copied him. He seemed satisfied.

Mr. Dempsey brought in the main course—chicken primavera. I took a few bites but couldn't force down much. The last thing I wanted to do was throw up. I set my fork down and watched Damian cut his chicken.

"Much better than the hospital cafeteria," I said.

He laughed. "So is burnt liver."

I bit my lower lip. "You're different."

"You're worth it."

"Are you happy, Damian?"

He curved up the corner of his mouth until he glowed. "I've never been happier."

"And the consequences of this happiness?"

He reached for my hand across the table and squeezed it. "Good, bad, I'll take it all."

Leslie's words rang in my ears: *If he falls for you, and you die, it'll kill him.* My voice shook. "And if…"

"No matter what happens Kate, being with you, right now, tonight, is *all* worth it."

I hoped he was right.

A tear slipped from my cheek as I gazed into his brilliant blue eyes.

And I suddenly realized that I loved him.

Chapter 12

After dinner, we moved to the den where a roaring fire burned in the stone fireplace. A blanket, surrounded by pillows, lay on the floor. Damian propped some up on one end and tugged me down next to him, wrapping me in his arms. I slipped off my pumps and tossed them in the corner with Damian's shoes.

He left a trail of little kisses from below my ear to my lips and nestled his nose in my neck. I giggled and leaned back against the pillows.

Damian's fingers danced up and down my arm. "How was it?"

I shook my head. "I'm…I'm speechless."

Damian caressed the side of my face. He tilted his head and teased my lips with his, tugging back when I wanted more. "Hmm," he whispered. "Let's keep it that way for awhile, shall we?"

I chuckled and drew his head down until I was kissing him. His hands glided over my face, slid down my neck and side. I ran my fingers down his back then up through his hair. He broke the kiss and started nibbling on my earlobe. His soft moaning in my ear stirred the butterflies in my stomach.

His fingers tightened over my hip. He lingered there for a moment then worked back up to my bare shoulder. His lips flitted down my skin until they reached the strap of my halter. On his way back to my mouth, I felt the tip of his tongue glide over my neck. A small gasp escaped me. Damian paused and looked at me, a sensual smile gracing his face. "Ohh, I like that."

He leaned in, his tongue playing against my lips. He didn't kiss me again, even though I longed for it. Instead, he sat up, locking onto my eyes.

"Katie, I don't ever want to let you go." I didn't recognize the emotion hidden deep behind his irises. Desire? Sadness? Love?

In response, I reached up, ran my fingers through his hair, and pulled him down, gripping his lower lip between mine. Neither of us noticed Dr. Lowell standing in the doorway. He cleared his throat. My eyes shot open, and my hands dropped to my sides. Damian didn't flinch. He took his time ending the kiss. Then he winked at me before turning his attention to his father.

"The hospital called," Dr. Lowell said. "I need to go in."

Damian nodded.

"The roads are getting slick. It's not safe to take Kate home tonight."

Something unfamiliar spread through my body. Was he saying what I thought he was saying?

Dr. Lowell continued. "I already called her parents. She's going to stay here tonight."

131

What?! My parents are allowing this? They must think Dr. Lowell's staying here, too!

Shocked and happy, I squeezed Damian's hand. I couldn't see the expression on his face, but his father instantly clarified.

"In the guest bedroom, Damian."

Damian shrugged. "Okay."

Dr. Lowell sent him a sideways glare and pointed at him. "I mean it, son."

"Yeah. Okay. Guest bedroom. I got it."

The doctor glanced over at me, then back at Damian. "I'll be back soon." He nodded once and walked away.

Damian didn't say anything about the exchange, which surprised me. I thought maybe he'd be happy that we'd be sleeping under the same roof. Instead, he got up and left.

"Be right back."

Confused, I sat up and crossed my legs. My racing heart started to slow down and the butterflies calmed. I didn't know what to do while I waited. I smoothed out the poufy skirt over my thighs and surveyed the den.

I didn't want to dwell too much on Damian's nonchalance at my staying. Still—did it have something to do with me sleeping in the guest room? That hadn't surprised me. What had me was Dr. Lowell's casual manner in catching us making out on the floor. Had it happened so often that it was commonplace in this house?

The black bra crossed my mind. *No. Not tonight.* I pushed the thought away.

Damian didn't stay gone long. He returned with

two flutes of champagne. Sitting beside me, he pecked my cheek. That's it. Just a peck. We sat in silence, sipping on our drinks.

"Thanks," I said. "So, what now?"

"Uh-huh."

Frowning, I sat the glass on the floor and slumped into the pillows.

The passion from before had dissipated, and I was disappointed. I didn't know where I had wanted it to go, exactly, but I knew I didn't want it to end. Without warning, a tear slipped out, and I turned my head to the fire, not wanting Damian to see. I wiped it away.

I scanned over Damian, who was concentrating on the doorway. His flute was empty already, and he tapped his fingers against the stem. I hugged my knees up against my chest, laying my head on my arms. What had I done wrong? Now, I realized, I felt unwanted. Damian wasn't paying attention to me. He looked…bored.

It crossed my mind to curl up on the pillows and fall to sleep. At least then, maybe, he'd lie next to me.

I fidgeted with the Celtic charm lying against my chest. It hadn't been removed from my neck since he gave it to me.

My stare drifted back up to Damian. His brow was furrowed. He leaned to the side and stuck his neck as far over as he could. The flames danced off his face, illuminating the indifference in his eyes.

I was about to focus my attention back to the fire and lie down when I heard a door close in the distance. A dimple deepened in his cheek, but he still ignored me.

A car engine purred to life outside. Damian's finger rolled over the top of his glass, making it hum. Headlights brightened the curtains then faded away.

Swiftly, Damian jumped to his feet and pivoted toward me. He offered his hand. "Come on." A glint had returned to his eyes.

I bit my lip and cautiously took his hand. He lifted my chin and swept his lips over mine.

"Your dad, he didn't seem to care that…has that happened often?" My voice trailed off.

Damian's Adam's apple rose and fell. "Uh. It's just you, you know that, right?"

I nodded.

"What happened before you, I—"

"It's okay," I assured him. "I don't really want to know."

Do I?

Damian's shoulders relaxed. His lips pressed against the side of my neck. "It's just you." After a few moments, he tugged at my hand. "Come on."

I followed him out of the den. Jitters washed over me as we ascended the oak staircase.

Suddenly, I was nervous. How far did I want to go? Was *that* what he was thinking?

The memory of the black lace lingerie on his floor flashed in my mind again. As much as it worried me, I never had asked him about it. Obviously, he had experience, and that brought up its own set of questions. How would I compare? *Would* he compare me? What if I wasn't any good? Would it hurt?

He led me into his room. Six candles, three on each side of the bed on nightstands, were already lit. Soft music from dinner played on the stereo in a corner. Dirty clothes, Xbox games, Blu-Rays, shoes, and a whole slew of other stuff were piled in the corners. The blankets on his bed had been pulled up over the pillows. Was this what he'd done when he left me earlier?

He didn't plan this.

The thought sent a tingle of anticipation through me.

His eyes searched mine. I still didn't know where I wanted this to go, but I reached up and stroked his cheek with the back of my hand. Slowly, I found my way into his hair and combed through it with my fingers.

I felt his steady breath on my forehead. He still hadn't said anything, he just watched me. Rising up on my tip-toes, I kissed him, my gaze never leaving his. He returned the kiss cautiously, hands at his sides.

I placed one of his hands around my waist. With it, he pressed me up against him. He ended the kiss, and I swallowed hard as he raised his other hand and traced his fingertips over my lips. He licked his own, his brow furrowing slightly. I wished I knew what he was thinking.

I glanced at the bed, then back up at him. "Damian, I've never...I'm a..." I let the words trail off.

He nodded, knowingly. "You tell me when to stop, okay?"

"Okay," I mouthed.

Damian's eyelids closed, and he leaned in. He cupped my head in both of his hands, and it was unhurried and deliberate. He took his time, considering every move before he made it. Part of me—a very small part—wondered if he thought he would break me like a porcelain doll. The rest of me drank it in, concentrating on every touch, every kiss, every ache in my own body.

I found myself fumbling with the buttons on his shirt, gradually unlocking them, revealing the soft skin underneath. Damian watched my face as I stared at my own hands. I'd seen him shirtless before, but this time I ran my hands over his hard chest, enjoying how the warmth radiated through my fingers and into my abdomen. When I undid the last button, I slid both of my hands over his stomach and up around his shoulders. He arched his back slightly, allowing his shirt and jacket to fall to the floor.

Swallowing, I glanced up at him before moving forward and kissing his chest over the Celtic tattoo. His hands glided over the bare part of my back. It tickled as his fingers caressed me, stirring tiny tremors under my skin.

His hands floated up my back to the straps of my halter fastened behind my neck. Holding them for a few seconds, he waited. When I didn't say anything, he unsnapped them, then started kissing my collar bone. He slipped the straps down, his mouth following. The room suddenly got hotter, and it was getting more difficult to breathe. I tensed as his lips pressed against the swell of my breasts. The sensation that soared through me shot thrilling pin-pricks up my spine. I gasped.

Damian stopped. "Do you want me to—"

I shook my head. "No," I managed through uneven breaths. "Don't."

He clamped my face in his hands, his blue irises searing with restraint. "I need more, Kate," he said, his voice deep. "Don't what?"

I ran my palms over his chest, unable to look him in the eye. "Don't stop."

It wasn't until the words came out that I meant them. I'd never wanted him more than I did right then. After touching his bare skin, I knew nothing else would satisfy me.

Letting go, hunger suddenly blazed in his eyes. He bent over, tucked his arm under my knees and swept me off the floor. I threw my arms around his neck, holding him close and sucking his earlobe into my mouth.

He laid me on his bed over the black comforter. The tantalizing smirk on his face made my stomach burn. I didn't want him to pause, but he did. He straightened up, slipped off his belt, and tossed it on the floor. My heart pounded, almost hitting my ribs.

Damian crawled in bed beside me, and I rolled to my side, facing him. He ran his hand over my cheek.

"You're so beautiful," he said, sliding his fingers over my bald head and behind my ear as if tucking away a lock of hair.

His lips pressed over mine then separated, sucking my lip into his mouth and massaging my tongue with his. I arched into him.

Passion fueled his kisses, but he still moved so

slowly. Every so often, he'd hesitate, squeezing his eyes shut and holding me a little too tight.

Heat from his breath rolled over my neck. "Oh, Kate. It's so hard to…"

The muscles in his shoulders tensed, and his fingers dug into my back.

"What?" I breathed.

His grip loosened, and the tension flowed out of him. "Nothing," he said against my lips.

Damian placed a hand on my hip and pressed it into his. Over my full skirt, he glided down until he reached the bottom hem and found skin. He hooked his hand around my knee and wrapped my leg over his. My breath caught as his fingers slithered behind my thigh and rounded the edge of my bikini line. I whimpered when they slipped under the elastic at my hip.

He grinned, his dimples sinking. "That's what I like to hear."

The corners of my mouth tried to curl, but it was so hard to concentrate on anything else. Damian gripped my bottom, squeezing, and I tilted my face to the ceiling and pushed my hips into him. His tongue tickled my neck, eliciting a soft moan from my throat.

"Yes," he whispered in my ear.

I squeezed my eyelids closed and felt Damian's hand move out from under my skirt and press his forehead to mine. Kissing me again, he lifted my arm over my head, leaving a trail of heat in his wake. He yanked on my dress at the side, unzipping it to my hip. Waves crashed inside my stomach, making me shiver as the front of the bodice fell open, and Damian traced over my skin.

He drew me closer to him. "Do you want more?"

My nipples had never been so hard. I was sure they were poking through my bra. The word was on the tip of my tongue, but I couldn't get it out. I nodded against his throat.

His lips pressed against my face, my neck, my lips. When I shuddered, he held me tighter. He hesitated then, taking in a deep breath and letting it out slowly. I kissed his eyelids and they opened, conflict brewing in his azure irises, and I didn't know why.

"Damian?"

With a small shake of his head, the clouds parted. "Shhh. It's okay."

He rose up a little and gently pushed me onto my back. His stare focused on me for a few seconds, waiting. I extended my hand and brushed my fingers down his cheek. He kissed them as they passed over his lips.

His eyes undressed me first, then he moved down on his knees, straddling my legs. I swallowed, both anticipating and dreading what was coming next. Every inch of me wanted to be against him, yet there was something almost embarrassing about letting him see me naked. Already, I felt exposed.

The ache for him won out.

Damian slid the dress down over my hips. I watched as his eyes danced over my body. The corner of his mouth curved up, and he leaned down, pressing his lips over my stomach. He moved to the side and sat up long enough to drop my dress on the floor.

Starting at my feet, he worked his hands over my legs and my outer thighs, then circled back up. At my knees, he looked up. My mouth went dry. He held my gaze for a few seconds, breathing deeply, before he dropped his eyes again. Gently, he separated my legs. My breath caught. I couldn't decide whether to close my eyes or watch him.

Ever so slowly, he ran his fingers up my inner thighs. The feeling was new and exciting. I reached my arms over my head and gripped the pillows in my fists. Whatever noises I let out made Damian smirk. When he reached the elastic between my legs, I tilted my head back. He moved his hands up over my hips, grabbing hold of my underwear at my hips.

Damian leaned down, kissing me right above the band. I gasped again. His tongue rolled from one hip to the other, then began to delve lower. I squirmed under him, unable to hold still any longer. He chuckled.

He kissed me on top of the cotton panties I now wished were silk. Lower and lower until I held my breath, and my eyes rolled back.

"Mmm," Damian hummed.

I let out the breath in a soft squeal.

His mouth began to climb up and over my stomach. When his lips reached the bottom of my bra, he glanced up. He tilted his head to the side in question. I nodded, and his smile grew wider.

He dipped his hands under me, and I arched my back. His lips pressed between my breasts as the hooks loosened behind me.

Again, he paused before he unclasped it

completely, this time longer than before. I watched as the muscles in his chest tightened. Was he holding his breath? When he opened his eyes, they met mine. He pursed his lips together and glared at the candles on the nightstand.

His struggle was starting to scare me. I scanned the floor for what I'd seen last time, but all I saw were the pieces of clothing that used to be on our bodies. No matter his reasons, I didn't think I could go through with it if Damian was so unsure.

"Damian?" My voice cracked.

His attention shot back to me. "Kate—I'm sorry. I...I can't do this."

He slipped his arms out from under me and rolled off the bed. My arms automatically covered my chest. Facing away from me, he tilted his head up to the ceiling. His fists loosened, and he ran his fingers through his hair, clutching handfuls of it at the top.

I watched his back as he walked to his dresser and yanked out a t-shirt. Expressionless, he tossed it to me, barely seeing me. His blue eyes seemed duller; the fire had burned out.

"You can put that on."

I stared at him, my lower lip trembling. With his shirt in my hand, I drew it to my chin and clenched it too tight. I fought the tears back; I couldn't let him see me cry. I'd allowed myself to let go in front of him, and he'd...

"I'm sorry," he said again.

The muscles in his jaw tightened as he made his way to his private bathroom. He slammed the door, and I heard the shower.

I sat up and re-hooked my bra. Holding the t-shirt to my nose, I breathed in Damian's aroma. Alone, I allowed the drops to pour down my cheeks and onto the cotton in my hands.

Moments later, I jumped at the sound of Damian swearing and something smashing the bathroom mirror.

Chapter 13

I didn't know if I should run to him, stay where I was, or creep downstairs and curl up on one of the sofas. My gaze stayed glued to the closed door. Other than the running water from the shower, no noise crept into the bedroom.

I slipped off the bed and gathered up my dress. Clutching it for a moment against my chest, I ended up draping it over a black chair. Out of the corner of my eye, I noticed a notebook on the dresser. I glanced up at the closed door, paused, then grabbed the notebook and a pen and hopped back in bed, sliding the blankets over my bare legs.

Since I didn't have my actual diary with me and I desperately needed the escape, I figured I'd jot down my thoughts on paper and transfer it later. My mind couldn't wait until I got home to get everything out.

December 18
Dear Diary,
I couldn't imagine a better Christmas

143

date. Well, before it began.

The night started like a dream. When he walked toward me singing, I could barely wait until he finished to throw my arms around his neck. He looked so gorgeous with the top button of his shirt undone. I've never seen his eyes so bright. I wanted to drink him in.

At dinner we danced, my head resting on his shoulder; I didn't want to let him go. I could have stayed there forever. I loved how he smelled, how he held me, how his lips pressed against my scalp. Why did it have to end?

I don't understand. I was ready, and he was...

I forced the tears back and stole a peek at the bathroom door. The shower was still running.

My stomach had an unfamiliar ache. Sobs began to sneak out, and I lost control. Not wanting Damian to hear, I hugged a pillow to my chest and cried into it.

I took a few deep breaths and lifted my head.

What stopped him? I thought I was doing everything he wanted. He said...

I scanned the bed. A lump formed in my throat as I envisioned our bodies tangled over the sheets. I closed my eyes, allowing the hurt to fill me. It burned, searing holes in my stomach. Chemo never made me feel this bad.

I gripped the pen again.

I opened up, and he rejected me. I thought that maybe, after tonight, after everything...that he might love me too.

The lacy bra invaded my mind again. Nothing made sense. I couldn't justify the bra on the floor with what happened tonight and still believe that he cared about me. But what I'd seen in his eyes couldn't be faked.

He didn't want me.

I didn't want to think about it anymore; it hurt too much. Numbing the pain would be easier. How did Damian take care of his? Oh, yeah—empty bottles sat on his nightstand.

I threw the blanket off and knelt to peer under his bed: shoes, clothes, books, junk. The thought crossed my mind to dig it all out. I'd probably find some girl's underwear I could throw in his face.

I searched the nightstands and came up with empty beer cans. In the far corner of his closet, I found empty bottles of Templeton Rye and Jim Bean.

He had to keep full bottles somewhere in his room. Where were they?

My body shivered. Frustrated, I sunk to the floor beside Damian's bed. Even if I'd found a full bottle, I probably couldn't have done it anyway.

Or maybe I could have.

I don't know.

Curling my legs to my chest, I rested my head on the pillow, avoiding the sight of the bathroom door. The shower stopped, and a minute later the door opened. I didn't glance up.

His footsteps drew closer. Was he surprised to still see me there? Disappointed? Never mind, I didn't want know.

When I didn't acknowledge him, he walked to the other side of the bed. I heard a drawer open, some shuffling, then it closed. He tossed a towel on the bed. My heart pounded as I heard him come back around and then sit next to me on the floor. He wore only a pair of pj pants. Without hesitating, he wrapped his arm around me and hugged me next to him.

He kissed the top of my head. "I'm so sorry, Katie."

Conflicting voices shouted in my head. *Don't call me Katie! Just hold me and kiss me and show me you care.*

"Come on," he said, standing. "I'll show you the guest room."

He offered his hand, but I didn't take it. I didn't want to touch his skin and have to deal with the consequences. By the look on his face, my gesture stung. Good.

I followed him down the hall, staring at the floor and walls; anywhere but his glistening wet body in front of me. Every time I caught sight of his naked back, the pit of my stomach tightened and fresh tears began to sting my eyes.

The guest room was at the far end of the hall, six doors down from Damian's. Good, I'd be that much farther away. I swept past him and climbed into the king size bed, which was decorated in ocean blue— the color of Damian's eyes. The darkness would soon blot out the reminder.

I rolled away from Damian. I couldn't give him the satisfaction of seeing how much he'd hurt me. He was still in the room. My fingers gripped the soft blue comforter, and I tucked it up around my neck. I curled myself into a ball with my eyes squeezed shut, listening for him to leave.

Instead, the bed sank next to me. The tears I'd been fighting dripped onto the pillow. At the same time, I wanted him to leave *and* hold me close. The confusion made me want to throw up.

He sat beside me, not moving, not speaking, not touching me. I tried to hold my breath and stop the whimpers I didn't want him to hear. The more I fought the inevitable, the tighter I gripped the blanket. Why wouldn't he just go?

Minutes passed like hours. The soft sounds of sobs faded away, and my eyelids began to drop. I felt Damian's lips next to my ear.

"Good night, Katie," he whispered and kissed my cheek. "I..." He sighed. "Oh, Fuck," he said under his breath.

He hesitated as he rose, then scooted off the bed. I waited until I heard the door click before I rolled on my back and stared at the ceiling. The pain overwhelmed me again, and without Damian's presence, I allowed my cries to echo off the cerulean walls.

I could smell Damian all over me. The scent filled me and made me long for him. I yanked his t-shirt off my body, wadded it up, and held it in my arms. I don't remember how long I cried before I finally drifted to sleep.

~*~

When I awoke the next morning, my body felt warmer. I could still smell Damian, but I no longer had his t-shirt clutched to my chest. My eyes hurt from the night before, and I wondered how I was going to make it through the day. Would I be able to say anything to him?

I heard a sigh beside me, and my eyes flew open. They drifted to the black chair in front of me, where my red dress hung from the night before. The blanket sitting around my hips was black, not blue. Suddenly, I felt naked, realizing that I was only wearing my bra and underwear.

What in the world?

Wide-eyed, I peered down to where one of Damian's arms was draped around my bare stomach, the other dangerously close to my breasts. I sucked in a mouthful of air. Damian pulled me closer to him, his nose nestled in my neck.

I didn't know how to respond. He'd damaged my pride, and I hadn't forgiven him. Sure, I was happy to be tucked next to him again, but I still hurt. Really hurt.

Gently, he rolled me onto my back. My lashes fluttered open, allowing his blue eyes to wash through me. He propped his head up on one hand. Leaning in, he brushed his lips lightly over mine. I lay there frozen.

Without dropping his gaze over my barely-dressed body, he drew the black blanket up over me, making me feel less self-conscious. My mind cleared, but only a little.

"Damian," I started.

"I have something for you." He twisted and reached down beside his bed. He handed me a leather-bound book with a red satin bow wrapped around it. "Merry Christmas."

I held it, staring at the slightly worn edges.

A few moments of silence surrounded us before Damian spoke. "It's *my* journal."

I swallowed, still gripping the leather.

He sighed. "You said it helps you, so I thought maybe I'd give it a shot."

"I can't read this." I shook my head and handed it back. He didn't take it. "It's your personal thoughts, and I—"

"Read it. Please," he urged, running his fingers over my cheek. "I know you're upset, and I... Damn it!" he muttered as he swept a hand through his hair. "I just...please read it."

"Okay," I replied, still not convinced. I had never let anyone read mine; it was too revealing.

He nodded. "The roads have probably been cleared off by now. I'll take you home."

His legs swung over the side of the bed. He grabbed a pair of jeans on the floor and pulled them over his boxers, standing to zip them. A lump formed in my throat as I stared at the way they hung low on his hips. He snatched a t-shirt from the closet and slipped it over his head. Glancing at me, he said, "I'll wait for you downstairs."

I stopped him before he could open the door. "Damian?"

He twisted around, pain overshadowing the gleam in his eyes.

"How did I get here?"

"I waited for Dad to get home and go to bed. Then I brought you in here with me."

"Oh."

"I'll see you in the kitchen." He closed the door behind him.

~*~

I tucked Damian's journal, bow still on, inside the drawer of my nightstand. No matter how tempting it was to sneak a peek, I couldn't. Some things were better left unknown. I feared what was inside.

I took a book with me to my treatment on Monday. Brennan was there, just finishing up. He smiled at me when I tousled his hair.

"Mom's taking me to McDonald's for supper."

I laughed. "Gourmet food at its finest."

"Bye, Kate," he said, running out after his mother.

"He seems happier," I observed as Leslie hooked the central line to the IV.

"I introduced him to the Commons today. He and another little boy played video games all afternoon."

I grinned.

"You used to enjoy hanging out in the Commons," Leslie noted.

I shrugged. "It's quieter in here."

"And gloomier."

"Easier to read." I held up my book.

"Hmmm." Leslie put her hands on her hips.

"Apple or orange?"

"Orange."

"You want Damian to bring it in?"

"Oh, uh." I paused. *Crap.* "No, that's okay. I'm sure he's busy."

Leslie's eyebrows rose. I cut to my book.

"I'll be right back," Leslie said, sweeping out the door.

I glanced up when I heard the door close. My shoulders relaxed, and I closed my eyes and leaned my head back against the chair. Gossip would be circling the nurses' station within seconds. Why did she have to ask that?

The door opened.

"Thanks, Leslie," I muttered, sinking deeper into the chair.

"I'm never too busy to bring you anything, Kate."

My eyes shot open. Damian stood in front of me, arms crossed with a hint of anger written on his face. I dropped my gaze.

Damian sat in the chair beside me. It hurt that he hadn't called the day before, and I still hadn't forgotten Saturday night.

"Look, Kate, there's only so many times I can apologize," he said. "Have you read it yet?"

I shook my head. "Why can't you just tell me?"

He shifted uncomfortably. "I can't."

I glared at him. "You can't, or you won't?"

"It's not that easy," Damian said, his voice rising.

"Sure it is. Don't make things hard."

"It *is* hard, Kate! That's something you don't

151

seem to understand."

"Then I guess you need to enlighten me." I crossed my arms over my chest and leaned back, challenging him.

Damian rose to his feet. "Life doesn't always fit into your candy-filled boxes. You're so fucking scared of the tough shit that you minimize it and brush it off your shoulder like a speck of dirt. Real life doesn't work that way."

"I'm scared? Me?" I shot out of my chair. "What have you been doing for the last two years? You lost two of the closest people in your life, and you're intent on pushing your father away too. You cope by dousing yourself in alcohol so you don't have to feel the pain, when maybe that's exactly what you need."

"Everyone deals with shit their own way."

"Yeah, they do. But you're hiding from it."

Damian threw his arms out to the side. "You get what you see, babe. At least *I'm* not pretending."

"Oh, yes, you are," I retorted. "You sink yourself into your bad-boy image so people will leave you alone. Everyone else might buy it, but I don't."

"I didn't ask you to buy anything. You've made up this bullshit story that everything is perfect in your little cancer-filled life—like it doesn't eat you up inside every second of every day. You put on this fucking façade that you're happy because it's easier to pretend it's actually true than have to deal with the reality of your disease."

My nostrils flared as heat boiled through my veins. "Get out," I growled.

"Happy to, princess." He slammed the door

behind him, and I fell back into the chair, tears burning my eyes.

I didn't look up when Leslie came in and asked if I was okay. When I didn't answer, she took the hint and left. I broke down.

At home, I stormed up to my room and refused to come down for dinner. I wrenched Damian's journal out of the drawer and glowered at the brown leather cover. What had he written that he couldn't tell me face to face? I squeezed the journal in my hands, almost folding it in half. After what he'd said today, the last place I wanted to be was inside his head. Anger filled me again. I screamed as I threw his journal across the room.

~*~

December 22
Dear Diary,

I keep staring at Damian's journal on the floor. It's been there for two days. I can't bring myself to pick it up, let alone read it. He hasn't called or texted or stopped over.

I hear his voice in my head. I feel his hand in mine sometimes, especially when I'm asleep. Last night I woke up actually thinking he was there, holding me. It was just my own arm draped over my stomach.

I stuffed all my blue clothes under my

bed. Every time I shuffled past a blue sweater, his eyes flashed in my head.

Maybe it's better that it's over. We can both move on, and...I miss him so much. How is that possible after today?

I can't stop thinking about what he said. Life isn't supposed to be hard. Isn't it always better to find the bright side of things? Always look for the good, my grandma used to say. That's what I've been doing, trying to stay positive.

So what, I have leukemia. It's just a part of life—well, my life. Is that simplifying it too much? Am I using it as an excuse to hide because I'm too scared of the possibilities?

He's wrong. I'm stronger than that.

Chapter 14

December 23
Dear Diary,

My last treatment before Christmas is almost over and Damian didn't show. I don't know if I expected him to or not. This whole thing is such a mess. And right before Christmas?

None of the nurses have asked me about Damian or the fight. I'm pretty sure they were congregated by the door listening in. When I came in today, I felt their stares on my back, but when I swung around, everyone seemed busy.

I didn't see Damian in the halls.

I had another headache yesterday. It hurt so bad I couldn't even cry over Damian. I missed having him there, holding me. His presence makes the pain more bearable. I sleep better knowing he's there.

I can't deal with the conversations in my own mind right now, much less explain to a real person why things between us were over. My mother asked if she should call him—I didn't tell her about the fight. I hate lying to her, but I still told her he was out of town.

I have to admit it to myself first.

~*~

The door opened, and Leslie peeked in. She straightened her uniform as she walked over and unhooked the medication.

"Leslie?"

"Yeah."

I hesitated for a few seconds. "Has…is Damian here?"

She nodded slowly.

I felt like someone punched me in the stomach. "Is he okay?"

She sat down on the chair beside me. "He's fine. He's doing his work and playing with the younger patients."

"Oh." Why couldn't she tell me that he'd called in sick? Or that his mood was depressing the whole floor? Or that he'd admitted he hadn't slept in days? "That's good." I dropped my gaze.

When I didn't elaborate, Leslie added, "You should go talk to him."

My hand clung to the necklace Damian had given to me, slinking the charm up and down the silver chain. "I don't think he wants to talk to the girl he dumped. Besides, I wouldn't know what to say."

"Well," she said grinning, "'hello' is always a good place to start."

Leslie stood and kissed my head. "I'll give you a few minutes."

"Uh, Leslie?" I said just as she opened the door. I hadn't intended to, but I felt a smile creeping across my face. "Were you all listening the other day?"

She laughed. "What do you think?"

"I think you're nosy."

"I prefer to call it 'staying informed.'"

I giggled. "Thanks, Leslie."

She nodded and walked out.

Alone, I paced the room trying to decide what to say to Damian. I thought about what Leslie said, then considered how it tied together. When I was ready, I checked myself in the mirror, put on my black knit cap—"the one with the, uh, little flower thing"—and applied some strawberry lip-gloss.

I frowned. Who was I kidding?

I grabbed my stuff and kept my head low as I passed the nurses' station. As usual, I had to wait for the stupid elevators. Why couldn't there be more of them in this place? I tapped my foot, stealing glances down the hallway every so often.

The elevator dinged. "Ugh, thank you," I whispered to myself. As the silver doors slid open, my breath caught. Damian, wearing his sky blue scrubs and looking as gorgeous as ever, stood inside, arms crossed over his chest. When he saw me, he dropped his arms.

"Hi," I managed. *Hi? Real smooth.*

He stepped out toward me. "Hey."

And my second line was? *Oh crap.*

"Um, I…I just got done." My voice sounded unrecognizable in my ears.

Damian glanced up at the clock then locked on me. "Yeah. Sorry. I, uh, had stuff Tammy wanted me to do."

"Oh, yeah, of course." We stood in silence, me shifting my weight and Damian staring at me.

"Are you done for the day?" I asked. "I mean, um, do you wanna, maybe, grab something to eat downstairs? My treat?"

Where did that come from?

"I can't tonight," he answered, not flinching. "There's some stuff I have to do."

"Oh! Yeah. Sure." Fighting the heat rising to my face took everything I had. "Well, um, have a good night then."

Damian's features softened, and for a split second I wondered if he would lean into me. I would've been fine with it, but he didn't. "You, too."

I nodded, forced a smile, then started for the doorway to the stairwell. Cradling the emptiness in my stomach with one hand, I reached for the handle and yanked the door open.

"Katie?" Damian stood in the same place.

The way he said my name, *Katie*, knocked the air out of me. I froze and held my breath. Slowly, I peered over my shoulder. "Yeah?"

The corner of his mouth curved up, and my heart

skipped a beat.

"I'll call you later."

"Okay." I couldn't stop the tears from escaping. Not wanting him to see, I ducked through the door.

I ran down the stairs and out to my car as fast as I could. I sat behind the wheel with drops streaming down my face. I didn't bother to wipe them away.

Seeing Damian, hearing him say my name, created a swell of longing in me. He'd hurt me, but I drove it right back at him. More than anything, I wanted to forgive him. To take back all the mean stuff I said, and have him wrap his arms around me and never let go. I needed to feel safe in his embrace again. Standing beside him and not touching him had turned me to mush. Yes, I still loved him.

After sitting in the parking lot for who-knows-how-long, I peered through the windshield. The windows of my Volkswagen Beetle were fogged over. I fumbled with the key and stuck it in the ignition. Almost immediately, the defrost kicked on and began to clear the clouds from the glass.

My head hurt from crying, and I hoped I'd be able to make it home before it blazed full force. Dr. Lowell had given me a migraine prescription, and I kept the pills in the bathroom with all the other meds I had to take.

When I got home, the headache hadn't worsened, but I popped the pills anyway, then crawled between my sheets.

I didn't want to think about anything. Not the indifference in Damian's eyes. Not the promise that he'd call. Not the conversation with Leslie. All I wanted was to drift off to sleep and forget everything.

The sound of my cell woke me. It almost slipped from my hand when I reached for it. I groaned, breathing heavily. Still lying on my stomach, I answered without checking the caller ID. Through the blur, I could barely make out the letters and numbers anyway.

"Hello?" I croaked.

"Hey." Damian's voice sounded soft on the other end, but it was amplified in my ear.

"Uh," I gasped and held the phone away. The pain seared, and I folded my free arm around my stomach. Struggling to hold the vomit at bay, I finally replied. "Hi."

"Katie, what's wrong?" His tone changed to concern.

"Um. Headache." I didn't move my lips when I spoke.

"I'll be right there."

I threw up in the garbage can.

When I awoke, it was morning. Sunrise, actually. Damian lay beside me, his arm draped over my stomach. A surge of happiness enveloped me. His hands gliding over my body and slipping my dress off flashed in my mind. I reached for his hand and drew it to my lips. The warmth from his skin filled me. He didn't stir. Gently, I tucked his arm between us and faced him. I ran my fingers through his hair and kissed his cheek. He twitched a little, a dimple flashing me. Adorable.

"I'm sorry," I whispered. "I love you."

I didn't remember him coming into the room the night before, but the soothing presence of his body had radiated through me as I slept. I giggled a little, wondering how much sweet-talking he had to do to convince my parents to stay all night.

I kissed him again, then swung my legs over the side of the bed. I glanced over my shoulder, making sure I hadn't disturbed him. Beams of sunlight streamed through the curtains, casting a glow on everything in the room. I crawled up on the window seat and peeked outside.

Cracking the window slightly, I closed my eyes and breathed in the freshness of the morning. Nothing smelled so sweet. I tilted my head back and imagined a beach sunrise in the spring. The coolness of the breeze surrounding me and the icy-cold water washing up over my bare feet filled my senses, and as always, Damian was beside me.

Pleasurable warmth against my back that spread like wildfire through the rest of me woke me from my trance. I swiveled my head to see Damian standing behind me.

"Did I wake you?" I asked timidly. Somehow, he being awake made my heart flutter in ways it hadn't when he slept.

"Yeah." The corners of his lips crept up. "I couldn't feel you next to me anymore."

"Sorry."

He crept up behind me, one leg on either side, arms wrapped around me. I leaned my head back against his chest, melting into him. It felt so good to have him close.

"It's amazing, isn't it?" I asked, gazing out the window. "No matter how dark it gets, the sun always rises eventually and starts a new day. The darkness is forgotten."

"Mmm," he hummed in my ear. "I'm sorry."

I nestled my head into him. "No. You were right."

"I don't want to be right," he murmured, his fingers stroking my cheek. "I just want to be with you."

My heart swelled, and I forced my pride away. "I'm sorry, too. I had no right to—"

He leaned down, cutting me off. "You had every right," he said against my mouth.

"New day?" I whispered.

"Darkness forgotten."

He kissed me again.

~*~

Damian stayed the rest of Christmas Eve with me. We put our baking skills to the test and whipped up a batch of sugar cookies. More sugar and flour lay in patches on the kitchen counter than what made it into the bowl. Admittedly, the flour wasn't exactly accidental.

Damian volunteered to mix up the frosting.

"What's 'shortening?'" He furrowed his brow and tapped the recipe card against the counter. The flour on his face and cookie dough in his hair made him look cuter than usual.

"This stuff." I tossed him a bar of Crisco. "Like

162

butter."

"*Like* butter?" His nose crinkled. "Why don't they just say butter?"

"To confuse you." I shrugged and watched as he plopped the whole bar into the mixing bowl.

"It's working, 'cause the next ingredient is actual butter."

Suddenly, Damian grabbed me around the waist."Hey!" I laughed.

He didn't listen, but tackled me lightly to the floor. He kissed my lips then my nose, and before he got up, the punk actually smeared Crisco on my head.

"You better watch your back, Lowell!" I said, wiping it off.

When his frosting was finished, it looked...uh...weird. And a little crunchy.

"Did you use *powdered* sugar?"

"I used sugar." He grabbed the container of regular sugar. "Like it said."

"Right." I giggled. "Why don't we throw this out and start all over?"

The next batch tasted better, and what didn't end up in the mixing bowel matched nicely with the cookie dough in his hair. Payback!

We didn't need all the frosting because we didn't have enough cookies. Mom retrieved two sheets of black snowmen—which Damian dubbed, *coalmen*—and Christmas trees from the oven while Damian and I were too busy making out on the sofa. After that, we stayed entangled in the kitchen—with one eye open.

"I need to use the bathroom," I said after setting

last batch on top of the oven. "I'll be right back."

Damian patted my butt as I walked away. Passing my parents' room, I overheard my dad talking. I stopped when I heard my name.

"Kate's lost weight, Marcy," he said. "And the headaches are getting more frequent."

"I know," Mom answered. "But look at her! I've never seen her happier than when she's with him. She glows."

"Yeah. We can't ignore it, though," Dad replied. "Any news on the donor front?"

"No. Nothing." Mom sighed. "I'll…I'll make an appointment after Christmas."

I heard them move, and I darted past the door and into the bathroom. I leaned my head against the inside of the door, focusing on the ceiling.

My hand automatically lifted my shirt and rubbed my stomach. I slipped my hand between my hips and the waist-band of my jeans. Since Damian had come into my life, I hadn't noticed how I could put them on and take them off without unbuttoning them. I walked over to the mirror and pulled my shirt over my head. The reflection of my ribs, easily defined, created a lump in my throat. I twisted and examined my back. Ribs there, too. They protruded more than they used to.

I picked my shirt up off the floor and put it back on. Then I leaned in closer to the mirror. The contrast to the rest of my body was easily recognizable. I'd never seen my eyes so bright and healthy. Even without makeup, my cheeks had color and my lips were the perfect shade of pink.

I shook my head. The weight-loss and headaches

had to be the chemo. *You're on the strongest dose,* Dr. Lowell had said. Stupid side-effects.

Making a mental note to buy some new jeans or a belt, I hurried back out to the kitchen.

Damian and I frosted about a dozen cookies before my mom walked in and almost had a heart attack. Her OCD in holiday decorations kicked into overdrive at the sight. Red frosting had made its way into the white, the black sat in clumps on the dining room table, and the green was splattered on her homemade glass ball Christmas tree that we forgot to take off the table. Besides all that, Frosty's silver buttons weren't perfectly aligned.

She tapped her fingers on her teeth, trying not to bite her nails. "Why don't you two go clean up? I'll finish in here."

I took a quick shower in the upstairs bathroom while Damian washed the frosting and dough out of his hair downstairs. Since Mom was OCDing over our cookies, we cuddled up on the sofa to watch *Miracle on 42nd Street*. We both dozed off somewhere in the middle.

Dad woke us up before dinner. As per Browdy family tradition, we went out for Chinese on Christmas Eve night. After a little persuasion, kissing him repeatedly and shooting him my best puppy-dog face, Damian finally caved and agreed to join us. Once there, he ate pizza—uh-huh, *pizza*— off the buffet.

When we got home, Mom pulled out the exquisitely decorated cookies. We gathered around the dining room table and played Rook, not bothering to keep score. Everyone smiling, everyone laughing, and for a few minutes, surrounded by the people I loved most in the world, I felt truly happy.

"What are you doing tomorrow?" I asked Damian as we stood by the front door at the end of the evening. "I don't want you to be alone."

"As of now, Dad's not working. We usually spend Christmas Day with my mom's folks here in town."

He ran both his hands down the sides of my face, then leaned down, kissing me slowly. I held him close, memorizing the moment.

"Merry Christmas, Katie."

Chapter 15

Christmas morning after I turned six, I remember bounding down the stairs at our house in Nebraska, eager to rip open the presents under the tree. My excitement got the best of me, though. Halfway down, I tripped over my nightgown and fell the rest of the way, breaking my ankle. Christmas morning was spent in the emergency room, and I needed help to open my presents when we got home. At the time, I vowed I'd never spend another day in the hospital.

This morning my alarm woke me before sunrise. I padded to my window seat and settled in. As the sun emerged over the horizon, the snow glittered like diamonds on the ground. Leaning back against the pillows and wrapping the blanket around my shoulders, I curled into a ball and simply enjoyed the moment. Until my mother came to wake me, I hadn't realized I'd fallen asleep.

"You feeling okay this morning, sweetie? We thought you'd be downstairs by now."

"I feel great, Mom. Just dozed off." I swung my

167

legs over the side, keeping the blanket snug around me. "What time is it, anyway?"

"Eleven."

"Are you serious?" I dropped the blanket. "Did I miss anything?"

Mom sat beside me. "Of course not." She hugged me to her side and kissed my temple. "Take your time and come down when you're ready."

Just as Mom closed the door behind her, my cell buzzed. I flew across my room and swept up the phone laying on my night stand. There was only one person who'd text me on Christmas morning.

Damian: Merry Christmas. I miss u like crazy.

Me: Miss u more.

Damian: C u 2nite.

Me: Can't wait.

I dressed quickly and tucked my cell in the back pocket of my jeans. Not wanting to relive the Christmas from when I was six, I descended the stairs at a normal pace, though I was dying to see what was under the tree.

My parents were sitting on the sofa sipping on coffee. One plate of pastries and a plate of mini-sausage biscuits sat untouched on the coffee table, along with a full cup of warm coffee for me.

"Good morning, sleepyhead." Dad handed me the mug, and I sat on the floor. "Half creamer, just as you like it."

"Thanks," I muttered, ignoring the disgusted face he made, and lifted the mug to my mouth. I let the liquid linger on my lips as if the warmth belonged to Damian.

My gaze wandered to the brightly wrapped packages in the corner. One caught my eye immediately: a small white box with a red satin bow.

"Stocking time!" Mom announced, slipping off the sofa and crawling on her hands and knees under the tree.

Since before I could remember, we each had a stocking overflowing with goodies and three gifts apiece under the tree. From the looks of it, the tradition continued.

Mom handed me my stocking first, then took hers and Dad's back to the sofa. I dug in before she'd sat down. Mine included the usual assortment of makeup, nail polishes, an iTunes gift card, and a couple new knit hats.

When we were done, Mom handed me a tiny package wrapped in blue snowflake paper and a shiny white bow. I sat it on my lap and waited my turn. Dad opened his first and pulled out an out-of-print book he'd been searching months for.

Mom shrugged. "I got lucky."

He kissed her, and I smiled. "Thank you, baby."

Inside Mom's box lay a new bathrobe from Victoria's Secret. I wondered if Dad had ordered it online rather than step foot into the store at the mall.

"All right, Kate. Open it up." Mom sat on the edge of her seat.

She didn't have to tell me twice. I tore it open

and flipped the lid off the black velvet box. A golden bracelet with my name engraved on it lay inside.

"Look on the back," Mom urged.

I lifted the bracelet and turned it over in my hand. *You're our blessing.* "Thank you," I said, fastening it onto my wrist.

Mom handed out the next round. On Dad's lap sat the gift I'd bought. It took me forever to decide on something for him, and I hoped he liked it.

I watched expectantly as he took his time with the tape. He liked to make it a challenge by not ripping the paper. When I was little, I thought he did it to teach me patience. I'm not sure it worked.

"Oh, Katie!" He held up the framed picture of Memorial Stadium in Lincoln, Nebraska, home to his beloved Cornhuskers and alma mater. "This is great. I know just where to hang it."

"I don't think so," Mom growled playfully. "I am *not* looking at that every time we go to bed."

"Above the television, then?"

"Attic?"

"Den?"

"We'll talk."

I giggled. I was definitely with Dad on this one.

Mom opened hers and gasped. I knew what it was because I'd helped Dad pick it out at the jewelry store. She picked it out of the box and slid it onto her finger. Dad held up her hand to examine the Mother's ring, a heart with my birthstone in the center.

"Looks better on you than in the box." He kissed her hand.

170

My next gift was long and heavy. I went at it like a cat with catnip and gaped at a brand new set of golf clubs.

"Seriously?"

"A girl on the varsity team needs a good set," Dad reasoned.

"I'm not on the team yet."

"You will be."

I blushed. "Thanks."

Mom gathered up the last of the gifts under the tree and handed Dad the white one that I was sure belonged to me from Damian.

"Why don't you go first, Marcy." Dad set the box on the end table beside him. I kept my eyes glued to it until I heard Mom's squeal of delight.

"Thank you, Katie!"

I'd bought her one of those craft cutting machines. I was pretty sure she'd find something to use it for by the end of the day.

"Okay, my turn." I opened the envelope in my hand. I yanked out the slip of paper.

Check the closet.

I glanced up at my parents. Dad smirked, and Mom nodded to the hall closet. I jumped to my feet and ran, throwing the door open. My jaw fell to the floor. I dragged out the orange golf bag and matching club sleeves. Each sleeve had an orange cancer ribbon embroidered on it.

"Best. Christmas. Ever!" I set the bag in the middle of the living room floor and reached down to fill it with my new clubs when Dad said, "It's not

171

over yet."

I paused and stared at him.

"I still have one gift left to open," he said with a knowing grin. "But I think you should have it."

I took the box from his hand and slipped off the red satin bow. My heart sped up with each piece of torn tape until it was thumping against my ribs. Carefully, I lifted the lid. Tucked behind red tissue paper lay two plane tickets to Orlando and two passes to Disney World. I couldn't breathe.

~*~

Damian came by that evening. I waited impatiently at the door, watching him drive up. He must have seen the giddiness on my face because he flashed me a flirtatious smirk and started walking extra slowly.

"Get in here!" I yelled, cracking the door open a little.

He stopped, put his index finger over his lips, and rolled his eyes to the sky, being a tease.

"Ahh!" I searched the floor for my boots, but seconds later the door flew open, and I was lifted into Damian's arms.

"Disney World tickets?" I exclaimed when he set me down.

"You said you wanted to go." He shrugged. "I planned it with your parents. We'll leave at the end of May, after school."

"Just you and me?" *My parents went along with that?*

His grin widened. "Just you and me."

I threw my arms around his neck, kissing him until I couldn't breathe.

"I have something for you, too." I led him to the sofa and grabbed the envelope from the side table and handed it to him.

"Get well. That's all I want," he said, setting the gift aside and scooping me into his arms.

"I'm working on it. But for now…" I put the envelope back in his hands.

He opened it up and slipped out the folded piece of paper. His mouth dropped open. "To record three of my songs in an actual recording studio?"

"Do you like it?"

His lips pressed together as he faced me. "Thank you." His voice was quiet, and when he kissed me, I understood how thankful he was.

~*~

December 31

Dear Diary,

I haven't suffered a headache all week. Nor has my mother mentioned me having a special appointment with Dr. Lowell. I've been trying to make an effort to eat more even though I'm not hungry. So far, it seems to satisfy my parents and Damian.

Tonight, Damian and I are helping with the New Year's Eve party at the children's hospital. Damian's in charge of the wheelchair races, and I volunteered to man the mini-mini-golf course. My mother even made a glittering paper ball that will fall at midnight for the event.

I'm not expected home until tomorrow afternoon. A whole night with Damian! YAY!

January 1
Dear Diary,
Just got home—it's 2:00pm.
We had a blast! With Damian's "help," Brennan got first place in the wheelchair races. His adorable toothy smile won my heart as Damian put the gold medal around his neck on the podium.

Mom's ball was a huge hit with the kids, but I only knew that because of the cheers erupting in the Commons. I didn't actually see it fall because Damian had pulled me into an empty room so he could kiss me at midnight. Best kiss ever! And that's saying something.

I don't know how I could love him more.

We stayed and helped the nurses clean up and take all the kids who had to stay back to their rooms. Finally, at four in the morning, Damian and I found an empty room and crawled in bed. Exhausted, I fell asleep before he had a chance to kiss me goodnight. When we woke up, it was past noon, so we went out for lunch—and not in the cafeteria!

Okay, gotta go. I'm heading over to Damian's for the day to swim in his indoor pool.

January 3
Dear Diary,

Today was the first day back to school— me to Roosevelt and Damian to Valley. I've thought about him all day, wondering how he's doing.

Several of my teachers pulled me aside after class to ask how I was feeling. Once, the girl whose locker is next to mine said hello between the bells, then gathered her things and disappeared into the crowd before I could respond.

After school, a dozen red roses waited for me in the office. The card simply said, Missed you.

Damian and I talked all through my chemo treatment at the hospital. He promised me he'd try harder this semester. I mean, he has to if he wants to graduate in May. I offered to help, and he dropped his math text in my lap. For the rest of the day, we ended up doing homework.

It sucks being back in school.

January 5

Dear Diary,

Had another headache yesterday, so I stayed home from school. I had to convince Damian not to skip. I'm not sure when he showed up, but he said he went a full day before coming over. I don't remember when he left.

January 6
Dear Diary,

Dr. Lowell showed up at the end of my chemo treatment today. He asked about the headaches. I told him that they were still painful, but I thought they were less frequent than they had been. He reminded me I only had three treatments left of the 12 week cycle and then there was the routine blood draw. I couldn't read his expression as he suggested that we should do the blood draw early—like today. Not only that, but he wanted to do a full work up.

Damian stayed as Leslie wrapped the tourniquet around my upper arm and drew the vials of blood. When she left, Damian asked why my blood was being tested early. Instead of the full truth, I told him his dad just wanted to see if the chemo was causing the headaches. How could I tell him the real truth when I don't want to think about it myself?

I put down my pen. It was late, after midnight, and I couldn't sleep. My mind had been spinning since Damian left.

I'd go for the scans and other tests tomorrow. I didn't tell Damian about those. The results would take about a week to get back, and I wasn't sure if I'd be able to wait that long. I didn't want to think about it, but it was impossible not to.

My parents had told me that they requested the early draw. The house was unusually quiet all evening, even with Damian here. It was in the backs of all our minds.

~*~

January 11
Dear Diary,
Dr. Lowell called today. He got the test results back. I asked that our meeting be held during school hours; I didn't want Damian there if the results were less than positive. It's tomorrow. How am I going to wait until then?

~*~

My parents and I sat in front of Dr. Lowell's large mahogany desk. He took off his glasses and set them down on top of my file. Then he leaned forward.

Déjà vu tugged at my memory. I recognized that

look. I'd seen it before. Three times before, in fact. I sank into my seat.

Dr. Lowell's gaze shifted from my father, to my mother, and then to me. I fidgeted in my seat and stared at my hands.

"I'm sorry, Kate." His voice was low. I heard him take a deep breath as if he were struggling with what to say next. When I glanced up, his cheeks were flushed. "Your numbers haven't improved. You're no longer responding to treatments, and the cancer is spreading into your organs."

My eyelids fell. I hung my head and balled up my hands. Even though I had expected it, it hurt to hear it said out loud. I worked to keep everything in, afraid of allowing myself to explode in front of everyone. I had to be strong.

"What are our options?" Dad reached for my mother's hand.

"Well," Dr. Lowell started, "she's still on the transplant list, waiting for a match. There's also a new experimental drug out. I can send a referral."

"What does that mean?" My mother's voice sounded like she was already shedding tears. I didn't look at her.

Dr. Lowell cleared his throat. "It means they only take certain cases and a limited number. You'll have to drive to Mayo, they'll do an initial evaluation there, see if you qualify."

"And if she does?" Dad asked.

"They'll do the initial treatments there, then send the medication here where she can finish the study. She'll have to go back every so often for follow-up evaluations."

Dad said my name. I don't know how many times. All I could think about was more tests, more medications, more hospitals. And for what? An experiment?

"Katie," Dad asked again, kneeling beside me.

I shifted my gaze to him. He looked as if he'd aged ten years since Dr. Lowell had called this meeting the day before. The creases in his forehead seemed deeper, and gray patches rippled through his brown hair.

"This is your choice, sweetheart. You've been through so much already."

My mother sobbed in the seat next to me.

I shifted my attention to the doctor without really seeing him. "What is the success rate of this new drug?"

Dr. Lowell pursed his lips. Before, he'd been upbeat and positive. I guessed I really was running out of options. I wondered if he was always this hesitant with bad news.

"There aren't any. Not until the study's finished."

"And how long is that?"

"Two years." Dr. Lowell averted his gaze and coughed as if he knew my next question.

I straightened up in my chair, forcing my voice to remain steady and confident. "And if I don't do it, and no donor is found, how long do I have?"

My mother choked back her tears. Stunned silence filled the room when Dr. Lowell answered. I nodded slightly.

"When does the study start?" I finally asked.

"I'd be happy to refer you anytime. I have the

paperwork right here." Dr. Lowell grabbed a manila envelope from a stack on his desk. "I can fill it out now."

"I'll think about it and let you know." My voice finally cracked.

From the look in the doctor's eyes, it wasn't the answer he'd expected.

Chapter 16

January 12

Dear Diary,

I've been staring at this blank piece of paper for hours now, trying to figure out how I feel. My parents were so quiet in the car on the way home. I don't want to disappoint them with whatever decision I make. Don't get me wrong, I'm glad they're letting me choose the next course of action, but it doesn't make it any easier.

I've been fighting for so long. How much do I have left in me? I'm tired.

I'm still hoping for a donor match, and I'll keep hoping for it. A transplant is the only guarantee of living a cancer-free life.

But an experimental drug? I don't know.

I'm going to finish out this round of chemo—hope to at least slow the spreading.

I don't know what to tell Damian. Sure, he deserves to know, but...why can't this be easier?

~*~

The weekend flew by without me making any decisions. At school I found myself studying my fellow classmates. The girl who sat next to me in math hid under long-sleeve hoodies to cover the bruises from her boyfriend. One of the star basketball players was out for the season with a torn ACL and might miss the opportunity for a scholarship. And the girl whose locker was next to mine was having a baby in two months. I'd take any one of their problems instead.

Before the class ended, I grabbed my things and ran out. I jumped in my car and drove. With no destination in mind, I still ended up at the hospital. Great.

Two hours early for my last chemo treatment, I sat in the cafeteria with a bowl of Jell-O. At least it wasn't red. I picked at it for fifteen minutes before dumping it in the garbage.

Brennan received his chemo treatment before me, so I wandered up to the third floor. He was sitting in the Commons playing Wii by himself, his mother preoccupied at the nurses' station.

"Hey." I tousled his golden head. "Want a racing buddy?"

His green eyes lit up. "Yeah!" he said, immediately handing me a remote.

He selected our courses and like Damian had, beat the mushrooms off me—pun intended. Must be a guy talent or something.

"I have my last treatment today, bud," I said, selecting a different character.

"Are you cured?" he asked.

I shook my head. "No, but I will be someday. Never give up, okay?"

Brennan cocked his head to the side. "Will your boyfriend still come here, even if you're not?"

I breathed out a laugh. "Yeah. He'll still come here."

Brennan's boyish grin widened. "Good. I like him."

"Yeah," I said. "I do, too."

He laid his controller on his lap, and his face got serious. "He loves you."

My breath caught. "How do you know that?"

"By the way he looks at you," Brennan said, shrugging. "Plus he told me."

He picked up his blue controller and chose a new set of races to beat me on. A lump suddenly materialized in my throat.

"Wait, he told you *what*?"

"Hmm-hmm," Brennan nodded. "Enough to marry you."

I laughed as I envisioned *that* conversation. His childhood innocence was adorable.

"Well, he's never told me that."

"My mom says it's hard for some guys to say. But it doesn't make it not-true. She always tells me how much my dad loved me, even though he didn't say it much."

Loved?

"Where's your dad now?" I held my breath as soon as I said it.

"He died three years ago. Motorcycle accident."

Oh.

"I'm so sorry," I said.

"It's okay. He's in Heaven now." The way he said it warmed me. Always looking up. "Are we gonna play?"

"Come on, Donkey Kong, let's start this race!" I said, sitting up into my primo racing position.

After four more races, I still lost. Brennan was doing a victory dance around the Commons. I was giggling at him when I suddenly started to feel dizzy. The laughter died out, and I leaned back on the sofa, wrapping my elbow over my forehead to block out the light.

I heard Brennan beside me. "Hey, Kate? Kate? What's wrong? Want me to get Leslie?"

I took a few deep breaths in and out. In and Out. Thankfully, the dizziness dissipated, but a headache would probably plague me that evening.

"I'm fine. Just got a little dizzy, that's all," I assured him, forcing a grin.

"Hey! Damian!" Brennan exclaimed, forgetting me and bounding to the doorway.

"Hey, dude."

"I beat Kate on eight races," the little boy bragged.

"Whoa! Next time, pick on someone your own size. She's a lightweight," Damian teased. He walked over and kissed me.

"Can I race you?" Brennan asked, standing at

184

Damian's side.

Damian was about to answer when Leslie poked her head in. "Time to unhook you, Brennan."

"Oh man!" Brennan sulked.

"Hey, next time, bud," Damian said, giving Brennan a high five.

"Bye, Kate. I hope you feel better." Brennan followed Leslie out the door.

I waved a hand over my head. "Thanks, kid."

Damian's brows furrowed. "What happened?"

"I had a little dizzy spell, that's all. I'm fine," I repeated.

He glared at me for a few seconds before he dropped it. Moving closer, he folded me against his chest, kissing the top of my head.

"I missed you," he whispered.

"Not more than I missed you." I wrapped my arms around his waist. "How was school?"

"A royal pain in the ass," he answered, but when I glanced up at him, he was smiling. "Help me again?"

To answer, I pulled him to my lips and kissed him.

"Hmm-hmm." A voice at the doorway interrupted us. We both turned.

Leslie stood with her hands on her hips. "G-rated room, you two."

"Well," Damian said, rising to his feet and offering me his hand. "In that case, I know an empty room we could..."

"Sit down, Romeo," Leslie teased.

"I'll be right back." I laughed and kissed his dimpled cheek.

I felt his gaze on my back as I followed Leslie out of the Commons and into the chemo room. Falling into the chair, I began to feel light-headed again. All around me the clear lines of walls and furniture, IV poles and medication, started to blur into a poorly replicated Van Gogh painting.

I didn't feel myself slump lower in the chair. Nor could I respond to the fuzzy sound of Leslie's voice calling my name. The blinding light shone even brighter, causing my eyelids to close. My throat tightened.

I thought I heard a thunder of footsteps run into the room. I was suffocating. Voices—I couldn't decipher how many—ripped through my ear canals. I tried to cover them before my head exploded, but I didn't know if my hands moved or not.

My head pounded, and I wanted to throw up. The heaving in my stomach increased as my lungs cried out for oxygen. I vomited.

I just wanted everyone to stop moving, stop talking. I wanted the lights off so I could sleep. The room felt smaller than normal, like the walls were closing in, crushing me. All over, my body got tighter and tighter.

Then it stopped. The burning quenched. The sounds dissipated, and the lights darkened.

Warmth cascaded through me. My muscles relaxed, and my stomach calmed as I drifted to sleep.

~*~

When I opened my eyes, my mother was sitting

next to me holding my hand.

"Hey, sweetie."

I rubbed my temples, trying to remember what had happened. I scanned the chemo room. It was just Mom and me.

"Where's Damian?" My voice cracked.

Mom's gaze dropped, and she shook her head. "Sweetie, I didn't know you hadn't told him yet."

Like a kick in the stomach, pain radiated from my gut through the rest of my body.

Finding a renewed sense of strength, I sat up. "What did you tell him?"

"That you were no longer responding to treatments. You're considering an experimental drug, and you'll stay on the bone marrow transplant list." She squeezed my hand. "I think he went to find his father."

"How long have I been out?"

Mom sighed. "Eight hours."

I swung my legs over the side of the bed. "I've got to go find him."

"Kate," she said, standing in front of me. "You passed out and—"

"Am I being admitted?" My tone sounded a little harder than I intended.

"Leslie—"

"Am I. Being. Admitted?" I repeated, getting to my feet.

Mom shook her head. "No, but—"

"I'm fine. Please."

Stepping aside, my mother patted my shoulder, guilt flooding her face.

"Thanks Mom," I said and kissed her cheek.

I hurried out the door, wondering where to start searching. As I passed the nurses' station, one of the night-shift nurses asked me how I was doing and if I needed anything.

"Is Dr. Lowell in his office?"

"I think so," she replied.

Without thanking her, I ran down the hall and rounded the corner to Dr. Lowell's office. The door was cracked as usual, but I still knocked.

"Come in." His voice sounded strained.

Slowly, I pushed the door open. Dr. Lowell was sitting behind his desk flipping through a stack of medical files.

"Kate," he said, taking off his glasses. "How are you feeling?"

"Better. Thank you."

"The migraines—"

"I'm not here about that, actually."

Dr. Lowell nodded.

"Where is he?" My voice hung in the air.

Dr. Lowell rubbed the stubble on his chin. "He came to me after your mother talked to him. I only confirmed what she said, nothing more."

"And now?"

"Probably home with a bottle of Jack. Here," Dr. Lowell wrote something on a piece of paper. "You'll need this to get into the house."

I took the key code, thanked him and walked to the door. When I got there, I swung around.

"You're okay with his drinking?"

My doctor sat back in his seat and crossed his arms over his chest. "Sometimes you gotta do what you gotta do."

I narrowed my eyes and opened my mouth to speak, then closed it, too disgusted to say anything. For emphasis, I slammed the door on my way out.

Because it was late, the parking lot was emptier than usual. I ran to my car and jumped in. Without allowing the engine to warm up, I threw it into drive and sped onto the street, heading to Lincoln Place Drive.

Visions of how I'd find Damian when I got to his house flashed in my mind. Fear flushed my face at each picture. I gripped the steering wheel tighter, wishing I'd just told him.

The traffic light turned red, and I squealed to a stop, jerking my body forward then back against the seat. I laid my head back against the headrest, reminding myself to breathe.

"Come on, come on, come on."

As I waited for the light, I tapped the top of the steering wheel with my fingers. I considered running it when there was a break in traffic, but my foot didn't leave the brake pedal until it changed to green. My tires spun before the car finally sped forward.

Pulling into the Lowells' driveway, memories of our Christmas date filled my mind. Tonight, all the Christmas lights seemed dim in comparison. The house itself loomed in despair. No lights graced the windows.

I stepped out of the car in less of a hurry than before. Now that I was there, I had to convince myself to keep moving. My arms ached to be wrapped around Damian's body, but all I could envision was the sorrow that would be behind his sea-blue eyes.

Standing on the entryway of the door, I paused, resting my forehead against it. What would I find inside?

If he falls for you, and you die, it will kill him.

I took a deep breath, remembering how I hadn't seen any full bottles of alcohol in his room the last time. My spirits lifted slightly.

I dug in my pocket for the key code and punched it in the pad. The little green light glowed, and I opened the door.

"Damian?" I said quietly.

Please, just be asleep.

The foyer was dark. I stopped and listened, hoping for some clue as to where he was in the massive house. Dead silence stung my ears. A knot formed in my stomach as I scanned the room.

Something else didn't feel right, though. Goose bumps formed over my arms.

I patted the walls for a light switch. After almost knocking over a vase, I found the switches and flipped them all on. I'm not sure what I expected with the lights on, but nothing seemed different.

My eyes drifted to the entrance to the den. Clenching my fists, I walked across the foyer. All I heard was the beating of my own heart and the heaviness of my breath.

I fumbled inside the doorway for the light switch, silently hoping not to find what I feared. Maybe Damian was just asleep on the sofa. And maybe this feeling in the pit of my stomach was my imagination. Then the smell of alcohol stung my nostrils.

When I flipped on the light, my stomach lurched. Beer cans littered the floor, most only partially drank and pouring out onto the hardwood floor and Persian rug. Half-empty vodka and whisky bottles laid on their sides on the end tables. It looked as though he'd opened them, drank some, then dumped the rest. Damian wasn't there.

I returned to the foyer. "Damian?" I hollered up the stairs.

A sense of urgency took over, making me dart up the stairs. My clammy hands balled at my sides. I hurried through the shadows. There was only one room I had in mind, and the more I thought about it, the colder I got.

My hand shook as it reached for the doorknob of Damian's bedroom door. I paused for a second before pushing it open. My heart pounded.

I almost turned around at the smell that wafted out of the room. Quickly, I placed a hand over my face, trying to breathe in some sort of freshness. There wasn't any. I lifted my shirt up over my mouth and nose and held on tight. My stomach churned, and I fought the urge to throw up and add to the horrific odor of vomit and alcohol already in the room.

Holding my breath, I turned on the light. Wide-eyed, I dropped my hand, letting my shirt fall back into place. A few seconds passed before I realized the scream filling the room belonged to me.

Chapter 17

I had expected to see Damian passed out. The rest of it, however, made my insides shake. Yanking the cell from my pocket, I dialed 911 as I strode over to where Damian lay on his bed, surrounded by a pool of his own vomit.

"911, what's your emergency?"

"I need...I need an ambulance."

Stunned, I knelt next to him, taking in his pale skin and sunken sockets.

"Are you injured, ma'am?"

"No. Not me. He's...he's passed out."

"And where are you, ma'am?"

I don't know how many times she repeated her question before I gave her the address and the key code Dr. Lowell had given me.

"I'm sending an ambulance now, ma'am."

"Thank you," I said, dazed. I didn't recognize my own voice.

"Ma'am? Stay on the phone with me, ma'am."

"Thank you," I repeated, not taking my eyes off Damian. Without hanging up, I allowed the phone

192

to slip from my hand and fall to the floor.

I took a couple of steps backward, staring at his lifeless body. Was he breathing? Holding my breath, I stood perfectly still watching until I saw his chest rise and fall slightly. Then I let the oxygen out of my lungs.

"Ma'am? Ma'am? Are you there?" The voice on the other end of my phone grew louder.

The words woke me from my trance. A bottle of Scotch, half drunk and without the lid, had poured out on his bed, a few beer cans lay on the floor covered with vomit, and an array of cigarettes were crushed into the carpet. I covered my mouth with my hand.

Squeaky whimpers sounded in my throat.

Blood had dried down the inside of his forearm. I glared at it, unable to process what I saw.

"Send two ambulances." The operator sounded muffled. "The girl who called..."

What? Me?

As if on their own, my eyes glided to the phone. I don't remember picking it off the floor and hanging up, but the voice on the other end stopped talking. With the phone still in my hand, I swallowed. It took everything I had to remember how to breathe. Heat flowed through my body, burning in my veins. I slipped the phone in my pocket on autopilot.

Listening to the sound of thick silence, I fixed on the way Damian's legs fell over the edge of his bed. His head lay cocked to the side with one hand over his chestnut hair, the other sprawled out over the blanket. Without thinking, I yanked the tourniquet off his arm and threw it as far across the room as I could.

"I thought you cared about me!"

I wanted to beat on his chest. "I thought you—"

Shaking, I reached down and took his hand in mine and squeezed too hard. With my lids closed, I lifted his hand to my lips.

If he falls for you, and you die…Katie, it'll kill him.

I dropped his hand as if it were on fire.

No. NO!

Talking a few steps backward, I locked on Damian's ghost-like face.

I should have told him. He should have found out from me. I should have been there.

"Damian, I'm *so* sorry!"

My whole body trembled as I stood against the closet doors for support. A mixture of anger, fear, and regret shot out in small gasps. Then I'd calm myself for a few seconds before another round began. No matter what I did, I couldn't look away.

Beads of sweat dripped from my forehead. Wiping them away, my knees buckled and I lost my balance, landing on the floor. I couldn't get back up; I didn't want to. Instead, I curled my legs up to my chest, and stared out in front of me.

That's how the paramedics found me. I never heard them come into the house or walk upstairs. I don't even remember them coming into Damian's room. One second my eyes were concentrated on Damian, the next, a bright light blinded me.

EMTs spoke to me, but I don't know what they said or if I answered. One took my blood pressure and another put an oxygen mask up to my face. I tried to shake it off because it blocked my view of what another group was doing to my boyfriend.

A paramedic picked something up off the bed beside Damian. He put it to his nose, a grimace appearing on his face.

"Heroin," he said, showing the woman taking Damian's blood pressure the needle.

"Bag it," she instructed.

I don't know what happened next because I started getting dizzy.

"Her blood pressure is sixty over thirty-five. We've got to get her to a hospital, now," someone said.

"Dami...Da..." I breathed.

"He'll be fine," a woman's voice assured me.

"But..."

I don't remember anything else.

~*~

When I awoke, I was alone in my hospital room. The sun sprinkled glitter through the window. My mouth felt like cotton, and I didn't see a glass of water anywhere. I thought about buzzing a nurse when the door to my room opened.

Dr. Lowell walked through quietly until he noticed I was awake. Then his shoulders fell, and he made his way over to my bed. He didn't have a hold of my chart, and his lips were pulled tight.

"Kate—"

"How's Damian?" I wasn't messing around. I had to know.

"He's fine. I'm more concerned about you right now." His eyes met mine on the last sentence.

"Me? Your son is falling apart and—" My nostrils flared.

"Kate." Dr. Lowell assured me with a hand on my shoulder. "I know. I'm taking care of it. Thank you for caring about him when I…"

His gaze dropped to the floor, sadness filling his aging features. He shifted his weight before resuming our conversation.

"I'm letting you go home today, but I need you to stay home and rest. You've overworked yourself the last couple of days, and your body can't handle it, Kate. Your mother is—"

"What do my parents know?" My voice was barely a whisper.

"No. They think it's alcohol poisoning. But if they ask, Kate—"

"They won't."

I took a deep breath, letting it out slowly. I gripped the edge of the blanket to ease the trembling.

"I'm not giving up on him," I said in the same tone as before. Then I glanced up at my doctor's face. "And neither should you."

His lines softened. He said nothing for a few seconds. "Take care of yourself, Kate."

Just before he left the room, I asked, "What room is he in?"

Hesitantly, Dr. Lowell turned around. "He has to sleep it off. It'll be another day."

He walked out before I could ask anything else.

~*~

I was dressed and sitting cross-legged on the bed when my mother came in. She said nothing when she saw me; she just walked over and took me into her arms. Her tears dripped down the back of my neck.

"There'll be other guys." She held me tighter.

I struggled to pull away and jumped to my feet. "What do you mean? Other guys?"

Mom wiped the moisture from her cheeks. "We liked Damian, too, sweetie. This surprised us all."

"What are you talking about? Is he…dead?"

"Oh, no, honey." She shook her head. "No, I didn't mean it like that."

I glared at her.

"I'm saying he *was—is—*a little rough around the edges, but I never pegged him as an alcoholic. Did he ever try to get you to take—"

"MOM!" I stepped away from her, shaking my head. "He messed up. That's all."

"Calm down, Katie. Guys like that—"

"Damian needs me. I'm not dumping him."

Mom's eyes drifted around the room and back to me. "We can discuss this at home." Her tone, however, said *This is over.*

Stiffly, she rose to her feet and flung my bag over her shoulder. Without saying another word, she crossed to the door, expecting me to follow. I did, but stayed ten feet behind.

Out in the hallway, Leslie's gaze followed me past the nurses' station. I jerked my head to the side at her. Slowing my pace to the elevator, Leslie caught up to me.

"What room is Damian in?" I whispered, keeping a keen eye on my mother ahead of me.

"Katie." Leslie shook her head.

"Please," I begged, tired of everyone blocking me. "I just want to peek in on him. That's all."

Leslie hesitated, glancing around the corridor. "Two-twelve, but you didn't hear it from me."

"Thank you," I mouthed.

Leslie patted my shoulder and ducked into a room to check on a patient.

I followed Mom into the elevator and stood with my hands on my hips. It stopped on the second floor then proceeded down to ground level. We filed out, and when Mom and I reached the automatic doors leading out into the chilly winter afternoon, I paused.

"Crap! I forgot my diary in the drawer upstairs." I hated depending on my acting skills; they were mediocre at best. I threw my arms out to the sides and slapped my forehead with my right hand.

Please buy it, Mom.

My mother's lips disappeared as she curled them in her mouth. "I guess we'll have to go back up and get it," she finally said.

"I'll go. You bring up the car." The words came out fast. Too fast.

Mom's eyes narrowed.

Smile like you're telling the truth.

I grinned. "Uh, I mean, it would be nice if the car was warm, as chilly as it is outside. I don't want to catch a cold. 'Cause that would suck." I stared at her, waiting.

Yes?

"Go get your diary and come right back down. Absolutely no detours." The tone in her voice meant business.

I nodded. "Of course. I'll be right back."

Before she had a chance to change her mind, I spun around and rushed off to the elevators. Inside, instead of pushing three, I followed the other patrons onto the second floor.

I noticed the number signs on the wall and started in the direction of room 212. Loud voices echoed through the hall and made my heart skip. I knew those voices. I hesitated. Taking a few steps closer to Damian's room, I leaned against the wall outside his door.

"How do you expect to help her like this, Damian?" Dr. Lowell's voice was harsh. "You say you care about her, then prove it!"

"I fucked up, okay?" Damian retorted.

"I thought things were getting better with you."

"Yeah, well, I thought she was getting better, too. I guess we all make mistakes."

"I'm doing everything I can!" Dr. Lowell enunciated each word.

I heard something crash against a wall as Damian shouted. "Then do more, damnit!"

"There is nothing more I *can* do."

"Why can't you do a transplant? She's on the fucking list!"

"It doesn't work that way, son." Dr. Lowell's voice lowered. He paused a few seconds, and I heard a chair screech against the floor. "There has to be a donor that matches her HLA."

"Test me. I'll do it."

"No."

"Why the hell not?" The anger in Damian's tone began to rise again.

"Look at you! You think the garbage floating around in your body is going to help her? It would probably kill her!"

"The cancer's already killing her!" he roared.

I squeezed my eyes closed, pain radiating in my stomach. A lump formed in my throat. I couldn't force it down.

"Clean yourself up, and I'll be happy to run your sample," Dr. Lowell yelled. Thick silence ascended on Damian's room. Then in a quieter tone, he added, "She has time, son."

"How much? And don't feed me any of that candy-coated shit you force on your patients."

"I can't, doctor-patient—"

"Fuck the doctor-patient confidentiality bullshit! I *love* her!"

I choked. Did he just say what I thought he said? *If he falls for you...*I should have been elated to hear his admission. Instead, I slid down the wall with my back pressed against it and buried my face in my arms.

Dr. Lowell spoke next, calmly and carefully. "This is nothing you don't already know. She's getting headaches because the leukemia has spread to her spinal cord. Chemotherapy is no longer effective for her. She has a choice right now. We can do a lower dosage with hopes that it will slow down the progression. It will buy some time until a compatible donor can be found. Or we can keep her comfortable and still hope for a donor."

Silence filled the room and cascaded down the corridor. I held my breath.

"What did she choose?" His voice shook.

"I think you should ask her, son."

Again the room was silent for a few moments when Damian spoke again.

"Please. I'm begging you. As my father, how long does she have?"

Dr. Lowell sighed. "A few months at most."

Chapter 18

I picked myself off the floor and ran down the stairwell, fighting the oncoming tears. Mom was waiting for me at the entrance. Opening the door, I slid into the car without looking at her.

"Where's your diary?"

I chewed the inside of my cheek, peering at the hospital through the blur. "I didn't bring it."

All I wanted was to go home and pour my heart out into my diary. Keeping everything inside ate at me the whole ride back. I didn't say anything, and my mother didn't press me. She seemed to be in her own world as well.

I dashed out of the car as soon as it came to a stop in the driveway. I didn't even grab my bag.

My mom hollered something at me, but I didn't hear her. I raced up to my room and slammed the door behind me. Flinging myself on my bed, the tears overflowed. I'm not sure when they ran dry.

I crawled over my bed and reached for the drawer on my nightstand. Fumbling inside for my diary, my hand glided over something smooth and soft, different from the cardboard cover I expected. I stopped. Air caught in my throat, and I lifted out the brown leather book. My jaw trembled as I stared at it.

As if in a dream, I scooted off my bed and floated over to the window seat, tracing my fingers over the cover of Damian's journal.

It was too personal to read. But, after all we'd been through, after hearing him say he loved me, I had to know.

Covering my legs with a blanket, I opened the journal to the first page. Inside the front cover, Damian had scrawled:

For Liam. I miss you, big brother.

I took a deep breath and turned the page.

November 16

I'm giving this a shot because Kate says it works. What the hell, maybe it'll work for me too? Can't be worse than going to Dr. Stuck-up-his-ass every goddamn week.

Kate's a girl I met at the hospital. She's beautiful, but she's got leukemia. She acts like it's a normal part of life, though, like going to school. I wish I were that brave. Dad diagnosed her when she was eleven.

Yeah, there's something about her.

We ate in the cafeteria today. She's a golfer. Figures, huh? I chickened out of telling her about you, Liam. I don't want her to feel sorry for me. I hate the memories and how they make me feel. Shit, I'd give anything to have you back!

You'd have kicked my ass if you knew that I walked out on her today. I would've deserved it—I was a fucking coward.

When I came back, she was staring at the hair that had fallen out of her head. I thought she was going to cry. She should just shave it all off in one day.

Yeah, that's at least something I can do for her. What do you think, Liam? Maybe I learned something from my big brother.

My breath caught in my throat. He'd written this because of me.

Something fell out of Damian's journal, landing with a small thud on my lap. Sitting on top of the blanket laid a small bag with a lock of auburn hair inside. I picked it up, examining it.

It was mine.

November 18

I wasn't sure if Kate would think it was

a good idea. I thought of what you would do, Liam. So I didn't tell her. I led her to an empty room and took out the clippers. Made it all dramatic. Unlike at the cafeteria, though, she cried, and it freaking hurt, man!

I can't describe the gleam in her eye. Well, yeah, I can. It's the same look Ellie used to give you. The one that said how amazing she thought you were.

I lost it in there with her, Liam. With Kate—I don't know, man. She's just different. It was so hard to let her go today. I didn't want to stop kissing her. I wanted to take her right there on the bathroom floor while she was hooked up to the IV. If she were anyone else, I would have. But she's sick, Liam.

Fuck it. I'm calling Ellie tonight. Where the hell did I put the vodka?

November 19

Ellie was fucking amazing as usual, but it didn't work. Every time I kissed her, I thought about how Kate tasted better. When I undressed Ellie, I was back in the hospital bathroom with Kate, pulling her to the floor. Ellie did everything right. Sorry, dude, but your girlfriend moves like an acrobat. So freaking good. I tried to concentrate on her. Really, I just wanted to get lost in her body. But when I sat Ellie on top of me, pushing her hips into me, all I could imagine was the look in Kate's eyes after I'd kissed her.

What the hell is this chick doing to me?

I sent Ellie home afterward. Having her here just messes with my head. Can you believe it, Liam? I think I'm feeling guilty. I'm screwing your girlfriend but picturing Kate. I can't get her out of my mind.

And I don't think I want to.

November 20

God! What did I do? Dad pissed me off as usual, so I took it out on him at the hospital. Kate was there. She fucking wasn't supposed to be there! God, the way she looked at me. I frightened her, man.

206

And then I really fucked up. Why did I ask her to come inside? I knew she'd do it! She wanted to help me. Comfort me. And what did I do? Liam, I treated her like shit. Fucking assaulted her! She'll probably never talk to me again.

I sent her a text. It was as lame as they get, and she didn't reply.

She gets me. Like REALLY gets me. In some twisted way, she understands. Kate doesn't expect me to be you. And now I've ruined it.

November 21

Ellie stayed over last night. Honestly, I don't even remember it. I can only think about Kate and what I did to her. Maybe I should call her and make sure she's okay.

Ellie's words keep repeating in my head. "Oh, that's where I left that bra."

I'm a fucking idiot. Kate probably saw it. No wonder she didn't answer my text.

And I'm pretty sure I pissed your girlfriend off too. She usually joins me in the shower in the morning for a quickie, but today, I locked the door on her. I needed to be by myself. She was gone when I came out, thank God. She took all of her clothes this time.

We're setting off to Grandma & Grandpa Lowell's today, as usual, for Thanksgiving. I won't even get to see Kate this week.

November 22

That was the best 6-hour drive to South Dakota ever. Dad drove, and I slept the whole way. Didn't say a single word to him, and I dreamt about Kate. I hope she likes the flowers I sent her. I didn't know what else to do.

Kate talks to me, like real conversations. Sorry, bro, but Ellie just talks about her girlfriends, college clubs and her new Gucci pumps—whatever those are. Who the fuck cares?

I laugh with Kate. I swear I smile when she's around—I don't fake it and pretend I'm interested. God, what I wouldn't give to have her naked body pushed up against me all night.

I hope she's not too pissed to come over

on Saturday. I want it to be perfect. She deserves an explanation. She needs to know who I am. I just hope she still stays afterward.

November 24

I found that tree in the back of the woods. You know, the one I fell from when I was eight and broke my arm. In all fairness, you warned me, but I didn't listen. I can't believe you actually tried to catch me and broke your arm too.

I hated living in your perfect shadow. Did you know that Dad blamed me for your broken arm? He said it was my reckless decision that forced you to miss the biggest swim meet of the year. If you hadn't played the hero, you'd have gone on to win gold in all your events.

Not my fucking fault.

But, dammit, man! I miss you.

November 25
Thanksgiving

I think I had too much of Grandpa's gin last night. I woke up with some girl's hair in my face—Amy? Not the neighbor girl from last time. I threw away her phone number as soon as she left.

Wow, dude. I thought I felt guilty for being with Ellie, but today, I might've thrown up over it. God, I miss Kate. Like really miss her.

She's been through so much. She doesn't take one second for granted. The hope she has, her determination, cuts at me. Even though she doesn't know the future, her eyes still smile.

Every time I close my eyes, I see her. What I wouldn't give to have her with me right now. She's fucking killing me.

I wonder if she knows how thankful I am to have at least met her. I want more, absolutely, but I'm not stupid. I know I may have ruined every chance I had with her. She deserves better than me.

I wish I could do her justice.

November 26

Everything's set. Dinner's ordered, and I even bought non-alcoholic wine—fucking disgusting, but tomorrow night is about Kate. I need to tell her about you and

Mom. About Dad. I don't think I can bring up Ellie, though.

She called, wanting to come over tonight. God, I can't believe I told her no. I've never told her no. Well, except that time when Allyson was here.

Just so you know, Ellie came to me, dude, the night of your funeral. She said she wanted to feel close to you again. We both needed the comfort. For a while, she always took the initiative, but eventually, I started calling her too. At some point, though, it stopped being about comfort. It was just a good time. Until Kate, I didn't really care. But now...now it's different.

His words cut through me like a soft piece of tofu, leaving my heart torn apart. I squeezed my lids shut as tight as I could and held my breath. Heat burned in my veins. My hands shook as I laid the journal down. A piece of my heart broke off each time I read something about Ellie. Jealousy swept through me. I *hated* her, yet, I felt sorry for her. She'd traded someone she loved for someone who just resembled him. So sad.

Reading, I understood why Damian didn't tell me. Even now, I didn't know if I wanted to know. It hurt so much reading the things he'd done with her—and the other girl. How many girls were there? My lips trembled as I fought to hold back the tears. One escaped and dropped onto the leather. I wiped it away, then opened Damian's journal and continued to read.

November 27

Kate came over last night, a bit hesitant, but at least she showed up. Gave me a chance, which is more than I deserve. God, she was beautiful. Her red lip gloss caught my attention, and I'm happy to know, tasted like strawberries.

Too funny. She'd never eaten lobster before, and I loved how she picked and poked at it, trying to be polite. I have to admit, I kind of hoped something like that would happen. It opened the door for me to move in and touch her, kiss her. She felt amazing, so soft and smooth. Damn, she drives me wild.

I told her what I could, leaving Ellie out. I just couldn't bring myself to tell her.

I think she forgave me. She kissed me back, anyway.

Liam, I could've held her all night. God, I wanted to. I never realized how much I needed her. The way she clung to me drove me crazy.

When Ellie holds me, it's just to quench her fire. With Kate, it's to feel the closeness of both of us—her to me and me to her. No one else belongs in my arms but Katie. And I never want her to leave them.

November 30

Kate's still out. I've been with her for two days. Last night, I dreamt that she didn't wake up. When I woke up, I was soaked with sweat. I laid my head on her chest just to make sure she was still breathing. I can't lose her now, bro. Not when I just got her.

December 4

I fought with Dad again today. Why the hell can't he wake her up? Her blood pressure dropped, and she turned white. I mean, yeah, I'm thankful that he got that under control, but now what? Just wait to see if she dies? What kind of medicine is that?

He's a goddamn oncologist, and it's his fucking job to fix her, so why the hell is he spending so much fucking time in his damn office?

December 6

Kate's not as pale today. This morning, I even thought I felt her squeeze my hand. When I asked her to do it again, she didn't.

I kissed her just now, and her eyelids twitched a bit. It's been seven days. Seven days.

She needs to fucking wake up!

December 12

Kate has a migraine today. Of all the stupid shit I've done, and even though Kate is in pain, somehow I'm blessed enough to hold her in my arms. How is that possible? I've fucked up so many times, but she's still here!

I want to take away her pain—hell, I'd take it all on myself if I could. Liam, I'd do anything for this girl.

December 14

Ellie crawled naked into bed with me last night. I was dreaming about Kate, and when Ellie started touching me, I thought it was Kate. It wasn't until I rolled on top of her and ran my fingers through her hair that I woke up.

She wasn't happy when I told her "no." Apparently she'd had a bad day and needed some love. I told her to take care of it herself in her own room. She didn't like that.

She asked me who the new girl was, but it's none of her business. Before she left, she said I could call anytime.

I won't.

December 18

I'm writing this alone in my room while Kate sleeps in the guest bedroom. Goddamnit, Liam! I'm shaking all over.

From the moment Kate stepped out of the limo tonight, I was hooked. She looked like an angel.

I worried my voice would crack as I sang to her. When she touched me and kissed me tonight, it was hard to hold back. I've never wanted her more.

The evening was perfect. Just as

planned. Her smiles, her awe, everything she did couldn't have been better.

I wish I could say I planned the blizzard and icy roads to keep her here tonight, but I didn't. More than that, I wish...hell, I don't know. I don't know if I fucked up or did the right thing. Either way, I just couldn't.

I couldn't do it, Liam, no matter how much I wanted to.

Dude, I didn't plan to bring her to my room. I didn't plan to make love to her, not that I haven't thought about it. I just...

She wanted to. Wanted me. I was ready, man, but then, I just couldn't do it.

Sorry, bro, but it's easy to fuck someone you don't care about. But with Kate...it's different.

I love her.

Chapter 19

I curled up on my window seat with Damian's journal hugged against my chest. I was drowning. Water rose higher and higher until it covered my head, leaving me gasping for breath. My body shook as I imagined Damian's arms wrapping around me, holding me close to his body, and lifting me to the surface. I still couldn't suck in air.

*If he falls for you...*Now his own words confirmed it. And if it wasn't for the last sentence in Leslie's prophecy, I'd be elated. He loved me!

I loved him too, but...

*If you don't recover...*God had yet to answer this part. The decision to try the experimental drug weighed heavily on me. There were no easy answers. Whatever I chose would affect everyone I loved.

I dry heaved into my hands. Shaking, I slid a blanket over me. The shivers, from cold or fear I didn't know, released goose bumps on my arms. I went back and forth; the best choice wasn't always the easiest or the clearest one.

It will kill him. I buried my head into one of the decorative pillows and finally lost control. Squeezing it as hard as I could into my chest, I sobbed until my head hurt and the sun began to set.

A few times, my mother shuffled up on the other side of my door, but she never knocked or came in.

When the sky darkened, I reached for my phone. Maybe Damian had tried to call and I hadn't heard it ring. Nothing appeared on the screen.

With a knot tightening in my stomach, I opened my diary and began to write.

January 18
Dear Diary,
I read Damian's journal today. I can't breathe.

It hurts. How could he love me when he's sleeping with her? She's his brother's girlfriend. I mean, who does that?

I'm so confused. He didn't have second thoughts about Ellie jumping into his bed. Is it me? Why doesn't he want me that way?

In his journal, he says she's not a part of his life anymore—because of me. It still doesn't stop the jealousy from boiling over. She had him in ways I may never get him now. It's not fair.

Oh what I wouldn't give to be in his arms. I want him to tell me everything will be okay, that it's only me, and that he...Pathetic, I know, but I want him to want me like that. Like her.

I want to go back to being wrapped against him before all of this. Back to when I was with him, I could forget everything else and feel comforted.

I stood up and walked to my vanity mirror. My whole face was puffy and red. After a few deep breaths, I dabbed on some makeup, put on my favorite knit hat, and grabbed Damian's journal. God, I hoped I wasn't too late.

I took my time descending the stairs. Halfway down, I stopped at the sound of my father's voice.

"I have to think about Kate and what's best for her."

"I understand, sir."

My breath caught in my throat as Damian's voice rung in my ear.

"And I guarantee we want the same thing. I made a huge mistake, and I can't take it back. But I'd like to ask for your forgiveness, and Kate's."

I leaned my back against the wall, waiting. For a few moments, no one spoke. I wanted to peek around the corner, but if I did, they'd see me.

"Mistakes happen, Damian. I get that. I've made plenty myself. But yours put my daughter's life on the line." My father's voice sounded calm, which surprised me, considering what my mother had said.

"I will spend the rest of my life regretting that. It was never my intention to hurt Katie. She...completes me."

Again silence dropped over the house. The sounds of cars driving by, dogs barking outside, the kitchen clock ticking filled my ears. I held my breath, listening to my heart pound against my ribs.

Finally, my father spoke. "I can see that. And I know she cares a lot about you."

"I'm asking you, sir, for a second chance. *Please*."

"I appreciate you coming over here, Damian, and talking with me. That took a lot of courage." He paused for a moment as if pondering what to say next. "I'm willing to give you that second shot…on a probationary period."

I let out my breath slowly. My feet moved me down a few steps on their own.

"Thank you, sir."

"And, of course, pending what Kate wants. Show me I'm not making a mistake."

That was my open door, and I didn't hesitate. Descending the last three steps, I made myself visible to the two men I loved more than anything.

Damian's eyes cut to me. He stuffed his hands into the pockets of his jeans then bowed his head. My stare didn't budge from him.

I felt Dad's hand on my shoulder.

"It's up to you, Katie," he said. He bent down and kissed my cheek before leaving the room.

I stood three feet away from Damian. His chestnut hair was disheveled, and his shirt appeared as though he'd run home from the hospital long enough to grab it off his bedroom floor.

Standing there with him, listening to him breathe, a mixture of longing and fear slowly replaced my anger. I swallowed.

I didn't want to speak first, and after a few

seconds of silence, I didn't have to.

"Katie," Damian murmured, his lashes hiding the splash of blue beneath them. "I...I let you down, and I'm sorry." He swallowed as water brimmed over his irises, making them glisten. "Please, give me another chance. I swear I won't let you down again."

Neither of us moved. Alone in my room, I'd forgiven him. All I wanted—no—all I *needed* was to be secure in his arms. I needed him to wash away my fear, tell me everything would be okay.

I held up his journal, digging my fingers into the leather. His eyes shifted to it, the color draining from his face.

"Is it true?" I asked unnecessarily.

He squirmed a little. His jaw trembled, but he finally met my gaze.

"Every last word."

I moved closer and tilted his chin so I could peer into his eyes. The pain and regret behind them almost made my heart stop. A tear escaped, and it was mine, falling down my own cheek. Damian raised his hand to wipe it away, but I grabbed his wrist before he could touch me.

His shoulders slumped in defeat. He blinked and let out a sigh. "Katie, I never meant to hurt you. It kills me to..."

He trailed off as I laced my fingers in his.

"Kate?" The shock in his voice made me hesitate a second.

Rising to my tip-toes and folding my other arm around his neck, pulling him down to me, I kissed him. It took a few seconds before he returned the kiss, but when he did, he let go of my hand and tightened his arms around me.

From somewhere behind us, I heard my father's hum, then it disappeared with his footsteps as he retreated down the hall.

When Damian let go, he wiped the tear away. He placed his chin on my head and crushed me into his chest.

"Shhh," he said, slipping my hat off and gliding his hand over my bald head. "Oh, baby, I've got you. I'm so sorry."

He held me until I let go.

"I should've told you," I said, looking at him. "I'm sorry, I didn't mean to—"

Damian shook his head. "No, Katie. What I did isn't your fault. It's the stupidest shit I've ever done. The pain I thought it would drown out was only made worse. I swear to you, it's never happened before, and it won't happen again."

I cupped his face in my palms. "I thought you were dead."

"Yeah, I thought I was too."

"I love you."

His dimples deepened. "Ditto."

He leaned down and kissed me, confirming his words.

~*~

Nestled together on the sofa, cuddled up in Damian's embrace, I felt safe for the first time since Dr. Lowell had told me the news. Damian and I held no more secrets from each other. A thousand pounds had been lifted from my shoulders.

"What about the new drug?" Damian asked after I admitted I'd overhead his conversation with his father. "When does it start?"

With my head on his chest, I was happy he couldn't see my face. I bit my lip.

"Katie?" he asked when I didn't answer.

I opened my eyes and tightened his arms around me. "I don't know," I mumbled.

Damian cleared his throat. "What do you mean?"

I couldn't look at him. "I haven't decided yet…uh, if I want to do it."

He tensed under me. His chest rose slowly before it fell again. "Why wouldn't you do it? What other option is there?"

"Well," I started. "There's always the transplant, and if—"

"Katie, there's no guarantee a donor will be found." He inhaled and clutched a handful of my shirt. "Without anything, you only have…"

I swallowed. "I know that." Loosening his arms, I sat up and straddled him. The suffering in his eyes was exactly what I'd wanted to avoid by not telling him. At the sight, my heart broke a little. How could I do this to him?

"The drug is still an option," I said, watching my fingers toy with the buttons on his shirt. "I'm just not sure if I can do it."

Damian's hands flew to mine, stopping them from fidgeting. He held them tightly against his chest.

"You're so strong, Katie. You can do it. I know you can."

223

I fought back the tears as I shook my head. "I researched the study. Damian, the side effects are, well, I'll be sicker than I ever have been before. And for what? A miniscule chance that it will work? I don't know…I'm scared." I raised my eyes to meet his as I said the last two words. Ever since I was a kid, I'd never admitted the fear. My diary knew, of course, but only I read it.

Holding my hands, Damian pulled me down on top of him. I snuggled into his neck as he traced his fingers down my back.

"I am too," he whispered. "I am too."

Due to Damian's new probation period at our house, Dad ushered him out at nine o'clock—way too early. Neither of us complained, though. We got lucky since my dad thought Damian had to be rushed to the hospital for alcohol poisoning, not the other thing. And I didn't exactly correct him.

Damian kissed me goodnight at the side door. When his lips parted and he caressed his tongue over mine, the familiar sensation of longing I had in the bedroom overwhelmed me.

"Here," I said, handing him his journal.

Damian sucked in his lower lip as he took it. "Thanks for reading it."

I touched his cheek and forced a smile.

After saying goodbye, I raced to my room and sat in my window seat so I could see him drive away. Cracking the window, I heard Damian with my father outside.

"I don't understand why she won't take the experimental drug, Mr. Browdy."

A few seconds passed before Dad spoke. "You have to understand, Kate's tired. She's been through this for over seven years of her life, and it's not easy on her body or her psyche."

"Don't you want her to do it?"

My dad was quick to answer. "Of course we want her to try it. Marcy and I are spectators, though. Kate has to suffer the treatments, not us. We hurt with her, but on a different level. Like you do.

"You see, chemo, radiation, medications—they serve their purpose. But they can only take her so far if she's too exhausted. Her mentality has just as much of a healing effect as the treatments themselves."

I shivered as the breeze wafted through the window. Dad's and Damian's voices carried on the wind. The truth of my fathers' words stung.

"You're saying the new drug won't work if she's too tired to fight."

"Yes, it's her job to fight this thing. It's our job to support her, no matter what she decides. We can't make this choice for her. As a part of this family now, Damian, I hope you agree. Love her. Support her. Encourage her when she needs it."

A part of this family. Wow.

"Yes, sir. But what if she chooses to wait? I don't want her to give up."

"Hmm." Dad shuffled his feet on the driveway. "You know, sometimes, what might seem like giving up is when we're in the midst of the toughest battle we'll ever face. Kate's a fighter. She'll keep fighting to the end."

Chapter 20

January 28

Dear Diary,

Funny, the conversation I overheard between my dad and Damian really helped me. For almost two weeks, I haven't had much else on my mind. Thanks to them, today I've made a decision about the experimental drug.

Since I've decided, everything I see is more vibrant. Even the sunrise this morning seemed more beautiful. All of the colors so magnificently blended together, yet still their own hues and shades. I imagine the mountains and the beaches, the splendor of the earth, and think, "God made all of this, how much more beautiful heaven must be." Like sunrise, all the time.

Being in Damian's arms lately, I can't describe it, but it's like my heart is free. I can breathe again. I smell the snow and

227

the ice on the trees differently. He sent me flowers this week, and they, too, smelled sweeter.

Last night, when his hands slipped under my shirt and I felt his fingertips gliding over my back—hmmm—even that felt deeper than it ever has. Then he kissed me. My whole body down to my toes responded. I'm smiling now, thinking about it.

You know, it's weird, but after Damian's heroin incident, something inside me clicked. Seeing him lying there, pale and wasted, suddenly made me realize how precious life is. You'd think living with cancer all these years I'd have a good grasp on that fact, but seeing someone you love slipping away right in front of you—well, nothing's more terrifying. Or jarring.

Tonight, at dinner, I'm going to tell my family, Damian included. I've made up my mind. It's all clear to me now.

~*~

I paced my room, stealing glances at the digital clock on my nightstand. The delicious smells of dinner wafted up the stairs and circled inside my bedroom. Unfortunately, the aroma mixed with my anxiety made me nauseous. All I thought about was

Damian and how he'd respond to my news.

The clock flashed six o'clock. He'd finished his shift at the hospital and would be on his way to my house soon.

I threw my head back, staring at the ceiling as if it wasn't there. Sitting on my bed, I gazed at the pictures of Damian and me covered in flour during Christmas that I'd stuck to my vanity mirror. Our happy faces made my heart flutter for a second before I fell back on the bed.

I stayed there until the buzz of an engine sounded in the driveway. Automatically, I jumped up and peered out the window. Damian stepped out of his black BMW, still wearing his sky blue scrubs with his backpack slung over a shoulder. So gorgeous.

He shut his door, spun around, and winked at me through the window. His dimples deepened, and his face lit up.

My grin widened by the second. Oh, how I loved him! Allowing the curtain to fall closed, I stepped back and took a deep breath. After straightening my skirt, I ran down the stairs to meet him at the door.

My mom had already let him in. As he rounded the corner, I flung myself into his arms, kissing him like crazy.

His arms tightened around me. "God, I missed you."

I pressed closer, not wanting to let go. He kissed me on the sweet spot of my neck, just under my ear, eliciting a soft moan from me.

"I'll take that as an 'I missed you, too,'" he hummed in my ear.

My dad fake-coughed behind us. We both turned, and I blushed.

"Hey, Mr. Browdy." Damian extended his hand.

"Good to see you." My father shook his hand, nodding. "Dinner in ten minutes, you two."

Damian winked at me again before heading to the bathroom to change. I went to the living room and sat on the sofa to wait. When he came in, I reached up to him, but instead of falling into me, he took my hand and shook politely.

"Katie, I presume?"

I laughed and yanked as I hard as I could, pulling him into me. Rolling, he scooped me up and buried his lips into my neck.

"Leslie asked about you," he said when I was securely enveloped in his embrace. "She wanted to make sure you're doing all right."

I played with his fingers, kissing them every so often.

"And Brennan says hi."

"How's he doing?"

"Kid looks good. Almost beat me in *Mario Kart* today."

I glared at him. "Is that what you did all day? Play video games?"

Damian feigned offended. "No! After an hour, his new chemo buddy showed up, and they kicked me out." He grabbed me in a bear hug.

My mother announced dinner, and my heart sank. I swallowed the lump in my throat, but another immediately took its place.

Here we go.

Damian offered his hand and helped me up.

"You're hands are clammy," he noticed.

"Oh, really?" I shrugged. "Go on, I'll be just a second."

I darted for the bathroom. In front of the mirror, my face looked pale. I took a deep breath and let it out slowly.

I can do this.

When I joined my family at the dinner table, everyone was laughing and talking, scooping chicken primavera on their plates. I took the seat between my dad and Damian and tried to join the conversation while thinking about what I needed to say when we'd finished the meal.

Through the laughing, the atmosphere was strained. Distracted by my thoughts, at first I thought it was just me. As I glanced around the table, it seemed everyone felt the apprehension. No one ate much, leaving over half of Mom's well-cooked meal in their serving bowls. My shoulders fell from the weight.

My mother fidgeted with her utensils. Dad studied her, some sort of unspoken communication passing between them. Damian's hand rested on my thigh. Whenever the conversation died down a little, he squeezed.

I watched the people I loved more than anything in the world. Resting on my father, I breathed a giggle. He had a bit of food caught in his goatee.

I'd always admired the way, after twenty years of marriage, my mother still gazed at him like there was no one else in the room. I wanted that, too.

And Damian. The way his eyes lit up when he saw me always made me shiver…in a good way. No

231

set of arms were more comforting than his.

My dad interrupted my trance. "Well, Katie. What is it that you wanted to tell us?"

My attention shifted from my father, to my mother, and my boyfriend. I cleared my throat and laced my fingers through Damian's for support.

Three sets of eyes pierced me. I inhaled.

"I, uh, wanted to tell you that I've made a decision about the new drug." Damian's hand held mine even tighter. My mother stiffened, and Dad gave me a nod of encouragement.

"Whatever you've decided, sweetie, we'll support you," Dad said, his voice cracking.

I nodded and glanced at Damian.

"It's okay," he murmured.

My eyes flashed to my mother.

"I love you, honey. No matter what you choose to do." Her tone softened as she spoke.

Bowing my head, I took another breath. I looked up, making sure to lock on each person when I spoke.

I said the words with confidence, holding my head high. "I've decided not to do the drug. I'll wait for a transplant if one becomes available."

Through the tears, Mom grinned at me. My father's mouth gaped slightly, his hand on his chin. Loving approval glowed in his brown irises.

Then Damian. It was the angst of his response that had taken me so long to decide. His nostrils flared; his face paled. Fear seemed to pour off him like steam.

Slowly, with his other hand, he caressed my cheek as if my parents weren't there.

"Katie." His voice trembled.

"It's what I want," I answered quietly. "I'm…"

"Don't say it. I'm here for you. Always."

I nodded as he leaned in and kissed me.

~*~

The tension lifted a little as the evening wore on. With my news, Damian's probation became null and void, and he was allowed to stay even after my parents went to bed.

Cuddled up on the sofa, Damian was unusually quiet. I glided my fingers down his arms, wanting him to speak first. He hugged me to him and kissed the top of my head. I didn't want to interrupt his thoughts, so I continued my motions on his skin.

"I don't want to spend a second away from you," he finally said.

"Me neither."

"This is really your decision, huh?"

I rolled onto my stomach, lying on top of his chest. "Do you remember our first conversation? When you asked if I was happy?"

Damian sucked his lower lip between his teeth then let it go. "I was wrong."

"I lied to you. I realized that I wasn't happy at the time. But I am now."

I ran my fingers through his hair and kissed him. He didn't kiss me back.

"Life is short, Damian. I'm not giving up on the hope of a donor. I'll still take the meds to slow down the progress. But I'm tired. Even with the drug, there are no guarantees. I could still only have a few months."

"But Kate—"

"Please." I swallowed, twirling a lock of his hair around my finger. "You told me once that I didn't know the outcome. Now I do, and I want to live it out.

"We all die, Damian. Before I do, I want to love with all my heart. Give all I have, experience all I can, and leave behind some piece of me that will never be forgotten. I want to enjoy the time I have left. I'm choosing life. Moments. Memories. For you."

A tear streamed down my face. Damian didn't hesitate in kissing it away.

"Because I love you," I whispered.

Damian cupped my face, bringing me down to him. His eyes sparkled amidst the fear. He kissed me with such passion, as if it was the last time he'd ever feel my lips against his. I clung to him, allowing his need to wash through me, his anxiety to be shared. His fingers gripped the back of my shirt, pushing me into him.

When he let go, he buried his face into my neck. I felt moisture slip from his cheek onto my skin. Slowly, I balled my hands in his hair.

I pulled back. "I do have some, uh, last wishes for you."

"Anything."

I smiled. "Five of them."

"Okay. Shoot."

"One at a time. When I'm ready to share."

Damian's brows furrowed as he tilted his head sideways. "A game?"

"An investment."

His tongue glided over his lips. "First one?"

"A visit."

"Hmm. To where?"

Inhaling deeply, I stared at him wondering what he would think. "I want to visit your mother and Liam's graves."

Damian's breath caught. "I haven't been there since…"

Silence thickened around us.

Finally, he raised his eyes to mine. "Okay."

Chapter 21

January 31

Dear Diary

For once, I want to be a regular seventeen-year-old girl. I don't want to think about cancer or treatments or donors or...yeah. I want my biggest worries to be things like the upcoming history exam I forgot to study for, and why my boyfriend hasn't asked me to the Valentine's dance yet, and whether or not the principal and the new music teacher really did it on the sofa in the counselor's office.

So I laughed at the look on Damian's face when I said I had school tomorrow. It was so adorable the way he raised one eyebrow and curled his upper lip. I'm not sure if he understands my reasons.

I also told him he has to go back too, and that I fully expect to see him walk across *the podium in May and receive his diploma. He made a cute grunting noise but agreed—eventually.*

Mom and Dad are trying to act normal. "Trying" being a loose term. In the desk drawer, I found a note Mom wrote listing all of my favorite meals, desserts, and restaurants. Gotta love her, I think that's her grocery list for the next few months. I wonder what Dad will think about fried chicken gizzards for dinner more than once a year? Sorry, Dad.

Dad allows Damian to stay as long as he wants, which of course means all night. We slept on the living room sofa last night, and when Damian's cell phone alarm went off, he, Dad, and I ate breakfast together before heading off for work and school.

Ah, life is perfect!

~*~

"How was your day?" Damian asked. He sat beside me at the kitchen table with what he liked to call a snack.

"That sandwich is like two feet tall," I said, scrunching my nose.

"Wanna bite?"

"I'm not sure how that's even possible."

Damian waggled his eyebrows and stuffed the food into his mouth. "Anything's possible."

"Apparently." I took a sip of my protein shake. "School was good. There's a new girl who got assigned as my new lab partner. She seems nice."

"*Seems* nice?"

I sighed, resting my chin on a fist. "She sat beside me the whole class, but we worked the lab separately. I'm not sure she even noticed I was there. When I said good-bye after class, she didn't even look at me."

Damian's hand rubbed my back. "They just don't know what to say."

"Something is better than nothing."

"It's hard to sympathize when you can't relate."

I buried my head into my elbow. "That's the thing! I don't want their sympathy. I just want to not be invisible."

Damian's finger glided over my temple. "I see you. And I'm sure they do, too."

"I guess I just thought…" I let my sentence trail off.

"Thought what?"

"…thought that after my decision, I'd feel like one of them—*be* one of them." My eyes met his, and I bit my lip. "I could be normal."

Damian chuckled. "Normal is overrated. Besides, invisible is totally in this season, I hear."

I laughed.

"Come on," he said. "I need help with Trig, so finish that impossibly delicious smoothie."

I dipped my straw into the pink slush and licked it off. "I thought you said anything is possible?"

He took another large bite out of his sandwich. "Yeah, anything except that atrocity tasting decent."

~*~

Damian and I were watching a movie in the living room when my head began to pound. Unbearable pain squeezed in on me from all sides. I dug my head into Damian's shirt and cried out.

"I've got you," Damian whispered as he carried me to my room.

A set of footsteps followed, their heaviness reminded me of my dad. I glimpsed the sky outside the window and realized it was already dark. Carefully, Damian laid me in my bed. My hands shook as I tried to pull the blankets up over me.

"I've got it, Katie," Damian said. "Go to sleep. I'll be right here."

I rolled onto my side and closed my eyes, feeling the warmth of the comforter surround me.

A chair slid up next to my bed. The bed sank a little as Damian rested his head on his fist. The bed sank even lower at the end.

"She'll have more of these days." Dad's gentle voice sounded soothing.

"I don't want to lose her, Mr. Browdy."

"Call me Jason."

"How do you do it? Remain so calm?"

My dad sighed. "Practice, I guess. When she was in kindergarten, she fell off the monkey bars. Instead of having the school call Marcy, Kate wanted me. She'll always be my little girl. I never thought I'd lose her to leukemia." He paused. "Now with you, I'm happy I haven't."

"I don't understand."

"I knew someday my Katie would find a man

239

who loves her as much I do. *That's* how I always imagined I'd lose her." My dad's voice cracked. Then the bed lightened.

I opened one lid to see my father pat Damian on the shoulder.

"Take good care of her, son."

Damian glanced at him. "I will, sir."

Dad nodded then closed the door behind him.

~*~

When I woke up around noon the next day, Damian was gone. I tried to sit up, but my head felt like it had welded itself to the mattress. Grabbing hold of the side of the bed, I forced myself up. Damian's clothes from the day before lay in a pile on my bedroom floor.

My vision blurred, and I fumbled for my blanket, collapsing back on the pillow. As my eyelids closed, I imagined Damian beside me.

~*~

Damian crawled into bed next to me, waking me up. Feeling his arms fold around me, I moaned softly. He felt so right cuddled up behind me.

"Hey, beautiful," he said, kissing my neck.

"Where'd you go?"

He chuckled. "School, as per your request. Then home to pick up some stuff."

"Hmmm," I murmured. "You smell good."

Damian held me closer. "How do you feel?"

240

I thought for a second. "Surprisingly good."

His lips pressed against mine. "Awesome."

He swung his legs over the side of my bed. I propped my head up on my elbow and studied him curiously. A large suitcase lay on the floor. Damian set it on my bed and unzipped it.

He winked at me, a dimple suddenly appearing on his cheek. "Care to help?"

I scrunched up my nose in confusion. "What are you doing?"

"Unpacking."

Sitting up, I crossed my legs on top of the comforter. I opened my mouth to speak, but when nothing came out, I closed it.

What is going on?

He took out a few pairs of jeans from the suitcase, stacking them in a pile on my bed. Beside those, he dug out some wrinkled t-shirts and attempted to fold them. I cringed as he gave up and rolled them around his arm, dumping them in a clump beside the jeans.

"Hangers in the closet?" he asked, holding a few pullovers. He nodded toward the tri-fold doors.

Stunned, I fumbled for words. "Uh…yeah."

With his back turned, I scooped up the slew of crumpled tees and folded them properly.

When he got back to the bed, he noticed the perfectly folded pile and laughed.

"OCD," I mumbled. "Um, so what exactly—"

"Do you have any empty drawers?"

My eyebrows rose. "Uh, girl?" I said, pointing to myself.

"Right." He suppressed a grin. "Can I empty

241

one?"

"Uh…um." I slid off the bed and made it to my dresser easily. The bottom drawer contained work-out clothes I never wore, so I arranged them nicely in the same drawer as my pajamas.

"Thanks." Damian smirked, holding his t-shirts and jeans.

When he got close, I stepped in front of the dresser and held my arms out.

"Not until you tell me why you're moving in."

The smile on Damian's face exposed his dimples. It almost made my heart stop. He dropped his armload on the floor and tucked his arms under mine. Kissing me, he picked me up and fell on top of me on the bed.

His lips worked their way from my mouth to my neck. "I'm all in, Katie. I get to fall asleep every night with you. And wake up every morning to your bad breath and your beautiful eyes staring back at me."

I clamped my hands over my mouth. "Bad breath? Really?"

He sucked my earlobe into his mouth. "Very bad." He took a hold of my wrists, moving them to my sides, and he kissed me full on the lips.

"I don't know if my parents—"

"Shhh." He covered his mouth over mine again, making me forget what I was saying.

"Didn't you hear what I said? I *get to fall…*"

~*~

242

Damian became a permanent fixture in our home. He woke up beside me every morning, sometimes early enough to watch the sunrise with me. We brushed our teeth together in the bathroom before heading down to breakfast. Because our schools were too far apart, I had to drive myself, much to Damian's disappointment.

So far, though, Damian had just held me in bed, careful to not let it go too far. Did he think I'd break if he went further? I gave him some subtle hints, but either he didn't understand them, or he still didn't want me like that.

After school, I went home, and three days a week Damian met me there. He'd cut down on volunteering at the hospital to two days—the days Brennan received his treatments. Sometimes I joined him, but I had to wear a medical mask. I played video games and caught up with Leslie and Tammy.

The time spent with Brennan and his new friend always made me laugh. Watching them play and seeing the glow in their eyes brightened my day.

With Leslie and Tammy, however, I felt different. They tried to hide their sadness behind fake smiles and cheerful voices. Leslie would reminisce about my initial treatments, then a distant look would cross her face, and she'd suddenly remember something she needed to do for a patient.

Damian took cover-up cues from Leslie when I asked about visiting the cemetery. He did just as well as she did being totally obvious. Two weeks had passed, and he still hadn't taken any initiative. He seemed to have a bag full of excuses: It's too cold. I have lots of homework. You were sick yesterday, today you should rest. Maybe after Valentine's Day.

On February 14th, Damian sent me a dozen red roses to school. On the card, he'd scribbled the words '*I LOVE YOU.*' That evening, a limo picked us up and took us to a restaurant downtown. Afterwards, we saw an off-Broadway show.

I was too busy kissing the dimples on Damian's cheeks to notice where we were until Mr. Dempsey opened the door to let us out. When I stepped onto the snowy driveway, the Lowells' house stood before me in all its winter beauty.

I glanced sideways at Damian. "What are we…"

"You're staying with me tonight," he said, unable to contain his grin.

"I…my stuff…I…"

"You think too much. I packed your bag yesterday. It's already in the house."

"But—"

Damian cut me off with a tug of the hand. "Come on."

His eyes blazed, much like they had the night of our Christmas date. The fireplace in the den burned, illuminating the make-shift bed on the floor.

"Your bag's over there." He nodded to the corner. "I'll let you get changed." Then he added matter-of-factly, "It's just us tonight. I'll be right back."

I froze, speechless.

Just us?

I jerked my head toward the foyer, staring at Damian's back as he ascended the staircase. Once in his room, I scanned the den, taking it in. The curtains were drawn, and Damian's black comforter covered the space on the floor. Pillows lined the perimeter of our bed. Suddenly, my mouth went dry.

Glancing back up at the empty doorway, my heart raced. We were alone. *All* night.

I stood, motionless, in the middle of the room. Jumbled thoughts flashed through my head in steady spurts. Was tonight *the* night? Did I want it to be? Oh no—what if it ended like last time?

I buried my face in my palms, taking a deep breath.

Calm down, Kate. Things are different now.

My heart raced. I grabbed my bag and unzipped it, trying not to think. Shuffling through some jeans and shirts, I choked on a giggle when I found a clean pair of underwear and a matching bra. Apparently moving in with me had given him confidence to go through my drawers.

I changed into the cami and shorts he'd packed as pajamas and eased myself down in the middle of our bed, peering at the fire. Even though the heat flushed my cheeks, I was shivering.

When Damian cleared his throat, I swiveled to the doorway where he leaned up against the trim. He had on a pair of plaid lounge pants, not unlike what he usually wore to bed. Tonight, though, he seemed different. I swallowed, allowing my gaze to work its way up his body. He looked…wow!

He sauntered over saying nothing, his eyes piercing into me with such intensity that my heart sped up with every step he took. I rose to my knees, nervousness sweeping through me.

Damian reached for me and lowered me onto the pillows. On the way down, I realized my breaths were shooting out in uneven spurts. The beating of my own heart vibrated in my ears. Ah, this was so overwhelming! Still, my fingertips moved over his back, feeling the muscles rippling underneath.

Sinking lower into the stack of blankets under me, I automatically pushed back a lock of his hair. For some reason, this particular image burned into my memory. A smile graced his face, and despite the heat pouring from the fireplace, goose bumps rose on my arms.

What had I done to deserve this amazing moment?

Damian held himself up over me, kissing the tip of my nose, then my cheeks. I closed my eyes, more than anything longing for his lips to touch mine. Instead, he bent down and ran his tongue down my jaw line and onto my neck. Instinctively, I arched my back under him as he kissed the sweet spot under my ear.

I held my breath, waiting for the tingles rushing over me to slow. They never did.

His mouth finally found mine, sucking my upper lip into his, letting go and repeating it with my lower one.

"You're so beautiful, Katie," he moaned into me.

He said it with such softness.

I opened my eyes to study him.

In one motion, he glided a hand down my side and hooked it around my knee, lifting it. He slid his fingers up the inside of my thigh, making my breath hitch again, but then he paused halfway up. His grip tightened over my skin. Letting go, he tucked his arm under my back instead. My gaze flowed to the fire, remembering his hesitation the last time. This time, I didn't want to be rejected.

I gasped when Damian nibbled on my neck.

Please don't stop this time.

Damian's hips pushed into mine, and the warmth cascading through my body made me shudder.

He toyed with one of my spaghetti straps, lowering it on my shoulder and kissing where it should be. His lips moved across the top of my chest, spreading tickles over my skin in their wake, before they moved back up to my throat. I whimpered and clung to him tighter, my insides turning to Jell-O.

Mixed emotions washed through me, blurring the lines of fear and desire until I no longer recognized them.

"Damian," I heard myself say. "Please."

He stopped, pursing his lips. "Ah, Katie." He averted his gaze to the fire and drew his lower lip between his teeth.

My heart sank immediately.

"You don't want me?"

"Oh, God, Katie. Yes, I want you. I want you so bad."

I swallowed. "Then, why won't you…"

"Because…" he paused, sighing. "I don't want you to regret it."

"I love you, Damian. I'll never regret that."

"You can still love me without…"

"I know."

247

I don't want to die a virgin.

With both hands, I pulled his face down to mine, kissing him with everything I had.

I needed to say it, not only for him, but so I could hear it out loud. "I want to."

"Are you sure?" he said, breathless against my mouth.

"Yes."

My answer was all he needed. His tongue separated my lips, entering. The way he pressed down over my waist with an eager grip created a whirlwind of need in my abdomen. When he reached the bottom hem, he lifted the camisole over my head.

Unlike last time, Damian didn't hesitate. He kept moving over me, wanting more with each touch.

His eyes danced over my naked breasts before his hands, his lips, covered them.

Oh God!

I curved into him, needing him closer. My nails dug into his back as hunger took over.

Damian controlled me, and all I had to do was respond, which I did without premeditation. My body knew what I needed—it did it for me. With each caress, each taste, and each breathless moan, I clung tighter, wanting to melt into him—lose myself in him.

Over my clothes, his hand swept between my legs. Somehow still shocked at the intimacy of it, a small noise exited my throat. Damian let out a small chuckle before he did it again.

"Just wait till I get them off." His breath tickled my ear, and I shivered at the thought.

Any nervousness I'd had from before evaporated in the heat of this moment. I'd never wanted him more. Just being close couldn't quench the thirst.

I need all of him!

My hands found their way down his waist and over his hips, looping my thumbs under the waistband of his pants. He'd never felt so good.

My eyes met his. They shone in a way I'd never seen before. Usually they gleamed with a mixture of fear, sorrow, and hurt, but tonight his irises were a lighter shade of blue. Behind them, the last trace of the walls Damian had built seemed to be crashing down. Tonight, he let his guard down, showing me all of himself.

I touched his cheek, and he leaned into me. Seeing him so raw, so vulnerable, captivated me.

Damian kissed my palm, trailing down my arm. He sat up a little and slipped his hands under the elastic of my bottoms. I swallowed, fighting to keep my gaze locked on him. The fire in his eyes blazed with desire, but he kept it controlled. Along with my panties, he glided my shorts past my hips, tossing them behind us.

Fully exposed in front of him, my mind began to race. Insecurity crept in. How did I compare with the others?

With Ellie?

I squeezed my knees together, constrained, but Damian's hold slid up my legs, separating them. The corners of his mouth curved slightly, revealing one of the dimples I loved so much.

His hands drifted all over me, leaving fresh trails of inexplicable warmth over my skin. I closed my

249

eyes. Letting the past go, I allowed myself to stay in the present.

I held my breath when warm palms arrived at my inner thighs. His lips pressed against my stomach, and my eyes shot open as a finger slipped inside my folds. My abdomen ached with need, and I tensed with each motion, biting the inside of my cheek.

Satisfied, Damian let go, and sat up, shimmying out of his clothes. I clutched a fistful of pillow in my hands as he lowered himself over me, kissing my neck.

"Damian?"

"Yeah?" he breathed, making his way back up to my lips again.

"Will it hurt?"

Damian's arms tucked themselves under me, holding me close. He said nothing for a few seconds, giving me my answer. "I'll take care of you. I promise."

Anticipation mixed with a sliver of fear made my insides tremble. I ran my fingertips over Damian's back, attempting to quench the anxiety. His skin felt like silk.

"You okay?" he asked, bracing himself over me.

I swallowed and took a deep breath. My eyes met his. "Yeah."

He leaned down and kissed my neck. I clung to him, my body tightening.

"Relax," Damian said against my mouth.

At his request, my muscles obeyed.

"Good girl."

He slid inside me, and I immediately clutched onto him. I tightened my thighs into his hips as the burning sensation consumed me. Wincing, I buried my face into his shoulder.

Damian stopped.

"Hey. You'll be okay. I've got you."

I bit my lip and closed my eyes. All I could think about was the pain.

Damian moved himself into me again, and this time, I whimpered.

Oh no! What does he think of me now?

"Katie."

My lids opened at the sound of my name.

"Focus on me," he murmured, pointing two fingers at his eyes.

I nodded, gazing up at him through my lashes. He rocked into me, slowly and cautiously. Each time, he paused before pushing himself forward. With each motion, the burn lessened, and his breaks became shorter until they were non-existent.

With the pain gone, I lifted my hips into him, eager to mold him into me. Damian moaned, kissing me harder, and I held onto him.

"Damn, you feel good."

At that moment, my mind went fuzzy. Damian's breathing increased, and I gasped as his body went rigid over me. He pushed into me one last time, sweat gathering at his hairline. His lids squeezed closed and when they opened, his irises seemed bluer.

He wrapped his arms under me, holding me tight. His face nestled in my neck. "Now you're all mine, Katie. All mine."

~*~

February 15
Dear Diary,
It kinda surprised me how easily Damian fell asleep afterwards. No matter how hard I try, I can't. I don't want to feel sorry for myself, but after tonight, I just...

I glanced at Damian. His chest rose and fell slowly, a soft snore escaping his throat. He shifted a little, wrapping the corner of a blanket in his arms. So peaceful.

Why? Why now? Why did Damian have to come into my life so late?
If it's possible, I love him more today than yesterday. I gave him all of me, and I don't want myself back. I'm his for always.
I just wish "always" lasted longer.

I cuddled up beside him, needing to be as close to him as possible. Finally, I drifted off to sleep.

~*~

Damian was already awake when I opened my eyes. His fingertips glided over my bare back, and my heart did a little twirl.

"You all right?"

Honestly, I felt more sore than I had the night before. But I nodded anyway. "Mmm-hmm."

Damian looked at me sideways.

I sighed. "Um." I squirmed under the sheet,

squeezing my thighs together.

Kissing me, Damian smirked. "I'll be right back."

His naked body rose from the bed and walked out of the room. I averted my eyes, but caught a quick peek of his back side as he left the room.

When he returned, he had a towel wrapped around his waist, a glass of water in one hand and two white pills in the other.

"Tylenol," he said.

I swallowed them both in one gulp. "Thanks."

"It'll be better next time." He lay back beside me. "Come here."

Next time?

My heart skipped a beat at his promise, and I smiled to myself.

With an arm under me, he held me close, and I took a few breaths to slow my heart. After a few minutes, I relaxed into him and folded my arm around his stomach.

I kissed his chest on top of the cross tattoo. Staring at it, I propped my head up on my elbow and traced the weaving lines with my index finger. I felt Damian's eyes on me.

"What does this mean?" I asked, still gliding my fingers over the black ink.

"My mother was Irish. Her faith in God meant everything to her. After she died, Dad went through the house and boxed up anything that reminded him of her. So I did this."

"What about the other one?"

Damian turned his body a little. Also in black, two interlocking shapes that formed one large triangle was inked into his bicep.

"For Liam," he said. "It means 'brotherhood.'"

Just as I had with the cross, I ran my fingers over Liam's memorial. "When are we going to go visit?"

He paused. "On Saturday."

Chapter 22

February 19

We're going to the cemetery today. Yesterday after school I stopped by the florist to pick up some flowers. I hope Damian doesn't mind.

He's been quiet all morning. He didn't stay over last night; in fact, he left before eight. I don't remember him even kissing me when he came in this morning.

I wonder if he told his dad what we're doing today. He said Dr. Lowell used to go to the cemetery every day and sit there until midnight, but Damian didn't know when the last time his dad had been out there.

It makes me wonder...who will visit my grave? When? Will I have a steady stream of flowers for a few years and then be forgotten? You know, I'd be okay with that. It would mean they're moving on, *like I have. Dying is just another journey, one which we all will take.*

I worry about my parents, though. Mom and Dad's lives have centered around me. They need each other.

And Damian. It's been two years since his mother and Liam passed away, and he has yet to cope. Leslie's prophecy can't come true. Whether or not Damian's ready for this, he needs to let go. The healing process has to begin—for them.

And for me.

"You ready?" Damian leaned against the door jamb of my bedroom. His hands were stuffed in the pockets of his jeans, his hair gel-less, and his blue eyes lighter than usual. From the stubble poking out from his face, I wondered if he'd slept at all.

I glanced up at him and nodded, tucking my diary under my pillow.

"No wonder girls take so long to get ready."

"I got dressed, just like I said." I grabbed my purple scarf from the bottom of my bed and wrapped it around my neck.

"Among other things," Damian teased, adjusting my scarf in the front. "You look beautiful." He kissed my cheek and wrapped his arms around me, holding me close. His chin rested on top of my head.

Against him, even through his sweater, his heart pounded in my ear. His arms tightened for a few seconds before he let go. Without a word, he took my hand and led me down the stairs.

I grabbed the flowers off the counter. When I spun around, he averted his gaze to the floor and reached for the doorknob.

In his BMW, I slipped off my gloves and placed my hand over his.

The trip to the cemetery was quiet. He didn't even have the radio on. His focus stayed on the road, and his lips remained taut.

I peered out the passenger-side window. The city moved in a hurry, yet I saw it all in slow motion. Cars didn't speed by. People didn't rush into the stores. I peeked over at Damian, the corner of his upper lip set between his teeth.

With all the cars on the interstate, the road seemed empty except for us. We made our way out of the city and onto a deserted county highway. The snow-covered fields glistened in the sun, and icicles hung from the trees like Christmas lights.

Damian made a right turn into the cemetery. He drove almost to the end of the lot before coming to a stop in front of the fence line. His lids squeezed shut as he took his hands off the wheel.

"I can't do this." He pushed his fingers through his hair, grabbing a fistful at the top.

I brushed the side of his face, the roughness catching a little on my gloves. "Yes, you can. I'm here for you."

I watched him sit motionless for a few moments. When he didn't put the car in reverse, I relaxed and scanned the surroundings.

The first thing that caught my attention was the large elder tree in the corner of the cemetery. Even without the shade of the leaves, the tree was spectacular. It leaned a little to the right and branches sprouted off everywhere, but something about it filled me with peace.

Two headstones poked up under the tree. Neither of them large or fancy, but the gray marble seemed to glow brighter than the rest. Somehow I knew they belonged to Nora and Liam.

My attention shifted back to Damian. His eyes were open now, staring straight ahead at the sea of snow.

"Hey," I said, taking his hand. "Ready?"

He didn't respond, so I reached for the door handle.

"Wait." Damian tugged at my hand, stopping me. "Just give me another minute, okay?"

I closed the door and leaned back against the seat. Remembering the flowers in the back, I twisted my body and scooped them up, laying them on my lap. My other hand never left Damian's hold.

Finally, Damian sighed. He looked at me, his irises cloudy. Letting go of my hand, he took the flowers from my lap and opened the door. I waited until he rounded the front of the car to follow him out.

He stood on the edge of the gravel path facing the elder tree. When I came up next to him, he slid his hand into mine and began to walk forward. The crunch of the snow under our feet echoed off the stones, filling the crisp air. Above us, the clear blue sky reflected the ice plastered to the tree branches.

Damian slowed his pace as we inched closer to the gray marble. The other headstones faced the entrance to the cemetery while Nora's and Liam's pointed toward the tree. Feet from them, Damian stopped and took in a deep breath.

"It's okay," I said, leaning my head against his arm.

He nodded and made his way around to the tree, keeping his head lowered. My gaze shifted up before Damian's. The almost identical stones gleamed back at me.

On the left was Nora's; on the right, Liam's. Along with their names, each stone had etched in the middle perfectly matched symbols to Damian's tattoos. The cross for Nora, the brotherhood arrow for Liam.

I studied Damian's expression. His eyes glistened in the sunlight, fixated on the symbols. His nostrils flared as he clenched his jaw.

"You didn't know, did you?"

He shook his head. "Dad did all of it. The arrangements. Everything." His voice was barely audible.

With the flowers still in his grip, he dropped to his knees, letting go of my hand. The flowers fell to the snow-covered ground as Damian buried his face in his palms.

I knelt next to him, not caring about the cold creeping through my jeans, and rubbed his back.

"I've started to come here so many times, but I always chickened out. I'm sorry, Mom. I'm so sorry."

We sat on the cold ground, staring at the gray stones. Every so often, Damian would lean his head on my shoulder.

"The tree is beautiful," I said, after we'd been sitting in silence for awhile.

"It's why Dad chose this place. The elder tree represents transition—moving on from this life to the next. Mom would have loved it."

Ten minutes later, he reached for my hand and smiled. "Thank you for making me come here."

We stood up, and Damian placed the bouquet of flowers on the ledge of his mother's stone. He kissed the top and whispered something I couldn't hear. For his brother, he fist-bumped the brotherhood symbol.

"Miss you, big brother."

The wind stirred up behind us, making us both shiver. Damian chuckled, leaned down and kissed me. The cold air gusted around us this time, circling its pleasant chill on all sides.

Damian pressed his forehead against mine. "I think they approve."

He winked in the tree's direction before we walked to the car and drove away.

Chapter 23

February 28

Sign-ups for golf qualifiers were posted on Friday while I was stuck at home with another headache.

They're more frequent now—as Dr. Lowell said they'd be. My good days are really good. But my bad days are getting worse. And lasting longer—two, sometimes three days. I can see it frustrates Damian; he hates going to school while I stay in bed.

Dad's been awesome, though. On bad nights, I hear the two of them talking in my room. I clutch the necklace Damian gave me against my heart. He wants so badly to fix the pain, but there's nothing he can do. We're still praying for a donor. Honestly, though, I'm not sure they'll find one.

She hasn't said it, but Mom doesn't want me on the golf course. I think she worries about me getting too hot or that I'll get a headache and collapse. From what I've overheard, they're working out a schedule so that one of them will be with me at all times while I play. It's a little overboard, but whatever. As long as I get to play, and they're happy.

~*~

I squealed and jumped into Damian's arms.

"I made it!"

Thankfully I'd finished the whole week of qualifiers without missing a day. That had been my biggest concern. The last day I felt a little drowsy and scored my worst game of the week: eighty-five. Luckily my qualifying average was good enough to place at the top. Number two, actually, behind senior Lizzie Cowden, our team captain.

"Congratulations!" Damian swung me around in a circle.

It was the end of the second full week of March. The snow had melted and the temperatures were rising. The change in the weather had done wonders for my health, in my opinion. My white blood cell count, however, continued to climb according to the last blood draw.

Damian opened the door of my car for me. "I think this calls for a celebration."

"I *couldn't* agree more." The smugness of my statement caught him off guard.

Damian cocked his head and knit his brows. So

cute!

"My second wish," I said. "And this time, I pick the date. Tomorrow. 9 AM."

Damian shook his head. "What's tomorrow?"

I smirked, hoping I looked as adorable as he did with the same expression. Considering our conversation in the hospital cafeteria back in November, I figured I needed the extra power.

"Willow Creek golf course. You'll need your clubs."

"Oh…uh, golfing?" He swept his hand through his hair. "Your second wish is to play golf?"

"Not just golf," I said. "Golfing with *you*."

Damian's tongue traced the corner of his lips. "You know I haven't played—"

"Since Liam died. It's time to change that."

"I think I told you that you'd kick my ass. And judging by the score you just put up, I have no doubt."

I jabbed him in the chest. "I'll give you a big handicap, even the playing field."

"One condition—"

"Nope. My wishes don't come with conditions."

"I get to take you to dinner tonight."

I suppressed a giggle and placed my index finger on my lips. "Hmm. I guess I can make an exception. Condition granted."

"Kiss on it?"

"When have you ever asked before?" I grabbed a hold of his shirt and pulled his head inside the car window.

Like he had since qualifiers began, Damian followed me home in his car. I ran into the house, barely able to contain myself. Throwing my arms around my mother, I jumped up and down.

"Guess who made the varsity team?"

My mom shrugged. "Tiger Woods." Of course, he was the only golfer she knew. She kissed the top of my head. "Congratulations, honey."

"Thanks, Mom."

I tried not to notice the worried glance she shot Damian, and I didn't acknowledge the way Damian's lips pursed together or his knowing nod in her direction.

After I got off the phone with Dad, I ran upstairs and got ready for our dinner date. Damian simply changed his shirt and was ready to go. I did the works and met him downstairs in a new record time of forty-five minutes. At least I didn't have to do my hair.

Damian met me at the bottom of the stairs. "You look amazing."

He led me to his BMW in the driveway. He officially had his own parking spot now. Opening the passenger door for me, he kissed the top of my hand.

"Miss Varsity-Golfer."

We ate Mexican food at a local restaurant and laughed at each other trying to balance salsa on our chips before eating them. Though the restaurant technically didn't have a dance floor, four men played Mariachi on a make-shift stage in the corner. With a mischievous gleam in his eye, Damian stood up and literally danced around the table and offered me his hand.

I pressed my palm over my mouth. "Uh, yeah.

You don't dance, remember?"

"Ah, seniorita. Baila conmigo."

"Wait! You speak Spanish?"

"Si, mi amor," he answered in an awful Mexican accent. "See, I learn stuff in school."

"You don't take Spanish."

"I learned about Google Translate in school."

I laughed.

Scanning the room for onlookers without turning my head, I felt all my blood flow to my cheeks. A small child turned in his high chair and pointed at Damian. Two teenage girls had their heads together, giggling.

"You're crazy!" I whispered. "Sit down."

"No fun in that," he said and swayed his hips salsa-style.

Ohh. Wait, no!

I bowed my head. Damian reached down and lifted my chin to meet his gaze.

"Come on. You only live once, and I've been practicing."

"No one else is dancing."

"So what?"

I browsed the tables again. More people were whispering as they checked out Damian's moves.

What has gotten into him?

"No. Way."

Damian shrugged. "Your loss."

With a smirk, he twisted his hips around and cha-cha'd over to one of the booths. My jaw dropped as I watched my boyfriend in horror. He offered his hand to a white-haired elderly woman. She glanced across the table at her husband, who nodded with a chuckle, then took Damian's hand.

As they danced, the patrons applauded. Another older couple rose from their seat and began similar moves to Damian and his partner. Before long, more couples joined in, and Damian allowed the lady to dance with her husband, who cut in.

His blue eyes hooked on mine, and he winked. He held out his hand again. Since he'd encouraged people to dance, I didn't feel as self-conscious, but dancing with him meant I wouldn't be able to watch his hips swiveling, and wow, that was hot.

When he reached our table, I stood up and took his hands.

"See? Fun."

I laughed and kissed his dimple. "See? Crazy!"

Damian hugged me to him and rolled his hips over mine. I tried to imitate what the other couples were doing, but all I did was step on Damian's toes.

"You may need to add Latin dance lessons to your wish list." He put both of his hands on my hips to move them himself.

"Yeah, I'll never dance again anyway."

"Not never. Prom is in less than two months."

I hadn't given much thought to prom with everything else going on in my life. Still, it was a high school rite of passage, an experience I didn't want to miss. I bit my lip.

A lot can happen in two months, though.

"Katie?"

I jerked my head up. "Yeah?"

"So, will you go with me?"

I swallowed. I didn't want to make promises I couldn't keep. Forcing a smile, I nodded. "We'll see."

Damian's shoulders dropped. "Not exactly the answer I expected."

"It's just that…two months…I don't know."

"It shouldn't take you that long to find a dress," Damian said. His dimples sunk deep into his cheeks. Then he frowned, his voice lowering. "You can't think that way, Katie."

Damian pulled me into him. I hadn't noticed that we'd stopped dancing until we started again, this time with my head on his chest.

"Okay, I'll go." I hoped with all my heart that I'd be able to keep my promise.

Damian hugged me closer.

When our meals arrived, we stopped dancing. Others continued, and the whole charade seemed to put extra pep into the band. By the time we'd finished our meal, however, the dance floor was empty.

The night air smelled fresh with a hint of rain. I shivered in the brisk wind. With his arm around my shoulder, Damian walked us to his car. I buried my face into him, starting to feel light-headed.

"What's wrong, Kate?" he asked after helping me into the seat.

I closed my eyes. "Dizzy, that's all. I'm fine."

Feeling his hand pressed against my forehead, I moaned softly.

"You're pale," he said. "Here." Damian lowered the back of the seat, and I felt him place something warm over me—his jacket.

I muttered something that was supposed to be "thank you." Curling up on my side, the heaviness in my head took over, and I fell asleep.

Chapter 24

When I awoke to the alarm clock, Damian's arms were around me. He groaned and slapped the buzzer, silencing it.

My head didn't feel like a boulder. A small sliver of relief washed over me. It was strange, though. I'd expected it to last a couple days like the rest of my headaches. I shifted in bed, rubbing my temples. The fuzziness remained.

"Damian?" I nudged him. "Wake up."

One of his lids rose. "Yeah, I'm up."

"Tee time at nine, remember?"

His other lid flew open. "We don't have to do it today, Katie. Not after last night."

"I feel fine. Please? I wanna go."

He glided the back of his hand over my cheek. "Maybe you should take it easy today."

I glared at him, and he groaned again, rubbing the sleep from his eyes. "All right."

I kissed him. "Thank you."

When I swung my legs over the side of the bed, Damian tugged me back to him.

269

"Did you say you feel *good* this morning?"

"No headache."

A smile crept over his face, his dimples pinching into his cheeks. His hands slipped under the back of my shirt, lifting it over my head. I reached for him, and he kissed me harder.

~*~

It was the perfect day for golf at Willow Creek Country Club. Damian was adamant about renting a cart even though I insisted on walking. He won, of course, and I pretended to be grumpy about it.

"Ladies first," Damian said, gesturing in front of him.

I studied him suspiciously and grabbed my three wood. To make it fair, I had told him I'd shoot from the men's tee box. After putting my orange tee in the ground, I glanced over my shoulder. Damian's head was bowed, and he tapped his fingers nervously on the hood of the cart.

Sighing, I set my ball and took a few practice swings before stepping up. I peeked back at Damian, who shot me a thumbs up. Readying myself, I swung, watching my ball until it bounced on the fairway.

Damian walked up behind me. "Well, well. I guess I'm up, huh?"

"Do you need some pointers? A refresher course? 'Cause, I mean, I don't want to totally blow you away."

Damian grabbed a club out of his bag and sauntered to where I'd just driven one of the best shots of my life. A sly grin spread slowly over his face.

"I think I can figure it out."

I stood back with my hands on my hips, trying to contain a smirk.

From his practice strokes, I'd never have guessed he hadn't played in years. His form was spot on. He stepped up, concentrated, and swung through.

We both watched as his ball rose into the sky in a perfectly straight arch. With my mouth still gaping, Damian came up next to me.

"How do you like them apples?" he whispered in my ear.

Still staring at where his ball landed, yards ahead of mine, I puffed out a breath.

Damian laughed. "You're cute. Come on."

We climbed into the golf cart and sped out over the fairway. I couldn't take my eyes off him and the gorgeous way his lips curved upward.

"You said...I thought..." I folded my arms across my chest.

Damian tilted his head toward me. "And yet the look on your face is priceless."

I scoffed and shook my head, unable to hide my amusement.

"Ah," he said, pointing. "I think that's your ball I see first. Hmm. Guess that means you're up."

I leaned over and kissed him to shut him up. "It's only the first hole."

"Whatever you say, baby."

My next shot landed on the edge of the green. But so did Damian's. Yeah, and his was closer—much closer.

I contemplated my play. To birdie this hole, I'd really have to be on my putting game. I scanned the layout from all angles, trying to analyze every possibility.

"Wake me up when you're ready," Damian hollered, putting his feet up on the dash of the cart.

I ignored him and set up. Taking my time, I hit the ball and cringed as it circled the hole and popped out.

Damian stepped up right behind me, his lips pressed against my neck. "Wanna reshoot? I can let that one slide."

"Shut up and go."

I smacked him on the butt with my putter on my way off the green.

He tapped his ball in for a birdie while I settled for par.

"You can shoot from the ladies' box," he said as we drove to the next hole. "It's only fair."

"Nah. I like the challenge."

Damian raised his brows. "Wanna wager?"

I sat back in the seat. "Depends. What're the stakes?"

"I win, you tell me your next wish *today*. I lose, I get to make a wish of my own."

I thought about it for a couple of seconds— longer than Damian would have liked.

He tapped a finger against his mouth. "Oh, come on! Deal or no deal?"

"I'm trying to see how you spun it since you tricked me the last time."

Damian laughed. "No tricks, no over unders. It's an 'I win, I lose' bet."

I repeated it in my head. *"I win...I lose..."* *Sounded fair.*

"Deal."

We kissed on it.

Damian cleared his throat. "Shall we?"

I started to follow him, then I stopped. "Wait a minute."

He turned around slowly, fingers pressed over his lips, trying to contain the coy grin.

"No! No deal!" I shook my head, stunned that he'd fooled me again.

"We kissed on it. Sealed the deal, baby."

"You win either way!"

Damian strode up to my side, hooking his arm behind my waist. "Will it make you feel better if I promise to return the favor tonight?"

"What does that even mean?"

"Wanna find out?" His breath tickled my ear.

My eyes widened. "Kiss on it?"

Taking my face in both hands, he leaned down and left me breathless.

Both of us scored par on the second and third holes. Somehow I managed a birdie on hole four after a horrible drive, tying up the score. My real luck, however, happened on the fifth hole when Damian cut it too far to the right, landing out of bounds. He ended up with a double bogie while I wrote down par—with a smiley face—on the scorecard.

During the cart ride, my head began to spin, but I kept my eyes forward, hoping Damian wouldn't notice. It wasn't bad, and I could deal with it. I *needed* to deal with it...at least until the tenth hole.

I did okay on hole six, considering Damian's ball landed in the sand trap. While Damian hit solid pars on holes seven and eight, I bogied them both. Normally, I played a tight front nine and tired on the back half. Today, though, the effects of the headache slowed me down.

One more hole. Hide it for one more hole!

"All right, Lowell," I teased. "Let's see what you've got!"

"Watch out, Browdy," he said, getting ready to swing. "I plan on tying it up right here."

It took a lot of energy to fake how I felt. With the way Damian glanced over his shoulder at me before he swung, I could tell he wouldn't buy it for much longer.

When I lined up, the ball blurred below me. I squeezed my lids shut, fighting to maintain control. My hands began to shake. Worried, I cut a stare to Damian for a second, but he was putting his club away and not watching me yet. Taking a deep breath, I swung.

Thankfully, the wind had picked up and caught the ball, pulling it to the left. I put on a flirtatious smile and batted my eyes at Damian.

"Nice shot," he said, his voice low. He wasn't smiling.

On the green, I focused harder. The sun stung my pupils, and I wished that somehow I could sink the ball with my eyes shut. I missed the hole twice and felt Damian's gaze on the back of my neck.

Judging by his stance and how his blue irises kept popping up to check on me, he putted his ball into the sand trap, missing the hole by a mile.

"Uh, Lowell?" I said pointing. "That wasn't even close." I winced at the pain.

He bit his lower lip and hurried to dig his ball out. Carelessly swinging, he took two more taps to finish the hole.

"Forty-three to forty—nine holes to go," I said, handing him the score card.

He didn't take it. Instead he took my hand and led me back to the cart.

"We're done." His voice sounded rough and irritated.

"Done? What do you mean?"

"I know that look, Kate. You've got another headache."

I adjusted my visor. "It's really not bad," I assured him. "Please. I can't let these control my life." I stared at him, hoping he'd relent.

Damian handed me a bottle of water, and I took a sip.

"More," he demanded.

I sucked down the rest and gave him back the empty bottle. "Please."

He sighed. "One hole at a time," he said sternly. "If it gets worse, or you pale—we're done."

I nodded. "Fine."

Damian studied me for a few seconds like he was trying to see inside me.

"Thank you," I said, taking his hand.

He lifted it to his lips. Then, he drove to the tenth hole.

I checked my watch.

He has to be there. He promised.

When I looked up, Dr. Lowell was standing at

the tenth hole with his clubs next to him, ready to play the back nine.

Damian's eyes flitted to me. "You planned this, didn't you?"

I shrugged. "An investment, remember?"

He said nothing.

"He's your father," I told him. "And it's time to make amends. For both of you."

"Kate." Damian voice cracked.

"I wanted to be here with you, and I will, but I don't think I can play anymore."

"Maybe we should—"

"No." The word came out louder than I'd expected, taking Damian by surprise. I swallowed. "Please, do this for me. I'll be fine."

Dr. Lowell walked over and shook hands with his son. I laid my head down in the cart, hoping I'd done the right thing.

~*~

March 22
Dear Diary,
I think my plan worked. Unfortunately I didn't get to be mentally there for the rest of the game, but Damian told me earlier today that his father asked us out for dinner tonight. He seemed genuinely happy about it. Damian's picking me up in twenty minutes. I haven't seen him all day, and I can't wait.

It's times like this when I regret my

decision to not try the experimental drug. Am I doing the right thing? If it would allow me to live just one more day, would it be worth it? Or would it just prolong the inevitable, allowing those I love to hang on to me and feel the pain a little longer?

No. I made the right decision. They've suffered enough. I've suffered enough.

I stuffed my diary under my pillow and headed downstairs to my parents' room. Dressed in a pair of black slacks and a pink and black frill top, I dug around Mom's closet for a matching pair of pumps.

"Mom!"

Her head immediately poked around the corner.

"Do you have anything that will go with this?" I asked, throwing my arms down my sides.

"You look amazing," she said, beaming at me.

"Yeah, well, I'm going to look dorky without shoes."

"Where are your black boots?"

"The heel broke, remember? You took them to the cobbler at the mall."

Mom scratched her head. She didn't remember. Just great.

From the top shelf of her closet, she grabbed a shoebox.

"You can wear these," she said, handing me the strappy rhinestone pumps she reserved for special occasions.

"Oh, Mom, they're perfect!" I exclaimed.

I sat on the edge of the bed and slipped them over my pink-polished toenails. Standing up, I admired my feet.

"Well, Cinderella," my mother said. "Same rules apply. Home by midnight, or they'll turn into pumpkins."

I laughed. "Yeah, that's not how the story goes. She gets to keep the shoes."

"She's probably still getting ready," my father said from the kitchen.

"Well," my mother said with a chuckle. "Your prince charming is here."

Throwing my arms around her neck, I kissed her cheek. "Thanks, Mom."

Damian's face glowed when he saw me. He wore a sky blue button-up shirt, casually untucked, and with the sleeves rolled up. As always, my eyes drew to his dimples. They definitely completed the ensemble. Super sexy.

Taking my hand, he kissed the back of it like a perfect gentleman. "Good evening, beautiful."

I blushed when his lips grazed mine.

We met Dr. Lowell at a Japanese steakhouse in West Des Moines. Damian squeezed my hand as we walked into the lobby where his father waited, sipping on a glass of wine at the bar.

Jackson Lowell grinned when he saw us. I peeked up at Damian. He returned his father's smile and the two embraced like old friends. My heart fluttered.

"You look lovely tonight, Kate," Dr. Lowell said, nodding at me.

"Thank you."

"That's a pretty necklace."

My hand automatically grasped the Celtic

symbol of hope I never took off.

"Nora would have loved it."

Dr. Lowell's lip twitched at his late wife's name. He and Damian exchanged glances.

"She was a wonderful woman. Her sons were the highlights of her life. I just wish..." His voice cracked, and he took a deep breath, his gaze passing from me to Damian. "I just wish she could be here to see what a great man you've become, son."

Dr. Lowell nodded at me. "She would have loved you, Kate."

Damian wrapped his arm around my shoulder and hugged me close.

"You remind me a little of her," he continued.

"Thank you," I said. "I wish I could've known her."

"I see her face every time Damian smiles." The dim light reflected off my doctor's eyes. I didn't know if it was my imagination or if moisture had gathered in the corner of one of them.

He slapped his son on the shoulder. "I'm proud of you."

A beeping noise sounded at Dr. Lowell's waist. Damian's shoulders slumped, and he shifted his weight.

Dr. Lowell excused himself and stepped outside to take the call. Damian leaned against the brick wall, his hands in his pockets. He focused on his shoes, not speaking. I slipped my arms through the small gap between his elbows and waist.

"Hey," I probed.

He didn't respond.

I kissed his cheek and laid my head against his

chest. The sound of his heart echoed in my ear, making me wish I could do something to slow the rapid beating.

The hostess announced our group before Dr. Lowell came back inside. Damian didn't flinch at the sound of his name. I walked over and told the hostess we'd be there in a minute.

Damian raised his head when his father came back in. "Hospital?"

Dr. Lowell nodded. "Yeah. Did they call our table?"

Damian's hands slipped out of the pockets of his pants. "Don't you have to go?"

Jackson Lowell clicked his tongue. "I told them Dr. Kepler could handle it. I'm spending the evening with my son."

Chapter 25

Damian lay in bed next to me, his fingers gliding up and down my arm. I held his other hand tightly against my chest, kissing it when I needed to feel closer to him.

It was the first day of April and a thunderstorm raged outside the windows. But it was nothing compared to the one raging inside my body.

Everything hurt. My head felt like it would burst at any second, and my stomach spun as if a whirlpool were dragging it in a downward spiral to the ocean floor.

I'd barely made it through my first golf tournament of the year before collapsing in Damian's arms. He drove me home immediately and put me in bed. Then he called his dad. That was two days ago.

I awoke several times in the middle of the night with dreams that would scare a zombie with a machine gun. Each time, Damian held me tighter, whispering comforting words in my ear until the fear passed.

After the last one, I didn't want to go back to sleep.

"Damian," I said, my voice shaking.

"It's okay. It was just a dream."

"Will you take me to the window? I want to see the sunrise."

Damian kissed my temple. "If that's what you want."

He slipped out of bed and threw on a t-shirt from the floor. By the time he made it to my side of the bed, I'd managed to sit up a little. Sliding his arms under me, he lifted me up and carried me to the window seat. With Damian behind me, I leaned up against him. He folded me into his arms where I felt safe, where nothing, not even death, could reach me. In the newness of the morning rays, peace spread over me, and I drifted into a restful sleep.

~*~

That evening when I woke up I was back in bed, and the tremors had stopped. Grimacing, I rolled to face Damian. He had a faraway look in his eyes. I caressed his cheek and ran my fingertips over his lips. His gaze shifted to me, the beginning of a smile forming.

"What were you thinking about?" I murmured.

Shadows clouded his irises. "Nothing."

I rolled a loose lock of his hair around my finger. "Hmm. Liar."

He laughed softly. "Yeah. I forgot about that."

"Now you *have* to tell me."

Sucking his lower lip between his teeth, he

hesitated.

"I love when you do that," I whispered.

He chuckled under his breath. "Dad said if…if a donor wasn't found soon, that," he paused, doing the lip-thing again. "Uh, that there'd be more of these days until..."

His head dropped, and he squeezed his lids closed, fighting back tears.

"Hey." I lifted his chin. "Open them."

They flitted open, two pain-filled sapphires glistening with moisture.

"Everything will be okay," I insisted.

Damian shook his head. "You don't know that."

"Sure I do." I kissed his lips, but he didn't return it.

For a split second, I thought I saw the faces of Nora and Liam flash in his eyes. Just when he'd finally begun to deal with their deaths, the tide had turned again. When I'd fallen in love with him, dying hadn't been an option. Now, it was staring me down.

"There's still time," I said softly, tracing the curve of his jaw.

Bravery. Hope. Courage. Yes, I did those things well. And whether Damian liked it or not, I did bedside manner just as well as his father.

"Damian, don't give up on me, because I'm not."

His eyes shifted up at the resoluteness in my tone. A chuckle escaped him.

"You're cute when you're serious. "He tucked his arm under my head and pulled me into him. "No way in hell I'm giving up."

~*~

A week passed, and I stayed in bed three of seven days. I drained of energy faster and faster. Coach allowed Damian to drive me in a golf cart during practices, but I only managed half the course. He started carrying a soda and snacks for me during golf practice—and everywhere else. I usually declined when he offered; he was my boyfriend, not my nurse.

During meal times, Damian's eyes bored into me when I pushed my food away, my toddler portion half-eaten. Even writing diary entries was exhausting.

Every night, Damian carried me upstairs and tucked me in before crawling under the covers beside me. Then, I laid my head on his bare chest, feeling the warmth of his skin flow through me before falling asleep in the only place I ever wanted to be.

On Saturday, I had to sacrifice some time with Damian to go prom-dress shopping with my mother. The glow of pure excitement on her face made up for it. Mom acted as if we were going wedding dress shopping. Exhibit A: she'd gotten her hands on numerous prom magazines and marked the dresses she liked before setting them on my dresser.

An overwhelming number of dresses attacked me in the first store. My mother danced around the racks, grabbing hangers off them at an incredible speed. Did she even stop to check the sizes before she swung them over her arm?

On the other side of the store, I spotted one through the masses of silk, satin, and tulle, and found an empty dressing room. Not long after I'd locked it, I heard my mom's voice calling my name.

"In here," I said, sticking my foot under the door and wiggling it around to catch her attention.

After one knock, I let her in. She barreled through the door with so many dresses I couldn't see her head.

"What the…? Mom!"

Within a minute, she had the gowns hung in an organized fashion on the pegs around us—a real Martha Stewart. I barely had room to move.

"Where do you want to start?" Her girlish excitement made me laugh.

"Um," I said, showing off the dress I'd picked out and already had on.

Mom stepped back to examine me. She made a funny face then shook her head.

I nodded. "Yeah, I wasn't impressed either."

An hour and a half later, only two gowns hung on the maybe peg. While I rested, Mom held up each remaining dress for my scrutiny; the last one being the most gorgeous dress I'd ever seen.

Where the strapless gown dipped in the front over grey sheer, beads and rhinestones were interspersed down the bodice. Gathered material, fading from grey to white, wove around the front to the back. Layers of soft, sheer fabric flowed into a pure white skirt with fish-wire creating waves at the hems. A slit in the left hand side of the front ran to the middle of my thigh.

The delight on my mother's face said it all.

I twisted to the mirror and gasped. It was perfect.

~*~

Damian studied me with a smirk when I walked through my bedroom door carrying the dress in a black bag.

"No peeking," I said as I hung it up at the far end of my closet.

He rose to his knees on my mattress, surrounded by homework. In one motion, he swept everything on the floor.

"I don't care about the dress. I haven't been able to concentrate since you left."

I stood at the edge of the bed with my hands on my hips. "You need to get your work done if you want to graduate."

"I put my name on the top of my math assignment. That's enough for today."

He took my hands and pulled me on top of him. His arms circled me, holding me close. Rolling me to the side, he kissed my neck, and I giggled. Slowly making his way to my mouth, he pressed his lips against mine. His tongue slid inside, and I melted into him.

My fingers tangled in his hair, and warmth filled me down to my toes. Just being near him set me on fire, but in his arms, kissing him, I was on a whole new level of burning. I kissed him back, allowing myself to absorb every touch.

Damian rolled me onto my back, stood up, and started for the door.

I frowned. "Where are you going?"

Without a word, he shot me a mischievous grin and turned the lock. The tingles cascading down my spine made me shiver.

Our clothes quickly found their places on the floor. Wrapped up in his embrace, the world faded away. It was easy to forget how quickly time ticked by with Damian's skin pressed against mine.

The room evaporated, and with it, all my medications on the nightstand, every reminder of how sick I was, and what the future held. In that moment, all that mattered was us.

"You'd better get some rest before the party tonight," he said afterward.

Oh yeah! I'd completely forgotten about Brennan's remission party the nurses were putting on.

Damian leaned over to kiss me. "Get some sleep. I'll be back up later."

He got up, swiping his clothes off the floor and got dressed. I watched him, the pit of my stomach beginning to tighten. He gathered his schoolwork off the floor and offered me a dazzling grin over his shoulder as he closed the door behind him.

Exhausted, and a bit frazzled, I lay back against the pillows, imagining Damian's lips against mine. I'd give anything to have them back, even for one more second. The pressure in my stomach dissolved into emptiness, and I scrambled to dig out my diary from under my pillow.

April 9
Dear Diary,
I wish I could go back. If I knew I'd feel

this way, maybe I'd have made a different choice. Taken the drug or something.

Time is running out, and I don't want to face the inevitable. Not because I'm scared to die, but because I can't wrap my mind around not being with Damian anymore. Not feeling his kisses. I don't ever want to be without him.

No, I can't let him go.

I thought if I could hang on for a few more months and not be sick, I could get enough of him to last a lifetime and be ready when death knocks. I thought I'd be able to say good-bye.

I glanced at my open closet doors. A piece of the dress bag stuck out from the corner. My vision blurred over, so I squeezed my lids closed. Sniffling, I wiped the tears away, opened my eyes and continued to write.

There's never enough time to say good-bye. Never enough time to say "I love you." Never enough time to let go. I could have been given a thousand years with Damian, and still not be able to do this.

I've tried to be brave for myself as much as for him. It's so hard to be strong, though, when I see his sadness, when he kisses me like there may not be a tomorrow.

I hate going to school now. It's so much time away from him. But if I don't go, he won't go. I can't have him give up his future. Him graduating is my consolation prize.

Dropping my pen, I looked up from my diary and took a deep breath. Sometimes it helped. I inhaled again, as deeply as I could, then let it out slowly. I picked up my pen again.

I love him. That's why, when the time comes, I need to let him go.

He can't fight this for me. It's the one thing I have to do on my own. When I close my eyes for the last time, I know it's Damian's face I'll see.

~*~

I didn't notice when Damian came back in. When I awoke, he was already dressed in a pair of jeans and a pin striped button-up shirt with the sleeves rolled up; the shirt was untucked as usual. He sat beside my bed, scratching his head over a math problem.

"You forgot to carry the one," I said.

He snapped his head up. "Where?"

"Second line."

His brow furrowed. "Damnit!" He ripped the paper out of his notebook and wadded it up, tossing it on the floor.

289

I chuckled under my breath. Damian stared at me for a second then started laughing too. He cupped my face in his hands and kissed me.

"God, I…" He shook his head slightly and kissed me again.

I took a quick shower and got dressed; a jean skirt with a white sleeveless polo. Damian waited downstairs, and before I met him, I opened the top drawer of my dresser and pulled out a white envelope I'd stashed under my socks. Glancing at the door, I slipped it into my purse.

Damian's hand never left mine during the drive to the hospital. The Commons was decorated with blue balloons in clumps sitting on the furniture. Blue and white streamers hung from the ceiling, and a table was set up in the corner filled with fruits and vegetables, nuts, mints, and a large blue-frosted cake with the words *CONGRATULATIONS BRENNAN* sprawled across the top in white icing.

When we walked through the door, Brennan ran toward us, throwing his arms around Damian's waist.

"Hey, buddy," Damian said, rubbing his back.

Brennan's smile could have been seen from Missouri; it was so bright. "Where've you been?"

Damian nodded apologetically. "Kate's needed me."

"Hi, Kate!"

I ruffled his head, where small bits of brown hair poked up now. "You did good."

"You will too." Brennan took me by the hand and tugged me into the room. "We're having a *Mario Kart* tournament. You've gotta sign up."

290

"Me?" I scrunched up my nose. "I'm not sure."

"Oh, come on," Brennan begged. "You'll be an easy win."

Damian snorted behind me. I glared at him over my shoulder.

"Please? You'll only have to race once before you lose. Well, unless you play my mom. Then you might have a shot." His puppy eyes pleaded with me. "Please?"

I sighed and put my name on the list. Damian followed suit, and Brennan clapped his hands in delight.

"This is gonna be awesome!"

"Right," I muttered.

Bouncing on his toes, he ran off to greet his other guests—and convince them to sign up, no doubt.

"How are you feeling, Katie?" Leslie's hand touched my shoulder.

I gave her a hug. "I've been better. This brings back memories," I said, scanning the room.

"I was really hoping to throw you a third remission party," she said.

"Maybe you'll be throwing me a successful transplant-party, instead."

Leslie dropped her gaze to the floor. "That'd be nice."

She nodded at Damian before she walked away.

Damian led me to one of the tables covered in a blue plastic tablecloth. We sipped punch and ate nuts, watching the party guests and waiting for our names to be called for the Wii tournament.

As Brennan so accurately predicted, I lost my

one and only match—against Tammy! Damian, of course, won his first match-up against a twelve-year old bald girl with a yellow headband. I slugged him on the shoulder.

"What?" he said, an eyebrow quirked.

During his second round, my stomach started to churn. Waiting until he was well into his race against one of the nurses, I slipped out of The Commons and hurried to the bathroom. I pushed open a stall door and fell to my knees, throwing up into the toilet.

A hand rubbed my back. I didn't have to look up to see who it was; I've known her touch since I was eleven.

When my stomach was empty, I dropped on my butt, leaning up against the side of the stall. Leslie handed me a glass of water.

"Thanks," I muttered.

I rinsed my mouth and spit into the toilet.

"Katie," Leslie said, her eyes focused inside the porcelain.

I shifted my gaze, and my heart lurched.

Blood.

I stared at it, understanding. "Don't tell Damian, okay?"

Leslie shook her head. "Katie, I can't just ignore this."

I nodded, my attention not leaving the scarlet-stained water. "I'm not asking you to. Just not Damian."

Pulling out her cell, Leslie dialed and held it up to her ear. "Dr. Lowell, are you here yet? Good. Come to the girls' bathroom. And be discreet."

Not two minutes later, the bathroom door opened, and Dr. Lowell knelt beside us in the too-cramped stall. He glanced into the toilet then at me. I'm sure my face was as white as the hospital bed sheets.

Dr. Lowell sighed.

"It's happening, isn't it?" My voice trembled.

Dr. Lowell nodded, his fist pressed against his mouth. Then he did something he's never done before: He wrapped his arms around me.

"I guess this means another pill?" I asked into his shirt. He smelled like Damian.

"Yeah. Yeah, it does."

I looked up at him. "Prom. I have to make it to prom."

Dr. Lowell nodded. "I'll do everything in my power."

We went back to the party in shifts so as to not alert anyone.

"Where were you?" Damian demanded as soon as I entered The Commons.

I kissed his cheek. "Little girl's room." I winked, and his shoulders fell.

"Let me know next time, all right? I was worried." He led me back to our table, and I laid my head in my arms.

The *Mario Kart* tournament came down to Brennan and Damian. A look of understanding passed between them before they began their five-race final. After each one, Damian's head pivoted in my direction. I smiled, and he went back to his game.

For the last race, Damian and Brennan were tied

two-two. Silence spread over The Commons as all eyes were on the 60 inch television hanging on the wall. On the last lap, Brennan hunched over a little further, determined. Damian had a mischievous grin on his face, and I was sure that on the last corner, Damian slipped off the track on purpose, allowing Brennan to pass him and roll over the finish line first.

The room exploded in cheers and applause as Damian scooped Brennan up on his shoulders. Damian jogged around the room, and everyone gave Brennan high fives as he passed.

Soon after, the blue cake was cut and Damian sat down with a piece for himself and one for me.

I took a bite before dumping the rest on Damian's plate. Ignoring the look on his face, I asked, "You let him win, didn't you?"

Damian couldn't keep a straight face. "Yeah."

I laughed. "You didn't even try to lie."

"What's the point? You know anyway."

"You made his day," I said, nodding in Brennan's direction.

"He deserves it."

As the party wore down, guests trickled out, and I slumped down on the sofa. Damian had promised Tammy he'd help clean up. My head had begun to pound after the trip to the bathroom, but it wasn't bad enough to call it a night yet.

Brennan sat down next to me, a huge smile on his face.

"Did you see me beat your boyfriend?"

"I sure did. Nice job!" I gave him a fist-bump.

Brennan's smile faded. "Are you okay, Kate?"

"Yeah. Yeah, I'm good. Hey, I've got something for you," I said, digging in my purse. Finding the white envelope, I handed it to him. "You have to promise me something though."

Brennan nodded. "Okay."

"No thank-you's."

Brennan's brows knit together. "Why?"

"Because thank-you's are like good-byes."

"Okay," he drawled out.

"Don't open it here."

"Okay."

"And send Damian a picture."

Again, confusion glazed over his boyish face.

I laughed. "You'll understand when you open it."

Brennan gave me a hug which was better than any "thank you."

I curled up on the sofa, my head on a pillow that Damian brought me. Damian's gaze shot in my direction every few minutes, and when it did, I offered a reassuring smile. The headache was getting worse by the second, and by the time the party ended, it had overtaken me.

The lights in the room blurred into fragments of gold, and the people were no more than fuzz. I tried to tell Damian I wanted to leave, but I'm not sure how far I got. Somehow, I still caught the fear in Damian's eyes before I fainted.

Chapter 26

April 23
Dear Diary,
Sorry I haven't written much. I've been so tired lately. I'm not going to golf practice, and I can only handle one class a day.

Tonight, though, is prom. And I feel like crap.

I've doused myself in meds and slept all day, determined to make this night special for Damian. I have a promise to keep.

He'll be here at six. I guess it's show time.

Showering went much faster without hair. After drying off, I slathered amber lotion over every inch of skin to cover up how pale I'd gotten. Dressed in a strapless bra and panties, I slipped on a pair of shorts and a button-up shirt to avoid getting blush on my dress.

I sat in front of the vanity, taking extra care with my makeup. Uncapping the black eyeliner, I squinted into the mirror. I always had problems putting this stuff on, but after wiping it off twice, I finally made the lines flawless above my lashes. Mom had bought me metallic eye shadow to match my dress. With three coats of mascara, the silver really stood out.

I rounded my lips with pink lip gloss then stuffed it in my purse for later. Studying my reflection, I added an extra coat of concealer under my eyes and tossed the compact in my purse too.

My headache began to disappear as I imagined Damian and me dancing. I unzipped the garment bag, the waves at the bottom of my dress poured out, cascading over the top. Gently, I pulled the dress off the hanger and held it up to my chest. I twirled, the skirt flowing out around me. I couldn't wait to get it on. When someone tapped on my door, I laid the dress back on the bed and sat down.

"Come in," I said, running my fingers over the material.

My mother held the last piece of the ensemble in her hand.

"What do you think?" she asked, admiring her work. She spun it around so I could see it from all sides.

I broke into a grin. "I think you've outdone yourself."

She set her masterpiece on the vanity and scurried over to pick up the gown. "Come on, princess. Gotta get you ready for the ball."

I laughed and kicked off my shorts. It took me a

while to get the buttons unfastened, but when I did, I threw the shirt on the floor and ducked under the gown Mom held up for me. With my arms raised above my head, I emerged out of the top, the bodice settling in place. She zipped up the side and stepped back to examine me.

"Absolutely magnificent," she said.

Her special pumps sat on the floor at my feet. I held onto the mattress with one hand for balance as she slipped them over my French-tipped toes and fastened them in the back.

Giddy, she took the final piece from the vanity and danced over to me. Her smile widened with each step.

I took a deep breath and sat on the bed. Mom crawled behind me and placed the wig on my bald head. The color was impeccable, matching my once-there auburn locks exactly. Then, she slipped off the bed and stood in front of me. She clasped her hands, her face lighting up.

"Oh, Katie!"

She led me to the full length mirror behind the door. I barely recognized myself. The wig had ringlets piled on top, and whips of bangs hanging over my forehead. A few curls swirled down, touching my shoulders. Pearls on bobby pins stuck out through the mass like glittering snowflakes.

"Mom!" I gasped. "It's…it's *gorgeous*."

She leaned across me, kissing my cheek. "No, *you're* gorgeous."

Slowly, I faced her. She was glowing, and I realized how much this moment meant to her. As I wrapped my arms around her neck, my heart sunk.

Again my thoughts went to how much she'd given up for me.

A small knock sounded at my door. "Katie?" Damian's voice sent ripples of excitement down my spine.

"I'll be done in a minute," I answered. "Wait downstairs."

"Do you need help—"

"No. I want to do it by myself."

I let go of my mom, her mascara running down her face.

"Thank you, Mom," I said.

She covered her mouth with her hand, inhaling a sigh. "I love you, baby."

I let her open the door for me. She wiped her cheeks and headed toward the stairs. A few steps down, she glanced over her shoulder and blew me a kiss.

I took a deep breath, brushed my hands over the flounce in the skirt, and pictured Damian's expression in my mind. It had been a long time since he'd seen me with hair, and I couldn't wait for his jaw to drop open. The wig already itched, but it was a small price to pay.

I stood at the top of the stairs staring down at the three pairs of eyes beaming up at me. The night of the Christmas date swirled in my mind. Descending, I held onto the rail, fearful I'd trip over the small train rolling behind me. I squinted through the flashes exploding from my mother's camera, trying to make out the look on Damian's face.

When I reached the bottom, I saw the pride in my father's eyes. He took my hand and kissed my cheek.

"You look beautiful, sweetheart," he choked out.

He patted the top of my hand before placing it into Damian's.

Damian shifted his gaze to the floor before meeting mine. A hint of disappointment glazed over his eyes—not what I'd imagined. He slipped a corsage of white roses and baby's breath over my wrist.

"Your dress...wow! I..." He pursed his lips together.

"You don't clean up half-bad, yourself," I said, brushing nothing off the shoulder of his black tux.

"We'd better get going, or we'll miss our dinner reservation." Damian shot a nod toward my parents and walked with me out to the limo.

"You sure you're feeling up to this tonight?" he asked once inside.

Puzzled that he hadn't mentioned my hair, I nodded and stared out the window.

He sighed. "You look amazing."

I nodded again. "You said that...sort of."

After a few moments of silence, he drew my face to him, peering into my eyes. "I thought you hated wigs."

I glanced at the floor. "I do, but I wanted to look perfect, for you."

Damian lifted my chin. "Oh, baby."

Putting his hand behind my head, he kissed me. With his other one, he pulled the wig off my head. He kissed my forehead, then sat back, admiring the view. A wide grin spread over his face.

"Here," he said, reaching for the sack next to

him. He drew out an iridescent butterfly and a small plastic tube.

"What's that?"

Damian puffed a laugh. "I saw this on YouTube; let's hope it works."

He unscrewed the lid and placed a streak of clear glue on the backside of the butterfly.

"Well," he hummed, examining me. He placed the butterfly on my head, just above my ear. Sitting back a little, he nodded. "*Now* you look perfect."

How is he mine?

Then I did something I'd never done before. Heat coursing through me, I took his face in both hands and crushed my mouth to his. Surprised, he stiffened a little before relaxing. I separated his lips with my tongue, then moved to straddle him in the backseat of the limo.

He chuckled. "I'm not sure if we have that much time, Kate."

I leaned into him, my head resting on his shoulder, and my lips pressed against his neck. My energy had drained that quickly. He held me close all the way to the restaurant, his fingers leaving trails of warmth over my bare shoulders.

At the Principal Building, Damian took my hand. Heads turned as the hostess led us to our table. Damian nodded in their direction, and I giggled.

"They think you're as dazzling as I do." His breath tickled my ear.

Conceding to my request of sharing a meal, Damian ordered for himself, and I ate his salad and a few bites of steak. It was more than I'd eaten in days.

After dinner, Mr. Dempsy drove us to the Marriot Hotel downtown. Dr. Jackson Lowell was waiting by the double doors, a camera in hand.

"Hey, Dad. Glad you could make it," Damian said, slapping his father on the back.

"Wouldn't miss it for the world," Jackson replied. "You look stunning, Kate."

"Thank you," I said, glancing up at Damian. Lights from over the Des Moines River flickered in his blue irises.

We posed for a few more pictures, then Damian shook his father's hand. Jackson embraced me, and kissed me on the cheek. Since Brennan's party, I had stopped viewing Dr. Lowell as my doctor, and more as my boyfriend's father. Well, actually, more than that. Like a second father. The proud gleam in his eye made me think that the feeling was mutual.

The ballroom swarmed with every color of the rainbow, from the gowns to the pulsing lights of the band. Tables surrounded the dance floor, glowing with flameless candles and purple bouquets.

Already, my eyelids began to droop. Damian found a table and pulled me onto his lap. I cuddled up to him, resting my head on his shoulder.

A few members of the golf team came over to say hello, but they didn't stay long. I assumed I was making them uncomfortable.

"It's good to see you here, Kate," Lizzie, the girl's captain said.

"Thank you."

Her eyes drifted to Damian and held his gaze for a second too long. He offered her a small nod, his lips curling between his teeth.

Lizzie continued as if nothing had happened. "We could have used your score on Tuesday."

"You pulled it out, though, didn't you?"

She rolled her eyes. "Barely. You two have a nice evening."

"Yeah, you too," I said as she walked away.

I glanced at my date. "What was that about?"

"What was what about?"

"That…thing. Between you and Lizzie."

"I didn't know there was a thing." The corner of Damian's mouth lifted, a dimple winking at me.

I narrowed my eyes at him, but he just laughed and held me tighter. We watched the band and the students dancing. Everyone seemed so happy; they'd dance all night without a care in the world.

The band started to play a slow song, and Damian nestled his nose in my neck. "Dance with me?"

I couldn't let him down. "Sure."

He led me to the middle of the dance floor and held me close as we swayed to the music. I closed my eyes. I didn't know the song; it didn't matter anyway. Damian's heartbeat was enough. I didn't even notice when the music stopped.

"Katie?" Damian said.

I opened my eyes and peered up at him.

He didn't say anything; he just nodded to someone off to the right. I followed his gaze and sucked in a lungful of air. The dance floor was empty. Everyone had formed a rectangle around the edge of the wood.

Suddenly, a few of the students created a small opening on the far side, and both the girls' and

303

boys' golf teams, our coach, and a few teachers walked out, creating a circle around us. Lights bounced off the skin of their heads where the hair should have been. I covered my mouth with my hand, unable to stop the tears.

Damian cupped my shoulders from behind me. "See? You were never invisible."

The ring of people sat down on the floor holding hands, and the band began to play. I stared at each person in the circle. I'd never known! They smiled at me, their expressions warm.

The band began to play a familiar song, and I turned to discover Damian standing beside me, holding a microphone.

There are no reasons
That you're searching for
I haven't left that door open long
Please don't stop skimming
I need your understanding
I need you to make sure that I land on my feet
Tell me that you love me
Tell me that you want me
Tell me that the world's not over me
The world's not over me
You'll find me
In my hiding place
At least I'll pray for you
I'm not sure if you'll follow through but if you do
I'll be waiting for you
To tell me that you love me
That you hate that the world
Isn't over me
The world's not over me

When he finished, the students cheered and applauded. Damian smiled at me, moisture glistening in his eyes too. He swept me into his arms. After he put me down, the golfers surrounded me, patting my shoulders and giving me hugs.

Overwhelmed by the attention, I let out the breath I hadn't realized I was holding. I tried to thank everyone, but I couldn't speak. Damian helped me back to our table before I buckled into his arms.

"You?" I murmured.

"I wish I could take full credit."

I shook my head. "What do you mean?"

"Most of it was Lizzie's idea. Something the team wanted to do for you." His forehead met mine. "I just added the finishing touches."

Amazed, I ran my fingers over his cheek. "I have no words."

"You don't need any," he said against my mouth.

Chapter 27

May 2

Dear Diary,

I can't stop coughing. Blood-stained washcloths keep piling beside my bed. I hate seeing them—such a horrible reminder that I'm shutting down. For days now, my stomach has felt like it's been eating itself from the inside. When I open my eyes, everything blurs together in a fuzzy haze.

I don't go downstairs for dinner anymore; everyone joins me in my room for meals now. It's kinda nice, them sitting around me. Though, it's impossible to miss the grief creeping in with them and settling on the edge of my bed. If they could leave it at the door, that'd be fine with me.

My favorite part of the day is when Damian crawls in bed next to me and *pulls me into his arms. There, I can forget. There, I'm not sick.*

Damian's birthday is in two days. He'll be eighteen. I want to find the perfect gift, but what do you get the person you love more than anything to say good-bye?

~*~

We sat in my room eating dinner. Mom had cooked something that smelled spectacular. I tried to eat a few pieces of the penne, but it was hard to chew and harder to swallow. Giving up, I sipped on the chicken broth Damian had made from scratch, insisting the canned junk wasn't nearly good enough.

"He didn't understand why he had to pay the deductible when it was clearly the deer's fault," Dad said, recounting some work incident. "He said the deer is the state's property, so the government can pay for it."

Mom laughed, gently touching his arm. After twenty-one years of marriage, she still gazed at him in the same way she did in their wedding photos. Dad kissed her cheek.

Yeah, they'd be okay.

Damian took my hand. "You sure you can't eat more?"

"No. I'm fine."

He bit his lip. "Try. Please."

I stared at the plate of food. Wanting to please him, I picked up my fork and poked at a tomato. My hand shook, so I dropped the fork.

"I can't."

I couldn't look at him. The pain clouding his irises would make my heart ache more than it already did.

"That's okay, honey," I heard my mom say. She swept the plate off the tray in front of me.

Dad cleared his throat. "Well, we'd better clean up the kitchen, Marcy. Katie needs her rest, and I'm sure Damian's got homework."

I heard the utensils clink against the plates as Dad stacked them in his hands. Mom bent over and kissed my forehead. Dad did the same, and I lifted my eyes to see them walk out, closing the door behind them.

Damian sighed then crawled in next to me. He draped his arm around my shoulders and tugged me close.

We sat in silence, listening to each other breathe. His heartbeat soothed me; I loved hearing it pound against my ear.

He kissed my temple, pressing his lips against me and allowing them to linger. I wanted to freeze that moment in time. Encase it in gold for eternity.

Then I started to cough. Damian rubbed my back and held a clean washcloth to my mouth. Scarlet liquid glared back at us when I'd finished.

"Katie," Damian whispered. "I'm scared."

Breathing heavily, I grasped his arm, pinning it to my chest. "It'll…be…okay," I gasped out.

The pain in my stomach imploded, making me cry out and double over. Somewhere in the distance, I heard Damian calling my name. Over and over again, his voice pierced into my heart. He seemed miles away.

I screamed again. Then crumpled over onto the bed.

~*~

Beep. Beep. Beep.
"Heart rate is eight-five."
Beep. Beep. Beep.
"Blood pressure is seventy over fifty."
Beep. Beep. Beep.
"Liver functioning at fifteen percent."
Beep. Beep. Beep.
"Kidneys at twenty-five percent."
Beep. Beep. Beep.

~*~

"Pneumonia." Dr. Lowell's voice sounded weak.

My mother's high-pitched sobs echoed in my ears.

It's okay, Mom. It's okay.

I imagined my dad holding her as she cried on his shoulder.

"Now what?" Damian's voice was barely audible.

Silence.

~*~

"How long?" my father asked.

309

"Maybe a week," Dr. Lowell responded.

"Any hope of a transplant?" Damian's voice was raspy.

"If a donor can be found, she'll need more than bone marrow now. Both kidneys are failing and her liver's damaged." He paused. "The best we can do is keep her comfortable."

~*~

I opened my eyes, blinking until they adjusted. Damian sat in a chair with his head lying on my stomach. The scene was all too familiar—I hated it.

The pain was gone. In fact, I felt warm and fuzzy all over. A morphine drip hung over the side of my bed.

Smiling at him, I rolled my fingers over a lock of chestnut hair. He reminded me of a sleeping toddler. So beautiful. So content.

I'd watched him before, noticed the subtleties that made my heart race. With a twist in my gut, I realized I'd never let them sink in. My gaze drifted from one feature to the next, memorizing each detail of him—allowing his face to etch into my mind.

No lines graced his forehead; only a stray tendril of hair fell across the smooth skin. Full eyebrows that knitted together once in awhile as he slept made me wonder what images framed his dreams: Good? Bad? Me? Liam?

His eyes, blue as the ocean when they were open, were just as breathtaking closed. Long dark lashes flowed from his lids like thick wisps of Makura

310

grass. Even his nose was stunning. The way it sunk between his brows and widened at the tip in a square. His high cheek bones were tinted red tonight. A small scar settled under his left eye and two moles under his right. The deep dimples on both cheeks depressed each time he swallowed.

My eyes wandered to his lips as they had many times before. Pink and soft, they looked as wonderful as they felt. I traced a fingertip over them, remembering the first time he'd kissed me, crouched in a hospital bathroom. Even in my state, a small shiver raced up my spine at the thought.

He had a small cleft in his chin that was most visible when he sucked his lower lip between his teeth. I glided my fingers over his jaw line, for the first time noticing the mole just under his left ear. Adorable.

As I touched the diamond stud in his earlobe, he flinched. I pulled my hand back, afraid to wake him. He sighed, shifted in his seat and relaxed, his breathing returning to a steady rhythm.

I wished I could watch him sleep forever. When the sun began to rise outside the hospital window, I raised my face to feel the rays that crept through the blinds. If only the window was open so I could see the full magnificence of the sunrise.

The next time I awoke, Damian was sitting in the same place, eating a sandwich.

"Hey, baby," he said, grinning through red eyes.

When he reached out to caress my cheek, I

noticed a cotton ball taped to his inner elbow.

"What's that?" I asked, panic filling my voice. Images of the night I'd found him passed out in his own vomit flashed through my mind.

"Oh, no. It's not…" He glanced at his arm. "Remember when I said if I won our round of golf, you'd have to grant a wish of mine?"

I swallowed, washing down the burn stinging my throat. "I remember."

"I'm sorry I didn't ask first, but I didn't want to wake you."

"Uh, huh."

He sucked his lower lip between his teeth, the cleft in his chin materializing. "My wish was that you'd let me get my blood tested to see if I'd be a match for you."

My breath caught. "No—"

Damian interrupted me.

"I know it's a long shot. And I had to clean up first, but I'm eighteen today, and that's what I wanted to do."

I studied the floor, letting his words sink in. It was too late to say "no" anyway. "Thank you."

"How about you?" he asked. "What's your third wish?"

I smiled, meeting his gaze. "Remember when we'd sit together at the window in my room watching the sunrise?"

"I'll never forget."

"I wanna see the sun rise with you every morning for the rest of my life."

What felt like minutes passed before he answered. His voice cracked when he did. "That's a whole lot of sunrises. Are you sure you can put up with me for that long?"

"That long and longer." I touched his face, wiping away a tear. "For always."

He buried his face in my neck. "Always isn't long enough."

Chapter 28

Sometimes I heard the voices of my parents and Damian. Other times I didn't, but I could still feel their presence.

Today, I woke up to Damian fulfilling my wish. Tammy had a hold of my IV pole, and Damian held me in his arms outside the hospital, facing east. It wasn't until the sun's beams filled the sky that I realized we were standing on the roof.

I closed my eyes, breathing in the rays. I'd never see the sun rise from the beach overlooking the ocean or from the top of a mountain, but in that moment, scooped up against Damian's chest, I didn't care. This was the most beautiful sunrise I'd ever seen.

Back inside, I drifted off with Damian's hand holding mine. Sometimes I heard him whisper in my ear. During the night, he crawled in bed next to me, clinging to me as tightly as he dared.

My parents camped out in the small room too. I'm not sure if any of them ever left. Each time my eyes fluttered open, the three of them were there. Smiling at me. Talking to me. Kissing me.

One morning, I asked if I could have a few moments alone with each of them. I'd been thinking about it during my few waking moments. If I didn't do it soon, well, I didn't know how much time I had left.

My mother was first. She lay down beside me, taking my newly polished nails in hers, admiring her work.

"You've always had the most beautiful nails, Katie," she said, playing with each one on my right hand. She kissed my fingers, one at a time.

"I love you, Mom," I said, wiping the tears from her face.

She sniffled. "Oh, baby. I love you. I love you so much."

Placing my hand gently on the bed, she put her arms around me. Wetness smeared over my cheek, making me feel like I was taking a small part of her with me.

"Take care of Daddy, okay?"

"You will always be with us, Katie."

I nodded. Slowly, I raised my hand and ran my fingers through her silky hair. It was the same color as mine used to be.

"Mom?"

"Yeah, baby?"

"Will you do something for me?"

"Anything." Her voice squeaked a little when she spoke.

"Check up on Damian."

"Of course we will, baby. Of course we will."

She held me again in silence, trying to stifle her sobs.

"And Mom?"

"Yeah."

"No wig, please. They itch."

She nodded, her hair tickling my bald head. "I promise, baby. No wig."

~*~

No matter how hard I tried, I couldn't stop dozing off. My body was too weak to stay awake for more than an hour at a time. Seconds ticked by at an alarming rate, and I hated losing them—each one so precious.

The sun had gone down when my lids opened again. My parents and Damian ate some sort of take-out by my bed.

I hadn't eaten in over twenty-four hours, and I didn't care to. It didn't smell bad, but I didn't have the energy to chew or swallow.

"Dad?" I managed.

"I'm right here, sweetie," he said, rushing over to sit on the bed and taking Damian's usual spot.

I glanced at Damian. He nodded, knowing what I wanted. Taking my mother's hand, he led her into the hallway to give me some time alone with my dad. I watched them leave, a deep sense of appreciation for Damian filling me. Oh, how I loved him!

Moisture glistened in my father's eyes. The color of Dad's irises were almost as blue as Damian's. Why had I never noticed that before?

He raised my hand to his lips and kept it there.

Saying good-bye to my father would be harder than my mom. I'd always been his princess.

Dad and I sat in silence, staring at each other. He held my hand to his cheek and kissed it constantly. His expression told me everything. How much he loved me. How much he'd miss me. How much he hated seeing his little girl in a hospital bed.

"Do you remember when you were six, when I bought you your first set of clubs?"

Of course I remembered. I nodded.

Dad continued, his voice heavy. "You begged me to take you to the country club right away." A snicker escaped him. "You had such a difficult time carrying those clubs. But you wanted to do it all by yourself."

"I couldn't get them in the cart," I said, my voice crumbling a little.

"No, you couldn't."

"You stood behind me, teaching me proper grips, how to position my feet, and the best way to swing the club for maximum accuracy."

"You caught on so fast. I should have known then how talented you were."

"Well," I murmured, "it was hard to discern those things with a concussion."

Dad laughed. "Who knew a six-year-old could swing with such force."

"You did. At the hospital afterward."

A moment of silence engulfed us before he spoke again.

"I'm so proud of you, Katie," he said. "You've grown into a beautiful young woman. I couldn't have asked for a better daughter."

"I love you, Daddy."

Dad sniffled, a tear overflowing. "I look forward to when I'll see you again, princess."

I smiled. "I'll be waiting for you."

~*~

Dr. Lowell and Tammy came in to check the meds in my IV. My eyelids were starting to fall again, but I forced them to stay open just a little longer. Tammy went to speak with my father as Jackson sat down beside me.

"You okay, Kate?"

Without answering, I reached under my pillow and handed him a white envelope I'd asked Tammy for a few days before. Attached to the front, I stuck a Post-it with instructions on it beside where I'd written Damian's name.

Jackson took it, nodded at me, and tucked it into the inside of his white lab coat.

"Don't lose him," I urged. "Please, don't lose him."

"I won't. I promise."

"Thank you," I mouthed and my lids closed.

~*~

"NO!" I shouted in my head. "Two more things to do. I won't go yet! I can't."

I was falling. Deeper and deeper inside myself. Brick after brick was piled over my body. I fought to breathe. Fought to think.

It didn't hurt, but I sank further and further asleep until I knew I'd never wake up.

"Please, God," I begged. "Please, just a little more time."

~*~

Sometime in the middle of the night my eyes opened again.

The room was so cold. *So* cold.

Damian lay asleep next to me, his arms wrapped around me. Running my hands through his silky hair, I let it wash over my fingers. I kissed him on the cheek and reached under my pillow for my diary. Somehow, a final surge of energy exploded inside me, and I began to write.

"Katie," he hummed.

"I'm here," I breathed out.

Damian's blue irises stared back at me, the color as pale as the morning sky.

"I love you," I said. "My first and my last."

He opened his mouth then closed it, tears brimming in the corners of his eyes.

"Any regrets?" I asked.

"Lots."

My finger traced the outline of his lips. "Are you happy, Damian?"

He glanced to the window. His hand, over my stomach, trembled. "With you, I've never been happier."

The lump in my throat made it more difficult to speak. "And tomorrow?"

Damian cupped my face in his palms and pressed his forehead against mine. The muscles in his face tensed. "I don't know what happens tomorrow. What I do know is that I'm happy to have had the honor of knowing you. Of..." He swallowed, choking back a sob. "Of loving you. I love you, Katie. God, I love you."

He buried his face in my shoulder, moisture clinging to my neck. My fingers flowed through his hair, remembering all the times he'd comforted me.

"I don't want to lose you, Katie." His breath cooled quickly against my skin.

"I'll always be with you."

I fumbled for the necklace he'd given me, the one that represented hope. Now, I was sure he needed it more than I. Gripping it tightly, I yanked. The chain broke and the symbol dropped into my palm.

I forced it into Damian's clenched hand. "I'll always be with you," I repeated.

He stared at his fist, clamping it tighter until his skin turned the same color as mine.

"I have something else for you," I said, handing him my diary. "Here. I've never let anyone read it. This one, or the others. I want you to have them, though. All of them."

Damian took the diary and squeezed his eyes shut, inhaling deeply. "You have two more wishes."

I forced a small laugh. "Yes, I do."

"So?"

"Graduate."

Damian's eyebrows furrowed. "What?"

"Graduate. Get your diploma. Do something

with your life."

"Katie, that's…"

"What I want. Please."

Damian nodded. "Okay. And what's the last one?"

I grinned. "The rules didn't change. When you fulfill this one, I'll give you the last one. Kind of like a security deposit."

"But—"

"It'll be okay. I promise."

Damian sucked his lip between his teeth. "Don't make promises you can't keep."

"I won't."

"Katie," he whispered.

"I love you, Damian. I'll always love you."

My time was almost up, my eyes getting heavy.

Damian lifted my chin, kissing me as our tears mingled. His lips moved slowly over mine, tasting every inch. The tenderness of his touch cascaded through me, melting my heart. It was by far the best kiss we'd ever shared.

Damian shifted on the bed, carefully resting my head on his chest. His hands smoothed over my scalp.

"I love you, my Katie," he said, kissing my head. "I love you."

Before tonight, he'd never said those words out loud to me. A swell billowed inside me. Content and ready, I closed my eyes and listened to him repeat those words over and over in my ear.

Chapter 29

May ?
Dear Dairy,

I'm not sure what day it is or how much time I've been in the hospital. That's the thing, though—we never have enough time.

There's nothing like being seventeen and dying to question your belief in God. I'm so young. I can't help but think that I'll never graduate from high school. I'll never go to college. Never get married and have kids. I'll never attempt to bake another pumpkin pie with my mother for Thanksgiving. Or have that round of golf with my dad on Hilton Head Island that we'd always talked about.

I will never fly to Greece. Or climb to the top of Mount Everest. I'll never see a volcano erupt. I'll never get to swim with dolphins. I'll never get to go to Disney

World with Damian. But it makes me happy to think of Brennan and his mother enjoying that trip for me. I'll watch him from Heaven.

And that's what makes it all okay. Of all the things I'll never be able to experience, I'll get so much more. I guess that's how God works.

Now, I'll get to see Damian graduate. See him fall in love and get married. I'll be there for my parents' fiftieth wedding anniversary. I'll get to see dolphins every single day; even what they're doing under the rolling blue seas. From Heaven, I'll experience everything and more, and not be sick for any of it. What more can I ask for?

But knowing that my family and Damian will miss me...that's the part I'm not sure I can handle. Especially Damian. He's lost so much already, and I hate that I'm adding to it. I hate what I'm doing to him. Maybe he'd have been better off not knowing me.

I keep going back to our first conversation. "What if." And the only ending I can come up with is: "What if I'd never gotten sick?"

If cancer had never invaded my body, I'd be golfing right now. Maybe in the LPGA, like I'd always dreamed. I'd be *graduating. Going shopping with my mom for new clothes. Considering colleges. Dancing at clubs. Washing my hair an innumerable amount of times. I'd be hanging out at a friend's house. Going to movies. On dates with guys. Planning a road trip with my best friends this summer.*

It all sounds so great, and yet...

If I were healthy, I'd have never grown this close to my parents. Never met Damian. Never loved him and known the joys of having him love me back. I'd never have gone to prom with him. Never watched my father treat him like a son. Visit his mother and brother's graves. I'd never have been showered in flowers. Or been serenaded on Christmas.

Without it, maybe I would've had a lobster dinner, but not in front of the fireplace in Damian's den. Not with him clinging to me; needing me. I'd have never fought with him and learned what it meant to really forgive someone and be forgiven by them.

I can't stop the tears now as I think about it. The scene still plays over in my mind and scares me just as much as it did when it happened; when I saw Damian passed out that night, sprawled out on his bed. I learned we weren't invincible. And that I loved him more than life itself.

If you're still wondering if I could do it all over again. If, somehow, I had been given the choice to have leukemia or not, I wouldn't have changed a thing. Nothing. My life has been so blessed, and it's my hope that through it, I've been able to do the same for those around me.

I can say without a shadow of doubt...it was worth it all. All the suffering. And all the joy.

I close Kate's dairy and set it on my lap. I've read it half a dozen times over the last three days since she gave it to me. Her chest rises and falls sporadically, the steady rhythm long gone. Oh God, it hurts to watch.

The skin on her hands is so thin and cold. I cover them with my palms, hoping my warmth will somehow sink into her. Swallowing the burn in my throat, I kiss her scalp and hold her against me.

"I love you, Katie," I whisper again, wishing I'd told her a thousand times a day since I realized what she meant to me. I'm a fucking idiot for not telling her until the other night. "I love you."

Kate shakes a little, then calms. I press my palm against her temple, gently pushing her into me where she used to feel safe. Now, she's fading away, and there's not a *goddamn thing* I can do about it.

She shakes again, and I hold my breath. This can't be happening.

"Jason," I say in the darkness. "Marcy?"

Kate's mother perks her head up, wide awake.

"You'd better come over," I hear myself say, but I don't recognize my voice.

Somewhere behind me, I hear them get up and rush over. I keep a hold of Kate's head, and her parents clasp her hand in theirs.

Marcy's quiet sobs hang in the air. It's the only sound.

Without me hearing the door open, Tammy and Leslie come in and stand at the foot of the bed. I barely notice my father next to me, his hand on my shoulder.

As day breaks, my gaze is drawn to the window. Golden rays stream into the room, and I realize I have a promise to keep.

Ever so carefully, I turn Kate's head. "It's sunrise, Katie. Can you see it?" I choke out the words. I take a deep breath, trying to calm myself; I have to stay brave for her. "It's beautiful, baby."

We watch the beams waft through the curtain. Kate's breaths are less frequent. She gasps for air, and I press my lips against her head. Tears that I've fought for days now overflow.

"I love you," I say against her.

Oh God! Please hear me!

Her chest rises again. Stops. Then falls slowly.

I whisper "I love you," over and over again, desperate to have her know. To me, she and I are the only ones in the room.

I wait to hear her inhale again, but her chest doesn't rise. She's gone.

I bow my head, grasping onto her. My dad hugs

me to him, but I can't let go of Kate. She's all alone, and she needs me.

No, I need her.

For me, time inches forward in slow motion. I don't remember getting out of her bed, or falling into my father's arms. Kate's parents embrace each other then hold me, Marcy's tears soaking my shirt. They shake my father's hand, and Marcy hugs him.

"We'd love it if you'd help us make the arrangements, Damian," Marcy tells me.

I nod once, not hearing anything else she says. My eyes glance back to the bed where Kate lays, and I have to force myself to walk away. It hasn't hit me fully yet. She's just asleep.

Kate's dead. She's not waking up.

Familiar pain takes over, and everything gets blurry. My father drives me home; that much I sort of remember. Alone in my room, I collapse onto my bed, clutching the sheets to my chest.

All I want is for Kate to be back in my arms.

Only because I said I would, I get out of bed the next day to meet Jason and Marcy at the funeral home. In a stuffy office I don't want to be in, we discuss the service with the director. I'm numb. I don't have much to add until I hear something about what time to hold the service.

"Sunrise," I say without hesitating.

The man beside me is caught off guard. "Uh, that's early, I'm not sure if people will—"

"Fine," I cut in, frustrated. This man has no

fucking clue, and I hate him for it. "Have the service the day before, but…" I swallow whatever it is that's rising in my throat, "bury her at sunrise." I barely get out the last part; it tastes bitter.

A strong hand grips my shoulder. "I love that idea," Jason says.

"Me too," Marcy squeaks out.

"Well, then," the director says. "I'll make the arrangements with the cemetery."

~*~

I sit with Kate's parents during the funeral services Monday afternoon. It's the last place I want to be. Dazed, I stare in front of me, avoiding the white casket surrounded by flowers. I'm sure everything the pastor says is worth listening to, but I can't. Hell, it *isn't* worth listening to. The whole thing's just a cruel reminder that she was taken away from me.

The song I wrote for her comes on over the speakers, and I can't take it anymore.

"I'm sorry," I mutter to Marcy, and escape to the bathroom.

I'm being a fucking pansy, but I don't care. I sit on the toilet, my hands squeezing into my head, afraid it will all pour out of me.

"Damian?"

I hold my breath.

Go away, Dad.

"Son?"

I see his feet, then his legs as he slides down the wall in front of the stall I'm in. And nothing. He just sits there, quiet.

After a handful of minutes, he finally says, "Why don't we go back in?"

I don't know why I nod. Why I open the door and follow him back out to our seats. I just do it. Then I sit there, staring in front of me but unable to see anything. This is a ruse. Yeah, it must be some cosmic-ass joke. It isn't real.

When the service is over, people make their way to the front to say their good-byes. I recognize some of her teachers from prom, her golf coach, and the whole team. Tammy is here, along with Leslie, who hugs me tight.

I don't feel it. I don't feel anything.

Marcy squeezes my hand and smiles weakly. Jason rubs my shoulder, and they make their way to the front after everyone else has gone.

Intentionally, I stay behind. I want to be the last one to see her before they close the lid, when she'll be lost to me forever. In seeing her, I hold on to the hope that she'll get up and fling herself into my arms.

I can't do this, Katie. You're the strong one.

She looks like an angel on a bed of satin. The butterfly I'd bought her for prom is stuck to the side of her head. Metallic eyeshadow is brushed to her lids as though she applied it herself. Even the black eyeliner she hated putting on is painted over her lashes. It's all wrong though. When she's asleep, her eyeliner is smudged. This isn't smudged.

Why the hell isn't it smudged?

Her white prom dress fills the coffin, and her mother's shoes sit in her hand.

"Yeah, that's not how the story goes. She gets to keep the shoes." I can still hear her voice in my head.

I squeeze my eyes shut, remembering when I carried her out to the limo after prom, the shoes hanging by their straps in her two fingers.

Opening my eyes, I glance at the flowers I'd bought. Shaped in a heart, one hundred red roses fan out among the greenery. A banner with the words "I LOVE YOU" is strung across the middle.

Carefully, I tug one of the roses from the bouquet. I kiss the petals then place it over Kate's heart.

"I love you, Katie," I whisper. "I'll always love you."

Chapter 30

Numbness consumes me during dinner. People come up to me, hug me, and tell me how sorry they are. I nod and thank them, but I don't care. They didn't know her like I did. Everything I ever loved is being lowered into the ground at the next sunrise.

I kiss Marcy on the cheek and tell her I'll see her in the morning. Kate's dad embraces me; I still don't feel any of it.

Kate's face is everywhere, and all I want is to forget. How she made me feel. How she spoke to me. The way she looked at me. Her eyes haunt me, and when the numbness subsides, pain will replace it.

Heart. Wrenching. Pain.

And I can't deal with it all over again.

I push open the front door of my house and drop my jacket on the floor. Yanking the tie, it releases from its knot, and I toss it on the floor too. I go into the kitchen, to the familiar cupboard. Not bothering with a glass, I grab a bottle of Jack Daniels and head to my room, tossing the cap as I walk.

331

The amber liquid burns my throat. I take another swig.

Heading to my bedroom, I see the door down the hall ajar. Anger pours into my bloodstream faster than the alcohol.

"Get the hell out of here!" I scream from the doorway of Liam's room. Not I, not anyone, has been here in two years.

Ellie spins around. She's clutching a picture frame to her chest.

I scan the room. It reminds me of Kate's—everything's in its place.

"What the fuck are you doing?" I say, glaring at her.

"Damian, I heard. I'm so sorry," she says and bows her head, that long blonde hair covering her face.

Fuck you.

I take another drink. "Is that what you came here for?"

A teardrops down her face, but I couldn't care less. "I miss him. Here, I feel close to him," she says. "It's…it's been awhile."

"Two fucking years," I mumble, tipping the bottle to my mouth.

"Actually," she says, "after you'd fall asleep, I'd come in here and sit."

I laugh. "Well, aren't you the perfect goddamn girlfriend."

She stares the floor. "I'm leaving tomorrow."

"Bye," I clip out, annoyed.

"I'm, uh, transferring to Florida State to study marine biology."

"Don't let the door hit you in the ass on the way out." I take another drink.

She steps toward me. I keep my eyes fixed on her, forcing more whisky down my throat. She's studying me. *Pitying me.* I swallow another gulp of liquid. The alcohol isn't working fast enough.

Ellie's directly in front of me now. She smells so sweet, like vanilla lotion, her favorite. Pressing her lips into a straight line, she wraps her arms around my neck. I consider taking a step back, but her hold is too familiar.

"I'm sorry, Damian. I really am," she says.

I close my eyes and breathe her in, barely hearing her. Her silky hair tickles my cheek, and I realize that the alcohol just isn't enough.

I dip my head down to kiss her neck, intentionally avoiding the spot under her ear. She tenses but doesn't say anything. I slip a hand under her shirt, gliding my fingers up her spine.

"Damian," she says, trying to pull away. "I don't think—"

"Exactly. Don't think." I unhook her bra, pressing my palm into her back.

"Damian, you just lost K—"

I swing her around, pinning her against the wall. "Don't *fucking* say her name," I yell. One of Liam's trophies falls from shelf at the force. I slam a fist to the wall by her head, and Jack splashes over my arm. Ellie winces and jerks her head to the side.

"I'm sorry...I—" she mutters, her voice so small.

The fear in her eyes subdues me, and I sigh. "I just want to forget, Ellie. For one fucking night, I just want to forget."

She faces me, the fear fading away.

"You remember," I remind her. "You, of all people, understand. This looks pretty fucking familiar to you, doesn't it?"

She bites her lip and glances to the bottle in my hand—the only difference from the night of Liam's funeral.

"You wanted to forget too," I say, cupping a breast.

She lifts her eyes to me again, and I can see her breaking. I take another drink before she grabs the bottle from my hand and sets it on Liam's dresser.

"It won't make it better," she says. "Or easier."

"I have nothing to lose."

She doesn't say anything for a few moments, glancing around the room. When she returns to me, her gaze is hard.

"Not in here," she says, placing the picture of her and Liam on the dresser beside my bottle of whisky.

"Fine," I say, grabbing her hand, and slamming Liam's bedroom door behind us.

As soon as we enter my room, I throw her up against the closet doors, kissing her mouth but not like I mean it. I don't love her. She doesn't love me.

I hook her leg over my hip and yank her shirt over her head. With her bra straps hanging off her elbows, she starts unbuttoning my shirt. Kate's fingers doing the same thing flashes in my mind, and I grab Ellie's wrists.

I take off my own shirts, then press myself harder against Ellie, my mouth moving over her breasts. She lets her bra drop to the floor and digs

334

her nails into my shoulders. I suck her lower lip into my mouth and cringe. Ellie doesn't taste like strawberries.

Suck it up, asswipe.

Waves of hair spill over her shoulders. I'd forgotten what a girl's hair felt like in my fingers. I push it away, hating it.

I jerk open her jeans, and she shimmies out of them, kicking them across the room. Then she unfastens my pants and pushes them down over my ankles. I like that she's quick and gets to the point. My hands grab at the back of her thighs, lifting. She gives a little hop, and I wrap both of her legs around my hips, pushing her harder into the closet doors. I'm not careful with her.

Her fingers weave into my hair, but not with Kate's tenderness. Ellie's not being gentle either. I puff out a snicker, happy about the difference.

When I push myself inside her, Ellie cries out. Her voice is so damn experienced; she knows what I like. A lump forms in my throat. I ache for the bottle of whisky to wash it down. I ignore it and turn us around so that I fall on top of Ellie on my bed.

Her moans don't excite me like Kate's. Tonight, Ellie's are just unnecessary noise. I try to drown her out. When I realize it's not working, I crush my mouth on hers to stifle the sound.

Come on, man! Just fuck her and forget.

Her thighs squeeze me tighter, and she pushes her hips into mine. I hear myself gasp. God, I hope Kate's memory erases itself from my mind. I close my eyes and see her hazel ones staring back at me.

"Katie," I breathe. "Oh, Katie."

My words won't faze Ellie, and I wouldn't give a shit if they did. I'm sure she remembers her own cries that night and the many nights afterward, until they finally ceased, fading to nothing more than Liam's ghost.

Ellie squeezes my biceps, her hand covering the tattoo reminder of Liam. I don't know if that's why she always grabs me there. It probably is. She was with me when I got it. Her identical one, only smaller, is on her hip. She hit me once for kissing it.

Ellie's moans grow louder, forcing me to realize it's almost over, and Kate's memory only increases. In my head, her arms fold around me, pressing herself into me as she comes. So different than this reality with Ellie's arms above her head, grasping the sheets.

Kate's voice smashes into me. *"Will it hurt?"*

"I'll take care of you," I'd said. *"I promise."*

Tears blur my vision as I cry out Kate's name a last time. Ellie reaches for me, but I don't want her sympathy. I roll to my side, allowing the guilt to take over. Maybe this was what I wanted; to feel more pain. Be reminded that Kate's gone, and that I never deserved her love.

Ellie wraps her arms around me and leans her head against my back. I let her because I don't have the energy to shove her off. Like I did for her, she'll stay. She'll rub my arms in compassionate circles until I cry myself to sleep.

~*~

I wake up to my cell phone alarm at four in the morning. Rubbing the dried tears from my eyes, I find Ellie still asleep beside me. Seeing her there makes my stomach hurt. She'd been right; last night hadn't made anything easier.

I get up and head to the shower. The hot water rolls over my shoulders and down my back, leaving my skin red. When I step out, I don't feel better. I drop to my knees and throw up in the toilet.

Clouds of steam fill my bedroom when I open the door. Ellie is putting on her jeans and pauses to look at me. She stands and walks over, wraps her arms around my neck like she did the night before.

"Letting someone go doesn't mean you forget them," she murmurs. "It means you love from here and move on with your life like they would have wanted."

She kisses me on the cheek. "Good-bye, Damian."

I don't watch her leave. Instead, I throw on a pair of khakis and the blue polo Kate loved so much, and get in my car.

Holding back the burning in my chest takes everything—which isn't much. I turn into the cemetery and see Kate's parents already here. They look weary but are holding it together. Better than I am.

I park behind their car and walk to the tent. Jason is speaking with the minister. He pauses to nod at me. Marcy hugs me to her and leans on my shoulder. Words can't comfort me, so I figure none can comfort her either. It's quiet, like sound-proof walls have popped up around us.

People slowly arrive. Kate's golf coach pats me on the back and thanks me for my help with Katie. I fake a smile. The last thing I need is someone fucking *thanking* me for loving her. It should be the other way around.

Tammy and Leslie stand under the tent with my father. Brennan and his mother are in front of them. Leslie's hands rest on the boy's shoulders. Other people, Kate's extended family, I think, fill in the gaps.

Just as the sun begins to rise, the pastor recites the same words from my mother and Liam's funeral. "Forasmuch as it hath pleased Almighty God of his great mercy to take unto himself the soul of our dear sister here departed, we therefore commit her body to the ground; earth to earth, ashes to ashes, dust to dust; insure and certain hope of the Resurrection to eternal life, through our Lord Jesus Christ; who shall change our vile body, that it may be like unto his glorious body, according to the mighty working, whereby he is able to subdue all things to himself."

I look to the west and close my eyes as Kate used to do. Holding my breath, I think of sitting with her at her window.

I hear her sweet voice in my ear as if she's standing beside me. *"It's amazing, isn't it?"* she says. *"No matter how dark it gets, the sun always rises and starts a new day. The darkness is forgotten."*

As the morning rays filter in, I feel her all around me like she's reaching down from above. But when I open my eyes, it all fades away. Before me is a blue vault, and Kate's shiny white casket.

The pain rushes over me, and I lose my balance. My father's hands grab me from behind, helping me hold it together. I roll into him and bury my face in his chest. Grabbing a hold of his shirt in the back, I clench my hands as hard as I can.

I feel hands patting my back as people begin to leave. My dad thanks them, but I don't let go of him until small arms fold around my waist. I peer down and see Brennan's bloodshot eyes staring back at me.

Kneeling down, I pull him into my arms. He coughs through a sob and lays his head against me.

"I miss her," he says.

"I do too, buddy," I say. "I do too."

We stay in our embrace until his mother pats him on the shoulder. He wipes his face with the back of his hand and sniffles.

"I'll send you a picture from Disney World," he says. "Kate made me promise I would."

I push my fist into my mouth, fighting to not break down. Through the stab in my gut, I smile. I love that Katie gave the tickets to Brennan; she was amazing like that. "Send me one with you and Mickey Mouse, okay? Have a good trip, buddy."

Leslie hugs me next. "You take care of yourself," she says. "You were good for her."

I scoff. "I don't know about that."

"You were good for each other," she says, a soft grin playing on her lips. "Don't be a stranger."

I wait until the cemetery is empty, even after the Browdys leave. My father stays with me.

"You can go, Dad," I say. "I know you need to

get to work. I'll be fine."

He shakes his head and squeezes my shoulders. "There's only one place I need to be today."

I take three roses from the heart wreath and place one of them on my mother's headstone and another on Liam's. Then Dad and I sit under the elder tree and watch the funeral home people take down the tent. I twirl the third rose between my fingers.

He hugs me to his side as I lose it. Kate's casket is lowered into the vault and placed in the ground. I watch, shaking, until the dirt is put back in place and the remnants of the flowers are set on top of the fresh pile.

The workers nod to me and Dad before they walk away. I stand and brush off my pants, the tears running dry. Picking up the rose, I press the petals to my lips, just as I did yesterday.

"I love you, Katie," I say.

I drop the rose on her grave, and Dad leads me to my car.

~*~

Back home, Dad offers me lunch. I decline and head to my room; I need to be alone.

Before I enter, I swing by Liam's room. I don't bother reminiscing, I don't pause; I just grab the bottle of Jack Daniels and hurry out.

I slip off my shirt and take a long drink, enjoying the burn. My gaze wanders to the closet doors, and I have to look away.

It doesn't take me long to reach the bottom of the bottle. Pissed that it emptied so quickly, I throw it against the wall.

Needing more to numb the pain, I run downstairs to the kitchen. Dad glances up from the counter and sighs. I know he smells the alcohol on me, but I don't give a damn what he thinks. He didn't stop me before.

I glare at him. "Old habits die hard, I guess."

"You got something in the mail," he says, flicking a white envelope down the granite.

I pick it up and open it without reading the return address. Only one sentence sinks in.

Your blood sample is 96% compatible to Kate Browdy.

I read the letter again. And again. And again.

A match. To Katie.

Dad stands behind me, reading over my shoulder and gasps. "Damian."

I allow the letter to flutter to the floor, and I walk over to my favorite cupboard in a daze. Throwing the door open, empty shelves stare me down. A note is taped to one of the shelves in my dad's handwriting.

I have a promise to keep for Kate, too.

"Oh, shit."

Turning away, I narrow my gaze at my father. Then I run at him.

Chapter 31

Come to find out, Dad had taken two weeks off. It's probably a good thing too. He needed some time for his face to heal. He's never been good at throwing punches, but he did manage to lay a good one into my left eye. Props.

Then, he confiscated my car keys. Asshole.

In the morning, I open my eyes to the most annoying sound I've ever heard.

BUZZZZZZZZZ!

I grab the alarm clock and yank it out of the wall. There's no way in hell that I'd set the goddamn thing. Five minutes later, Dad pounds on my door.

"Time for school," he shouts.

"Not going," I yell back.

Dad opens the door, letting himself in. Shit! I'd forgotten to lock it the night before. I roll around, my back to him.

An air horn blares, and I jerk up, throwing my pillow at him.

"What the fuck?"

"Language, son. Time to go. First day of finals,"

342

he says, way too fucking chipper.

"In case you didn't get it, I'm not going. Now get out."

The horn goes off again.

"Damn it, Dad!"

"If I remember right, you have a promise to uphold to Kate. Now, get your ass out of bed. I'm driving you."

When I don't move, he sounds the horn again.

"I've got all day, son."

Fuming, I grab my stuff and stomp into the bathroom, hoping to lock him out. Instead, he catches the door with his foot.

"You're gonna watch me *shower*?"

He shoots me an arrogant smile. "If that's what it takes."

"That's fucking messed up," I mutter.

~*~

After school, I run to my room, ready to crawl back into bed. I grab for the door, but somehow I miss and swipe at air.

Turning, I glare at the empty hinges. My bathroom door is gone too. I poke my head down the hall—every goddamn door has been removed.

No fucking way.

Screaming, I punch my fist through the drywall.

I fling myself on the bed, not caring that the blood from my knuckles smears over my sheets. From under my pillow, I pull out Kate's diary. I read it, letting her words envelop me until I fall asleep.

~*~

Dad doesn't bother with the horn this morning. He does stand over me, though, as I get ready. Then he drives me to my last day of high school.

When we get home, I head to my room and sprawl out on my bed, thinking of Kate and feeling the knife slice through me over and over again until sleep relieves me.

I don't see my dad for two days because I stay in my room. Friday morning he walks in with two trays filled with eggs, bacon, pancakes, and juice. He doesn't say anything; he just sets one of them in front of me and sits on the edge of my bed with his own tray.

I poke at my eggs as I watch him cut up his pancakes. He nods at me, and I notice his black eyes seem less swollen, and the cut on his lip looks healed shut. I force a smile at him, and he grins back, the apology accepted.

We finish our breakfast in silence. Dad sighs and pats my leg.

"Ready to get out today?" he asks.

I shake my head. "Nah. Not really."

"Well, it seems you have a coping tradition that needs performed. I figured I'd drive you."

"What?" I stare at him, having no clue what he's talking about.

Dad chuckles as if something is funny. I don't get it. "Shower. Shave. Get dressed. Then I'll show you."

He gathers the dishes and heads downstairs without looking back. I toss back the sheets and head to the bathroom. His whole staying with me this time has me tripping a little.

I walk downstairs, feeling better after the shower.

"Now what?"

"Now, we leave the house."

"Splendid," I mutter but follow him out the door.

I peer out the window as the city flies by. How can everyone go on with their lives?

Dad parks the car in a strip mall and faces me.

I sigh, resigned. "Lead the way."

To my surprise, I follow Dad to a tattoo parlor on the corner.

"What's this?" I ask.

My dad takes a few moments before he answers. "I think this helped you grieve last time. Maybe it will again."

I stare at the door, close my eyes, and swallow. My hand automatically goes to the pocket of my jeans. I pat what's inside and open my eyes.

"Yeah," I say. "Maybe."

Dad winks. "And you can do it legally this time."

I reach back into my pocket and pull out the pendant I'd given Kate. "I want this," I tell the artist.

He takes it from my hand, studies it, and nods. "Yeah. No problem."

I slip my shirt off and lie on the table. As I feel the burning sensation sink in over my heart, the memory of the night I'd given it to her makes me smile.

~*~

A strange feeling pierces me on the morning of my graduation. It doesn't have anything to do with the diploma I'm receiving. No, it's Kate. She's the reason I'll be walking across the stage, not only because I promised her I would, but because she believed in me.

That's not what hurts today, though. Me graduating had been her fourth wish. She had five. And as I dress in my orange cap and gown, I realize that I'll never know the fifth. She took it with her.

I shoot one last look in the mirror and grab the keys my dad has given back based on good behavior.

"See you after the ceremony, son," Dad says, hugging me. "I'm proud of you."

"Thanks," I mumble and walk out the door.

The ceremony drags on, and I count a thousand other places I'd rather be. Passed out on my bed with a bottle of Jim Beam tops the list.

The putz handing out diplomas starts calling names. Those with their last names beginning with the letter A make their way to the stage. Their worthless slip of paper is handed to them, then a lady at the end gives them a red rose. Lame.

I stand with the Ls, oblivious to the crowd of happy parents around me. I know I should be excited; I'm doing this for Kate, after all. But I feel empty.

"Damian Lowell."

I walk up the steps and shake hands with the guy in the suit.

"Congratulations, Damian," he says.

"Thanks," I mumble. That guy doesn't care.

346

The lady hands me the red rose with a smile. I take it and stare at the petals. Somehow, it didn't dawn on me until then that the red rose was Kate's flower. I'd always given her red roses to match her diary.

"You can step down now," the lady says.

"Uh, yeah," I say, swallowing the lump in my throat.

At the bottom of the stairs, I lift my head to the sky. Of all the flowers in the world, I hold a red rose on graduation.

Thank you, Katie.

I choke back a sob and notice all the other students in their seats already, clutching their diploma and their rose. My gaze rises, and I scan the crowd. I see her on the bleachers, third row up.

Taking Kate's flower with me, I jog around my fellow classmates. I cross the track and unlatch the gate. Eyes from the crowd follow me, but I pay no attention to them. Taking the bleacher stairs two at a time, I finally stand in front of Marcy Browdy.

I kneel, and she wraps her arms around my neck. Jason grins at me and pats my shoulder.

"You did good, son," he says.

"Kate would have been so proud," Marcy says through her tears.

I nod and hand Kate's flower to her. "I know."

Chapter 32

I sit beside Kate's tombstone after graduation. Placing my cap on top of the light gray marble, I imagine it on her head and smile.

I trace my fingers over her name. Kathryn "Katie" Browdy. Under it, the Celtic heart knot for hope is etched to match the symbols on the stones beside hers. Kate's parents had loved the idea, and we all knew Kate would have wanted nothing else.

Tears roll down my face when my fingertips reach the words under the dates of birth and death. *You are worth it, Katie.* No regrets cross my mind.

"I did it, Katie," I choke out. "I graduated. So now what?"

My gaze hangs on the marble as if it will answer my question.

"You said you had five wishes. That I had to wait until I finished each one to get the next. I'm ready now."

A breeze blows through the elder tree behind me. I bow my head, tears spilling onto the new slivers of grass poking out of the dirt.

I look up when I hear tires crunch the gravel. My dad parks his car behind mine and steps out.

"I figured you'd be here," he says and sits beside me. He takes in a deep breath, raising his head to the sky. "After your mom and brother passed, I came here every day. Sometimes, I slept out here between them."

I stare at him, waiting for him to get to the point.

"It's hard, son, but it does get easier. Though the pain never completely goes away, it lessens over time."

I don't know if I believe him. We sit together in silence for a few more minutes. Then he pats me on the back and rises to his feet.

"Come home when you're ready," he says.

"I will," I mumble, watching him walk to his car.

He drives away, and I turn back to Kate. I shift my hand on the grass and feel a wrinkle beneath my palm. A white envelope lies on the grass. I glance up at the dust left behind my father's car.

Swallowing, I pick up the envelope. I recognize the girly handwriting that had scrawled out my name. My stomach lurches as I rip it open. I unfold the paper, and my heart melts.

Dear Damian,

Congratulations! I always knew you could do it. Just like I know you'll do well in college and pick some amazing career. Maybe you'll be a musician; I love hearing you sing.

This letter isn't easy for me to write. If you're reading it, it means I'm gone. I know you're hurting. And I'm sorry. I wish I could take it away somehow. But then again, I don't. Pain has a purpose. It makes us stronger. More compassionate. Able to love more deeply than we thought possible. If we let it, it makes us better people. That's my hope for you.

You know, I used to think that being strong meant not getting emotionally involved. Becoming separate and passive. Unattached. Damian, I was wrong.

Being strong means allowing yourself to cry over the things you can't change; laugh when things are funny; smile when you're happy. It means understanding where your breaking point is, and yet, going further and still remaining whole. Strong people push themselves to the limits of pain and joy. They fall to their knees in agony, then they lift up their faces to find the beautiful morning rays shining down on them, and they rise to their feet. Being strong means never giving up, no matter how crushed you are, and finding happiness in the smallest parts of life.

I learned that being brave is the hardest thing in the world. That it hurts. That it tests everything you believe in and more. I realized how unbrave I actually am and how that's okay. I'm so glad you are next to me right now. You give me courage.

I'm scared when I think about you reading this. I imagine you in your room, in your cap and gown, in two weeks. That's as far as I can see, though.

But, Damian, I was wrong about something. I thought death was a journey I'd have to take alone. You have no idea how happy I am to know it's not. I see your face, feel your touch, and I know how much you love me. Because of you, I'll never be alone.

I promised you five wishes; do you remember? I said you'd get the last one after you graduate. So here it is. My fifth wish.

This one might be the hardest one because it may seem like you're doing it alone. You won't be; I'll be with you.

My last wish, Damian, is that once you've read my diary, you'll put it in a box. Place it in the attic somewhere and leave it there. Let it collect dust.

That's not all, though. You have a whole life in front of you. Don't waste it. Don't dwell on the past. Move forward.

Life isn't about merely surviving. It's about living.

Damian, my love, my final wish is for you to let me go.

Love Always, Kate

Love Always, Kate

Discussion Questions:

1. In the first scene of the book, Kate is in Dr. Lowell's office and finds out her leukemia has returned for the third time. How does this first scene set the mood for the story?

2. Kate's first response to learning she's out of remission is to buy a new diary. What purpose does her diary play in the development of the story, Kate's character, and Damian's character?

3. Kate deals with her disease first-hand, but it also affects her parents. How do Mr. and Mrs. Browdy handle Kate's illness this time around? How does that affect their relationship with their daughter?

4. Damian and his father have a much different relationship with each other than Kate has her parents. How is Damian's relationship with Dr. Lowell different?

5. Kate is on a first name basis with the staff of the pediatric oncology unit. Describe her relationship with Leslie, Dr. Lowell, and other patients. How do those differ from Damian's relationship with them?

6. Leslie warns Kate to stay away from Damian. Do you think her reasons were justified?

7. When Damian comes into Kate's life, her response to his good looks is immediate. But after she learns more about him from Leslie, she doesn't slink away. Why does she pursue him and insist on seeing him differently than others see him? How does this affect her feelings for him?

8. There are five stages of grief: denial, anger, bargaining, depression, and acceptance. What stage is Damian in, and why do you think that? What stage is Dr. Lowell in?

9. Damian asks Kate two questions early in their relationship: Are you happy? Are all the treatments worth all the junk that comes along with it? These are repeated themes throughout the book. How do the answers to these questions change for Kate from the beginning of the story to the end? How do they change for Damian?

10. Damian's attraction to Kate is slower than hers to him. What keeps Damian coming back to her? Does his response to her fit his character? Why or why not?

11. Ellie is Liam's girlfriend, and Damian's bed buddy after Liam's death. What was your initial opinion of Ellie? Did that change by the end of the book? Why or why not?

12. Damian went all out for the Christmas dinner. Why do you think he pulled out all the stops to make that night so special?

13. The Christmas date ended with Kate feeling rejected, and the reader seeing Damian struggle with his growing feelings for her. How does this night change Damian's outlook? Kate's? Was Kate's response natural?

14. Damian accuses Kate of being so scared of the reality of her disease that she minimizes it as to pretend it doesn't bother her. Kate then accuses Damian of pushing people away and drowning in himself in booze to hide from the pain he desperately needs to feel. Are they right about each other? Why or why not?

15. Kate learns about Ellie when she reads Damian's journal. What is Kate's response to Ellie after learning about her? What's her response to Damian? Why does she choose to overlook his past behavior? Would you have made the same decision Kate made?

16. Kate's cancer progresses throughout the story. How does that affect her relationship with Damian? With her parents? With hospital staff?

17. Brennan is a little boy who's just beginning chemo treatments. What is his purpose in the story? Why does he relate so well to Damian?

18. When Kate finds out the chemo isn't working and her only options are to wait for a transplant or try a new experimental drug, she takes some time to think about it. Do you agree with her parents'

decision to let her decide? Do you agree with Kate's final decision to wait for a transplant? Discuss how the story may have been different had Kate's decision been different.

19. Hope is the overarching theme of this book. In what ways did Kate give Damian hope? In what ways did Damian give Kate hope?

20. Kate comes up with five wishes for Damian to fulfill. What were her purposes for each wish?

21. Kate's dad says, "Sometimes, what might seem like giving up is when we're in the midst of the toughest battle we'll ever face." What did Jason Browdy mean by this? Is he right?

22. Kate doesn't want to die a virgin and eventually sleeps with Damian. How does this act make her doubt her previous choice to not try the drug? How does it change it her feelings for Damian?

23. Even though Kate knows she's going to die, she stays strong for Damian and for her parents. How does this show her growth as a person?

24. Kate is a strong female character, yet she's quiet and content. How does she show strength throughout the story?

25. Before she dies, Kate requests a few minutes alone with each of her parents and with Damian. Do her conversations fit her relationship with each

person? How?

26. Most of the story is told from Kate's POV. Then, at the very end, it changes. The tense of the story also changes from past to present. Why do you think the author made this shift? Did the story change for you after the shift? If so, how?

27. Damian never said the words "I love you" to Kate until the very end. Why do you think he never said them before? How do those words affect Kate?

28. After Kate's death, Damian slips back into his old habits. When he finds Ellie in Liam's bedroom, he uses her again to drown out his pain. It's also the only place where Ellie makes an appearance. What do you think the author's purpose for this scene was? Why do you think Ellie indulged him? Afterward, Ellie tells him that letting someone go doesn't mean you forget them. It means you love them from here and move on with your life like they would have wanted. Why do you think she says this?

29. One of the biggest heartbreaks in this story is when Damian receives a letter from the lab saying he is a positive HLA match to Kate. Why do you think the author did this? How would the story have been different had the test been negative?

30. Kate's final letter to Damian tells him everything she's learned, as well as gives him her final wish. If you were to write a letter to give

someone after you are gone, who would you write it to? What is the one most important thing you'd want them to know?

Acknowledgements

Behind every great writer is an amazing team of support: family, friends, beta readers, CP's, editors, marketing people, cover designers, formatters, submissions teams, and everyone else at the publishing house. This is my chance to say 'thanks,' and I sincerely hope I don't leave anyone out!

First and foremost, I thank God, for without Him, none of this would be possible.

Secondly, my family. To my husband, David, for his encouragement to chase my dream, his analytical thoughts when I had problems figuring something out, his willing ear, and the fire he lit under me to start sending out query letters. I couldn't have done this without you!

To my children, David Michael, Brennan, Natalie Anne, and Abigaylle, for making me smile when the story wasn't moving like I wanted, and for finding things to do while Mommy worked. You four are the best!

To my parents, siblings, and-laws for being among the first readers and for being there when I had good and bad news to share. Thanks for letting me count on you!

Thank you to my friends and various beta readers who read through my stories with a keen eye. Your thoughts have been very helpful, as well as your encouragement and kind words. Holly Hendrian, Tonille Burrows, Heather Jelsma, Kim Jackson, Landon King, and I hope I'm not missing anyone, I appreciate you all very much. Your insights have been invaluable.

A special thanks to Heather Jelsma and Angela Rothfus for helping me put together my website! Seriously, I wouldn't have one if it weren't for you!

I've been blessed with some amazing critique partners (CP's), and I can't even begin to express my thanks for the hard work they put in making my stories shine their brightest. Sunniva Dee: You were the first non-family/non-friend to read my work, and not only did you fall in love with it, it spawned a great friendship. Your honesty and thorough eye has made me a better writer, editor, and has made my manuscripts look more polished than I could ever have done on my own. Temperance Elisabeth: You know how to ask the right questions in the right places to make my stories come alive even more. I appreciate your fine eye for details. Your comments always make me smile! I'm so grateful for our newfound friendship! Laura Carlson: I don't know how you do it, but you seem to always know what my story needs to make it sparkle! Thanks for loving LOVE ALWAYS, KATE so much. You are a gem, friend. Virginia Pierce: You've inspired me! And your comments on LOVE ALWAYS, KATE were perfect! They meant the world to me, and I look forward to growing as friends and writers.

Thank you to my editor, Toni Rakestraw, for going through this novel with a fine-tooth comb! It's much appreciated!

Thank you to *Limitless Publishing* for taking a chance on me! Jennifer O'Neill, Jessica Gunhammer, Dixie Matthews, Olivia Oswald, and everyone else who had a hand in getting my book out there, you're all amazing!

And of course to the readers! Without you, there'd be no books! So a huge, sincere, round of applause for each and every one of you! You're the best!

Love Always,
D.

About the Author

Born and raised in Iowa, d. Nichole King writes her stories close to home. There's nothing like small-town Midwest scenery to create the perfect backdrop for an amazing tale.

She wrote her first book in junior high and loved every second of it. However, she couldn't bring herself to share her passion with anyone. She packed it away until one day, with the encouragement of her husband, she sat down at the computer and began to type. Now, she can't stop.

When not writing, d. is usually curled up with a book, scrapbooking, or doing yet another load of laundry.

Along with her incredible husband, she lives in small-town Iowa with her four adorable children and their dog, Peaches.

Facebook:
www.facebook.com/dnichole.king

Twitter:
https://twitter.com/dNicholeKing

Website:
www.dnicholeking.com/

Pinterest:
www.pinterest.com/dnicholek/

Goodreads:
www.goodreads.com/author/show/7762889.D_Nich
ole_King

Made in the USA
Charleston, SC
11 September 2016